THE MAYA STONE MURDERS

THE MAYA STONE MURDERS

M.K. SHUMAN

ST. MARTIN'S PRESS NEW YORK

Design by Jaye Zimet

Library of Congress Cataloging-in-Publication Data

Shuman, M. K.
    The Maya stone murders.
    I. Title.
PS3569.H779M38 1989   813'.54   88-29812
ISBN 0-312-02608-0

First Edition

10 9 8 7 6 5 4 3 2 1

To
the real
explorers
of Ek Balam:
Will Andrews and
his students, past and present.

I stood on the hot sidewalk outside the Crescent City Cultural Center looking at the exhibition poster, but I was thinking adultery. Why else would he have asked for a meeting here at the museum, instead of in his Tulane office?

Located a block south of Poydras, the Center is a simple brick building with flags sticking out from the facade on poles, and unless you look hard when you pass, you might mistake it for the consulate of some third-rank country. It was ten in the morning, yet the air was already steamy, the way it gets only during a New Orleans summer, with the moisture thick in the air from the previous day's rain. My guayabera already wanted to stick to me, so I was glad to go through the glass door and into the air-conditioned lobby.

The posters said it was a special exhibition from the Mayan city of Ek Balam, on the Yucatán Peninsula. The middle-aged lady selling tickets told me they would be open in just a few minutes if I wanted to wait. I thanked her and gave her my card.

"I'd like to see Dr. Thorpe," I said. She smiled and handed the card to a black man with a white shirt and bow tie. It was one of my plain cards, with just my name, *Micah Dunn,* no address, just the box number of a fictitious insurance company.

The man led me through the gift shop, where a worried-looking young woman was arranging imitation Mayan curios in a display case, in anticipation of the day's visitors. We passed through a door at the rear and into a narrow passage whose shadows seemed an ominous contrast to the brightly lit rooms outside. Ahead was an open doorway and the man with me halted and knocked.

I heard voices inside and he handed in my card. A second later he gestured for me to enter, then faded back into the corridor. I stepped forward and found myself in a richly furnished office dominated by a large oak desk.

"Mr. Dunn," said the man behind the desk, peering up at me through thick bifocals. He held my card as if it might be unclean and then laid it in front of him on the glass surface. Perhaps fifty, he looked much older, with a skewed bow tie under a long face, thin nose, and sandy brows. The muscle of a former athlete was long gone, but there remained a certain tenacity in his features. He nodded at the doorway, not offering to shake hands. "Would you please close the door?"

I did as he asked and then waited.

His eyes went over to my left arm, as if he had hit on an interesting problem. I was used to it by now, but most people's eyes left again, quickly. His stayed. "Is there something the matter with your arm?" he asked.

"It doesn't work," I said evenly. "A war wound."

"Vietnam?"

"That's right."

"Don't you find it a hindrance in your occupation?"

"No more so than in any other. There's not much strong-arm stuff to being a detective, Dr. Thorpe. Most of it involves examining documents, typing reports, and waiting. Lots of waiting."

"I see." His nose wrinkled as if he'd smelled something unpleasant. He played at squaring my card on the tabletop and I guessed he was having trouble finding the words to explain how he had sunk so low as to require my services. I started to tell him that it was a symptom of our times, but I had a feeling he didn't need to be reminded.

Finally he made his decision and looked up. "Mr. Dunn, I have a problem and I can't go to the police."

So it was blackmail. "Do you want to tell me about it, Dr. Thorpe?"

He gave a jerky little nod. "But this can go no further," he insisted. "You have very good references." He cleared his throat. "The Tulane police chief said you were the best."

"Chief Butler's very kind."

"Naturally, I didn't tell him about this. I, ah, just, obliquely, approached him about private detectives and security services in general . . ."

"Of course."

"But this must be completely confidential."

"It always is," I told him, a little tired of standing. "Although, if there's a crime involved . . ."

"A crime?" Thorpe looked up, shocked. "Of course there's a crime, or else I wouldn't . . . Oh, I see. You mean, if *I* . . ."

I nodded.

He shook his head vigorously. "Mr. Dunn, I am a

tenured, full professor at Tulane University. I can assure
you that the very insinuation is . . ."

"No insinuation," I said. "I just wanted to get the
ground rules straight. Now what *is* the problem exactly,
Dr. Thorpe?"

Thorpe leaned forward as if about to impart a terrible
secret. "Mr. Dunn, the excavations at Ek Balam carried
out by the Middle American Research Institute, or
MARI, as we call it, are among the most important ever
conducted in Central America. They prove, beyond the
shadow of a doubt, that Maya civilization continued in
northern Yucatán at a time when it had collapsed in
Guatemala, to the south. This exhibition brings to the
public the results of a five-year program of investigation
that I, myself, directed. I cannot—*archaeology* cannot—
afford to have the fruits of our efforts destroyed."

I got tired of standing and pulled up a chair. So it
wasn't blackmail after all. "May I assume, Dr. Thorpe,
that you have a problem with artifact smuggling?"

He nodded eagerly. "Yes. That's exactly it. It could
wreck everything we've done."

"I understand. How many artifacts have been taken
from the museum, Dr. Thorpe?"

He shook his head violently and his thin brown hair
went from side to side like the plumage of a bird. "No.
You don't understand at all. It's just the opposite."

"The opposite?"

The jerky nod again. "Yes." He half-rose from his
seat, his eyes angry. "You see, Mr. Dunn, they're not
smuggling artifacts *out*. They're smuggling them *in*."

I must have dropped my usual poker face because
Thorpe's own expression changed to one of chagrin. "Do
you find something amusing, Mr. Dunn?"

I straightened out my smile. "No, Dr. Thorpe. It's
just that it's generally the other way around."

"Agreed. And that's why I half-suspect that this is

someone's perverted idea of a joke. An attempt to make a fool of me." He gave a hopeless little shrug. "I know I'm not the most popular person at the Institute."

I said nothing.

"But if it's a joke, it could have horrible consequences. It could ruin this entire exhibition, cast a shadow on the integrity of our excavation, prevent us from obtaining funds in the future. Any hint whatsoever of fraud can be disastrous."

"What, exactly, is being brought in, sir?"

In answer, Thorpe shot to his feet, a marionette without strings. "This way," he indicated. "And if any of the staff asks, you're an insurance appraiser."

He led me through the doorway and back down the dark hall into the shop, but this time, instead of turning right, to the lobby, we went left, into the display area, where muted lights highlighted the showcases. My feet sank into thick carpet.

He took me to an exhibit of tiny clay dolls. "Here, the figurines. You see?"

I looked down. Four small figurines were propped upright. Each was perhaps three inches high, and two bore pronounced male genitalia. It took me a minute to see what he was talking about, but when I went from the dolls to the signs describing them I understood: The descriptions were of three figurines and yet there were *four* on the other side of the glass.

"Three days ago, that's when I noticed them. It was horribly embarrassing. I mean, a woman came to one of the guides and pointed it out. Naturally, the guide was terribly confused and called me." He shook his head again. "I removed it immediately. I was sure that it was some kind of mistake, but none of the curatorial staff would admit it. Then, when I checked the accession records, I saw that the piece wasn't listed, and yet it was so

similar it might have come from the same cache of artifacts."

"You mean it could have come from Ek Balam?" I
asked.

"Could, but *didn't*. Mr. Dunn, I know what came
from my own site. Most of the artifacts, of course, are
stored in the Mexican National Institute. National pol-
icy, you understand. They let us take these out specially
for this exhibit."

"I see."

"In any event, I replaced the figurine in this case
when I came in this morning to give you an idea of the
way it was. It was the second doll from the left." He
indicated one with an exaggerated penis.

He walked quickly over to a case in the center of the
room, tiptoeing as if someone might be listening. This
case bore a display of Mayan pottery, some only fragments and others whole bowls, decorated with kings and
plumed warriors.

"Then, the day before yesterday, there was an extra
polychrome bowl, next to the one in the center. I have it
in the office. Again, it was so similar it might have come
from the same site. But it had not come from our excavations, according to the records. I removed it and ini-
tiated an inquiry. I called in every member of our staff,
but no one knew anything."

He hurried over to a third case, this one with some
spear points of black, glasslike material.

"The final blow was yesterday," he declared. "Here,
in the display of obsidian blades. There was a fifth blade
that nobody had ever seen before."

I bent down and examined the display glass, then
walked over to the wall and checked the connection. It
was a vibration-type alarm system, and like all such sys-
tems it had its strengths and weaknesses. "How many
people have a key to the control box?" I asked.

"Myself; my secretary, Katherine Degas; my graduate student, Gordon Leeds. And that's all, except for Jason Cobbett's people."

"Jason Cobbett?"

"The director of the Center. I don't work here, you understand. Cobbett's putting on our exhibition. I only borrowed his office because I knew he wouldn't be in this morning and I wanted you to see everything in situ, as it were. Quite frankly . . ." He lowered his voice and looked around. "There's been some friction between our two groups. I believe Cobbett and his people thought we should just have handed them everything and walked away. I insisted that, since we were responsible for the artifacts, we should have daily access to them and should work with displaying them. Naturally, after a few weeks we could have faded out, but this is the first week of the exhibition and I wanted to make sure there were no foulups. If you want it done right, I say do it yourself."

"So there's another whole crew with access to the alarm system."

"I suppose. Certainly Cobbett and his assistant, and the security guards, have them. They didn't want us to have keys, of course, but I insisted. *Entre nous,* Mr. Dunn, I think you might want to look in their direction."

"Why wasn't the exhibition put on at the University?" I asked.

"Well, no space, of course. Who'd climb four flights of steps to the top of Dinwiddie Hall? But down here, near Riverwalk, during the tourist season, well . . ."

I walked back to the exit and examined the infrared barrier. It looked fairly secure, but, then, I've never cared for that technology: A bird or a bat raises hell with it and after a while it gets turned off in frustration, which means no protection at all. Vibration alarms, on the other hand, are harder to set: Too much sensitivity causes false alarms and not enough makes them useless.

I always recommended something like Sonitrol, which gives you an ear in the alarm room, but in this case it was academic because it was clear to me that this must be an inside job.

"One other thing." Thorpe sidled up to me. "About your fee . . ."

"Three hundred dollars a day and expenses," I said. "And you get a written report every week."

He flinched. "That's a lot."

"It's the going rate."

"Well, I don't suppose I have much choice. I can't let this go on." He bit his lip, the light from the displays reflecting from his glasses. "You wouldn't have any idea how long this will take?"

"With luck not more than a day or two. Depending on what you want, of course. Discreetly letting the guilty party know that somebody's looking into this will probably make them stop. But if you want to know who it is, that could be a little more difficult."

"Yes, I'd already come to that realization. I really need to know who it is, of course. I have to be sure it isn't one of my own people."

I nodded. "All right. If you'll give me a list of your associates and also of Cobbett's, I'll get on it right away."

We started out the way we had come and suddenly the archaeologist gave a little shriek. I whirled, afraid he was going to collapse, but there was no danger of that. Instead, he was facing a display case on the left, his eyes glued to the glass and his skin the color of dead fish. I followed his gaze to the cluster of small green jades that were arranged in a semicircle on a creme background. Each one bore the likeness of a Maya warrior, with almond eyes, hooked nose, and giant earrings. I read the labels, already knowing what I would find.

"My God," Thorpe stammered, unable to control his trembling. "He's done it again."

SOPORTA HASTA · HOLDS UP TO
30 lbs.

25 PCS | PZS

FOR | PARA
Drywall
Paneles de yeso

NO PRE-DRILLING

Zip-It Patented

Drywall Anchor

HILLMAN

0 08236 90069 9

INSTALLATION | INSTALACIÓN

Includes #6 x 1-1/4" Screws
Incluye tornillos N° 6 x 1-1/4 pulg.

Ideal for hanging electrical fixtures, drapery supports, bathroom/kitchen accessories, pictures and more!
Ideal para colgar accesorios eléctricos, soportes para cortinas, accesorios para baño o para cocina, cuadros y ¡muchas otras cosas!

Easy to remove
Fácil de quitar

* **Load value on front is the MAXIMUM ALLOWABLE LOAD in 1/2" drywall.**
* El valor de carga indicado en el frente es la MÁXIMA CARGA PERMISIBLE en paneles de 1/2 pulg.

PERFORMANCE GUIDE | GUÍA DE UTILIZACIÓN

Screen Size Tamaño de tornillo	Screw Allowable Load *Máxima carga permisible	
	1/2" Drywall Panel de 1/2 pulg.	
#8 X 1-1/4"	50 lbs.	
#8 X 1-1/4"	30 lbs.	

Fixture thickness not to exceed 1/4".
El grosor del accesorio no debe ser superior a 1/4".

Not recommended for ceiling applications.
No se recomienda para uso en cielos rasos.

Do not over tighten.
No ajuste excesivamente.

* **Maximum Allowable Load is based on a 2:1 (in 1/2" drywall)** safety
factor using an average of ultimate tension and shear loads. **Maximum Allowable**
Load is a guide only and cannot be guaranteed.
La máxima carga permisible se basa en un factor de seguridad de 2:1 (paneles),
promediando las cargas de rotura a la tracción y al corte. La carga máxima permisible
es solo orientativa y no puede garantizarse.

Pound ratings are based on the anchor only. Effectiveness can be diminished
based on the material and conditions of the base material.
Las clasificaciones en pounds se establecieron tomando en cuenta solo el ancla de
expansión. La eficacia del producto se puede ver afectada por el material y por las
condiciones del material de base.

INSTALLATION TIPS | CONSEJOS DE INSTALACIÓN

76226

WARRANTY | GARANTÍA

The sale of this product is "as is" and without any express warranties. Liability, if
any, is limited to refund of purchase price only upon return of product and package
to manufacturer's plant.
Este producto se vende "en el estado en que está" y sin ninguna garantía implícita.
La responsabilidad, de existir alguna, se limita a la devolución del dinero abonado por
la compra, solo en el caso de que se devuelva el producto, en su envoltorio, en las
instalaciones del fabricante.

HILLMAN
CINCINNATI, OHIO 45231
www.hillmangroup.com

I walked back out into the sunlight and stood for a few minutes at the intersection of Constance and Poydras, trying to convince myself that Gregory Thorpe was going to get his money's worth. Three hundred a day was a steep price to pay for unmasking somebody's joke. On the other hand, someone had gone to a lot of trouble if the only object was to make Thorpe out a fool. I took his list out of my pocket and glanced down the names. One of them was almost certainly the culprit, and odds were I could shake loose an admission without too much trouble. I stuck the list back into my pocket and walked toward the river. The '84 World's Fair had been a disaster, declaring bankruptcy before the last tourist had bought a ticket, but the city had salvaged the old wharf area where the fair was held, transforming it into a multi-level mall of shops and restaurants called the Riverwalk. One of the stores had a cash-flow problem just now, and the manager suspected the flow was into his cashier's pocket. I had a woman planted there as a clerk and I drifted across the plaza now and into the first level, where already a healthy summer crowd was beginning to build. The air smelled of popcorn and candy, changing to fresh croissants as I walked. I went up a stairway, past a clown with balloons, and found a table at a little doughnut shop where I could look into the doorway of the shop in question. I ordered coffee and beignets and sat quietly for twenty minutes, watching the people pass. Then I got up slowly and meandered out, down the hall, confident that I had caught the eye of my operative.

I was standing at the rail, looking out at the river, when she appeared at my elbow. A thin, attractive black girl, Sandra can go from Newcomb coed to Butterfly McQueen in five seconds, as the situation demands.

"It's the morning cashier," she said with just a hint of satisfaction in her voice. "I saw her making out the sales report for her shift yesterday. There was a lot of erasing to make it come out right. Then, just half an hour ago, she palmed a ten-dollar bill she'd stuck up on the register to make change."

I nodded. I like doing a good job but it always saddens me to learn the worst about people.

"Was it our money?" I asked.

"Sho' were, honey. When I ask her to change a twenty later on, I'll get it back and I'll give you fifty to one the serial numbers are the same."

I shook my head. "You worry me, Sandra. You like your job too much."

She gave me an enigmatic smile and blended into the mosaic of strollers. When she was gone I stared back out at the river, toward Gretna, a mile away. A string of empty barges bored upriver, barely making headway against the current. For a moment I was seeing another river, one with sampans and junks and a rickety ferry crowded with people, pigs, and chickens. A vapor trail overhead told of another load of body bags headed home, and from somewhere in the distance came the painlike throb of rotors as a chopper skimmed by just over the rooftops. I reached for the rail to steady myself, then remembered where I was.

It was eleven-thirty when I got back to my office, a second-story walk-up on Decatur, a stone's throw from the Old Mint. The first floor is a voodoo shop owned by a man who calls himself Lavelle, but whose real name is David Erikson. His voodoo charms are as phony as the state budget, and it's an open secret that his real revenue comes from flogging pre-Columbian artifacts. I'd known when I'd taken the suite six years before that he'd come in handy one day. When I entered he was busy explaining a gris-gris to a skeptical-looking woman with two thousand dollars' worth of necklaces hiding her neck wrinkles. I let him do his thing but as our eyes crossed I caught a look that said he was wasting his time.

I slid through the strings of beads with the bamboo wind chimes at the top, reminded that anybody coming up would make enough noise to wake the dead. I opened my door and went inside, turning on the window unit and flopping into my chair. It's a plain, white-walled office; just a typewriter, a couple of filing cabinets, an answering machine, and an obsolete computer with a modem attachment. One window looks out onto a balcony, and on the other side is a doorway into a sitting room that faces the patio and fountain, with my efficiency-style living quarters next door. I punched the automatic dialer and waited and when a voice answered I asked for Lieutenant Mancuso. When he came on I gave him the names on Thorpe's list. "Any priors, including DWIs," I asked him. "And run Gregory Thorpe, too."

"Thorpe? You mean the guy at Tulane? Is this something we ought to know about?"

"Not at this point," I said and leaned back as he made the usual growls of protest and allowed as how jarheads liked to give orders, but the Aircavs had relieved us more than once. My eyes came to rest on the photo on the wall, the one with the members of Second Platoon. It was crooked, I noticed, resolving to straighten it when I got off the phone. Mancuso promised to get back to me by late afternoon, tomorrow morning at the latest, and I hung up. There were a couple of messages on the machine, two from people looking for security work, and one from an insurance salesman who wouldn't go away.

I unlocked the bottom drawer of my desk, levered out my album with one hand, and dropped it before me on the desk. Then I reached into my in-basket and withdrew a large, stiff manila envelope. I turned it upside down, so that the contents slid out through the slit I'd made when it had arrived earlier.

I caught the pictures by the edges and laid the accompanying note to one side. Then I leaned back and savored the colored photos.

They depicted a yacht, grandiosely named the *Excelsior II,* a throwback to the J-boats of prewar days. It was owned by a billionaire from Miami, and it was supposed to have a good crack at the America's Cup. The pictures had been taken by the owner's nephew, whom I'd helped with a racing problem of another sort. The photos were the final installment in a bill it had taken him six months to pay and I was pleased to see he was a man of his word. I opened my album, took the glue from my top drawer, and carefully pasted the photos to the pages, covering them with a sheet of clear plastic. Then I leafed back through the earlier entries, to all the great Cup winners: *Constellation; Intrepid; Courageous; Freedom; Australia II; Liberty.* I even have a painting of the first winner, *America,* from 1851, and a sepia print of *Defender,* from 1895. And there were a lot of boats that didn't win the Cup, but gave it a good try.

I made a mental note to drop a thank-you to my erstwhile client and carefully replaced the album in the drawer. I stuck a cassette in the stereo—Brahms's Second Piano Concerto—then got a beer, half a French-bread loaf, and a hunk of Longhorn cheese out of the refrigerator in the next room. I went out onto the balcony and took a seat in the lawn chair overlooking the patio. I settled back, slicing off pieces of cheese with my pocket knife to make a sandwich. Sometimes, in the late evenings, with the faint sound of traffic coming over the rooftop and the smell of exhausts in the heavy air, I have the sensation of being somewhere else. It's one of the benefits of the locale, watching the water playing up from the fountain and now and then catching just the right light, so that there's a rainbow in the center of the yard.

I knew pre-Columbian artifacts brought high prices on the collector's market. But Thorpe's problem was just the opposite. I sighed, finished my sandwich, and went back down the stairs to my car, parked just off the street, behind the green wooden doors that led to the patio. I headed uptown, for Tulane, keeping to a steady thirty on most of St. Charles and only hitting a couple of lights until I reached the University District. It was a test of skill, driving in New Orleans with just one hand. At first I'd rebelled against the turning knob on the steering wheel, but common sense finally vanquished any residual machismo.

You can do without the special blinker bar, the rehab counselor had said. *But you have to accept the fact that things won't be as easy.*

He was right. They weren't. But I managed. I just made sure all my cars had automatic transmissions and I reluctantly gave up my accustomed high speeds. I scaled back my sailing and became a spectator. Most people who saw me, with my left hand in my pocket, seemed unconcerned. Thorpe was an exception.

I found a place to park on Calhoun, about a quarter of a mile from the school, and walked the rest of the way.

The University was founded in the 1830s as a medical college. Later, a millionaire named Paul Tulane left it a fortune and it began to cultivate an image as the Harvard of the South. The image was enhanced by the Gothic architecture, an elite student body, and a board composed of more old money than politicians. Most of the city's doctors and half the lawyers are products of Tulane. I didn't know about archaeologists.

Thorpe's offices were at the top of Dinwiddie Hall, a forbidding gray stone structure within sight of the streetcar tracks. I found the building and clambered the four flights to the top, where a sign said MIDDLE AMERICAN RESEARCH INSTITUTE. I stopped beside the sign to examine the alarms. They were Honeywells, which meant that someone had given Thorpe good advice. I emerged into a narrow, dimly lit hallway, with display cases on either side and what appeared to be a Mayan temple on the right, at the end. To the left I saw a classroom and, somewhere beyond, an office, where I heard a typewriter at work. I made a pass by the display cases. One contained a human skull, its teeth inlaid with flakes of jade. Another bore some pottery from the Classic Maya period. I stopped before the temple, which was really a plaster copy of the sculptured facade of the real thing. Then I passed along the other wall, checking the cases there. I'd thought for a moment that the artifacts might have been taken from the displays here, but I could see now that none of the cases bore comparable items. And besides, Thorpe would certainly have known his own displays, wouldn't he?

I started for the classroom and at that moment a woman emerged, a pad in her hand.

"May I help you?" she asked pleasantly. She was in her early forties, with glossy black hair pulled back severely, and a pencil behind one ear. Her clothes were tasteful—white frilly blouse and a neat gray skirt and heels. I wondered if she took off her shoes to get up the stairs every morning.

"My name is Dunn," I said, handing her one of my appraiser cards with a phony company but the right telephone number. "Dr. Thorpe has asked me to assess the value of some of the artifacts in the current exhibition for insurance purposes."

The woman smiled. "My name is Katherine Degas. I'm Dr. Thorpe's administrative assistant. That's a fancy term for secretary, editor, and dogsbody. I'll be happy to show you anything you need to see, Mr. Dunn."

"Thank you, Miss Degas. I think mainly I'd like to ask a few general questions."

She started to reply and that was when a voice cut her off.

"I can handle it from here, Katherine." A young man with a black, closely cropped beard emerged from a passageway between the display cases. He wore a white sports shirt and dark slacks and I caught a faint whiff of English Leather.

"My name is Gordon Leeds," he said with an accent I placed as midwestern. He stuck out a hand and I shook it. "I'm Dr. Thorpe's assistant. I'll be glad to answer any questions. Where did you say you were from?"

"The insurance company," I told him.

He frowned slightly. "Really. I suppose it's about the exhibition?"

"That's right. I've already been to the Cultural Center and I wanted to come here and get some background.

I'm sure the items displayed are just a small amount of what was recovered."

"Absolutely. If you'd like, we can walk over to the other side of the campus and I'll show you the lab."

"That would be fine." We went down the narrow stairway and into the sunlight again. Walking away from St. Charles, we came into a shady quadrangle formed by a mixture of old stone and wooden buildings. Squirrels scurried across the green and on the far side two professors walked, heads down in discourse.

We went around the new Biology Building and came out on Freret Street. Leeds was quiet all the while, as if something were puzzling him. I let him work it over in his mind, figuring it would come out when he was ready. We passed the library, turned down a side street, and came to a two-story white stucco structure.

"This is where we actually do the analysis and restoration," he explained. "The first floor is the Anthropology Department."

"I assume you were in the field with Dr. Thorpe?" I asked.

"I was the field supervisor," Leeds said quickly. "For the last three seasons I was there every day. Dr. Thorpe was the principal investigator, but he spent a lot of time in Mérida and Cancún. That's not a criticism," he added hurriedly. "I mean, the PI isn't *expected* to be in the field all the time."

"Are you a graduate student?"

"I'm working on my doctorate. This dig will be the basis of my dissertation."

He held the door open for me and we went into a hallway and down a flight of steps into the basement. I saw a large room with cardboard boxes stacked along the sides. In the center of the room was a long table where a slight, dark man with a hooked nose bent over the fragments of a broken pot. "Artemio is Dr. Thorpe's personal assistant. He bossed the Mayan crew and came back from Yucatán with us. He's working on analysis and preparation of artifacts. You can see that we really don't have any place to store the things. This is only one of several buildings on campus where we have them stuck away."

"How many people were on the dig?" I asked.

"Well, the fieldwork lasted for five seasons. A season is generally from January through May, the dry time of the year. There were different graduate students at different times and the Mayan labor force fluctuated, too. Usually there were seven to ten workers. Then there was the ceramicist, Astrid Bancroft. I was there as a shovel hand the first two years. Then I started my graduate work and was promoted to field supervisor. I guess Artemio, Astrid, and I were the only ones that were there for all three past seasons. As I said, Dr. Thorpe came and went."

"The dig is over now, though."

"Yes. We've been working all this last year on analysis and writing. Of course, the published monographs won't be out for three to five years, but Dr. Thorpe thought it would be in order to have an exhibition."

"The discoveries were that spectacular?"

Leeds let me have a quick, almost embarrassed, smile. "'Success breeds success,' Dr. Thorpe likes to say. If you put on a good show, you stimulate interest and there's a good chance donors will come forward for more work." He gave a little shrug. "It's kind of a game. See how long you can stay in the field. I'm lucky I don't have to get involved in that part of it." He lowered his voice to a near whisper. "To tell the truth, this exhibition is sort of a nuisance. I'd like to get my dissertation written."

"Then the project didn't really cast any new light on Maya civilization?"

"Of course it did. They all do. And they raise new problems for the next project. We learned more about what was going on in eastern Yucatán after A.D. 900, when Maya civilization collapsed in Guatemala. And we recorded a number of glyphic inscriptions that bear on Mayan ideas of astronomy, which is a special interest of Dr. Thorpe's. I don't think any of it will change any ideas, though."

I stared at the clutter of potsherds. "In any case, there seems to be enough to do," I observed.

Leeds chuckled. "That's for sure. People think the fieldwork is difficult, but the real problems come in the lab. Show me any batch of sherds two ceramicists would sort the same way."

"What about frauds?"

"It's a problem, but more to collectors than to archaeologists. I mean, who'd want to stick fake potsherds into an excavation?" He gave a little chuckle. "On the other hand, there are some quite good forgers who can manufacture replicas that even the best museums will buy, and most archaeologists say good for them."

"Really?"

He smiled at my surprise. "Yes. After all, archaeologists have little to do with collectors. Collectors are in it to either make money selling artifacts or to have items to adorn their living rooms. They couldn't care less about what archaeological knowledge is destroyed when the artifacts are plundered. A good forger will divert them from real archaeological sites."

"There must be ways to detect forgeries, though."

"There are. But most, like thermoluminescence, require that the artifact or part of it be destroyed. Otherwise, if it's a very good replica, and the forger hasn't let the paint run, you can sometimes fool anybody."

There was a noise on the stairway and a young woman stood staring at us, her brow furrowed. I realized then that she was letting her eyes adjust to the darker interior. Leeds nodded. "Mr. Dunn, this is Astrid Bancroft, our project ceramicist. Astrid, Mr. Dunn's from the insurance company."

The girl squinted at me from behind thick, not very stylish glasses. She would have been attractive, even pretty, had she made an effort, but her mind seemed elsewhere. She squeezed out a quick smile, mumbled something, and then I caught a flash of jeans, tanned skin, and brown hair as she turned around and vanished back up the steps.

Leeds gave a little laugh. "Don't mind Astrid. That's just the way she is. She lives in her own little world. Believe it or not, she was even worse before she got engaged to her oil broker."

We went back up the stairs and into the afternoon. I took a deep breath, sucking in as much water as air, and Leeds shook his head. "Nothing like a tropical climate to leave you wrung out by three o'clock." We started toward Freret Street and when we got to the library he stopped. "I'll leave you here. I have some work to do in the library."

I thanked him and went back across the quadrangle. He was right. There were times when the only thing a sane person would do was take to his hammock with a rum and Coke. I was mulling over the prospect as I approached Dinwiddie Hall and that was why I didn't see the form until it stepped out of the shadows.

"Mr. Dunn?" I recognized Katherine Degas, Thorpe's secretary, and halted.

"Have you been waiting here long?"

"No. I called over to the lab and they told me you'd just left." She fixed me with good-natured gray eyes. "Gordon can get very officious at times. After all, he'll have his doctorate in a year or so and I'm only a secretary, as far as he's concerned. But I've known Gregory Thorpe a hell of a lot longer. There's not a lot he holds back from me, if you understand. So if there's any way I can help you, just let me know."

"Thank you, Miss Degas."

"Mrs.," she corrected. "I never got liberated. My husband was killed in Nam."

"I'm sorry."

"It's okay. It was a long time ago. Gregory was good to me. He and his wife took me in. When Roberta died, it hurt him so badly. I'd do anything to keep him from being hurt again."

"If someone's trying to hurt him, I'd like to know."

"So would I, Mr. Dunn." She gave me a quick smile and then offered her hand. She looked down at my class ring and a light went on. "Of course. I knew I recognized your ring. Annapolis. You were a naval officer, weren't you?"

"Marines," I said. "You're very perceptive, Mrs. Degas."

"No. I just saw you looking at my hands and returned the compliment."

"Touché, Mrs. Degas," I told her and felt her eyes on me as I walked away.

I went back to the office in time to get
a message from Sandra saying they had
caught the Riverwalk embezzler. Some-
thing about her glee left me depressed and I broke out
another beer, even if it was only three o'clock. I went
downstairs where I found that Lavelle had already been
working on his sherry.

"How's witchcraft?" I asked him, sliding into a
wicker chair under some hanging garlic.

"Bad." He shook his head. "Tourism is off fifty per-
cent. I don't know how I'm going to stay in business." A
small, dark man with a spade-shaped beard and darting
eyes, he talked quickly, as if each sentence had to be
uttered before it was too late. "And do you know the
bastards actually cut the tourism budget this year? I
mean, what else have we got in this state? What else?"

"There's always pre-Columbian artifacts," I said.

"Tougher all the time," he declared. "Used to be

Houston was half the market. Oil money. Now look at 'em. Do you know John Connally's *broke*?"

"Is that where most of the buyers are? Private individuals?"

"A lot of them. But museums are a big market. Or they used to be, before the laws were tightened up. Now there's a reciprocal agreement with Mexico, and with a lot of the other countries down south. So the museums have to be careful that what they're getting is legally in the country. Papers can be forged, of course, but it's a big risk. No, the money's definitely with the private buyers."

"Tell me something. Where do you get the items you sell?" We had never discussed the subject and I knew I was taking a chance.

He gave me a dark look. "You have your secrets, I have mine."

"Oh, come on, David, I'm not going to screw up your action."

"I told you not to call me that. Not here, anyway. The name is Henri."

"Sure. Now about your sources . . ."

He shrugged. "Various. Some tourists, but mainly from some people in the various countries who know what they're doing. Some have diplomatic cover, so there's no problem. Salvador is another good market these days. They don't have any laws down there about export. Now please don't ask me to name names."

"Of course not. But how do you know they aren't selling you fakes?"

He scowled. "How do you know your car has genuine GM parts?"

"I don't know. So how *do* I?"

"Feel. Appearance. Dealing with reputable people. Sometimes, of course, you have to get an appraisal by an expert."

"Where would you go, Tulane?"

"Tulane?" He snorted. "Those bastards won't lift a finger. It's against their *ethics*. I go to Jason Cobbett, the director of the Crescent City Cultural Center."

"The man responsible for the Maya exhibition?"

"That's right. He knows his artifacts, especially ceramics."

"And it's not against his ethics?"

"He's a *museologist,* for Christ's sake, not a damned archaeologist. Don't you know they fight like cats and dogs? Archaeologists accuse the museum folks of being collectors, and museologists accuse the archaeologists of trying to be high priests that hide their knowledge from the public."

The door opened then and a middle-aged woman in designer jeans walked in, accompanied by a man in shades and Bermudas. Lavelle's glance told me to get lost, so I went back upstairs, which was as well, because my phone was ringing.

Somehow, before I even lifted it, I knew it was the Captain.

"Micah!" It was more a bellow than a statement, and I wondered what effect it would have on the fiber optics of the long-distance lines.

"I'm here," I told him.

"It's about damned time. I thought I was going to have to talk to that goddamned thing of yours, that recorder. I'll be damned if I will, too."

I sighed. They were an hour ahead of us in Charleston, so it was almost four, which meant he was well into his third cuba libre.

"Well, I'm here now," I said evenly. After all, he *was* my father. "What's up?"

"I want to know when you're coming home, that's what. I've been reading about that state in the paper. It's all going to hell. I can't for the life of me see why you'd stay."

"Just mean, I guess. How's Mrs. Murphy?"

"She's fine. But don't try to change the subject. She may just be the housekeeper, but she's of the same mind as I am."

"Well . . ." I began, but he cut me off.

"By the way, I saw Arnie Robbins the other day. He's a captain now. Waiting for sea duty. He says you weren't at the class reunion in May."

"That's right. I had some business to take care of here."

"More of that private-eye stuff, eh? Boy, when are you going to grow up and get into something worthwhile? I could get you a vice presidency at B. L. Davis. With your background, education, you could be on the board in five years. They just got a contract from the Navy to—"

"Thanks, but I really don't see myself in that kind of job."

"Well, what about security then? You could head up their security division. I was talking to Bert Davis the other day and—"

"Dad, listen: I don't *want* any strings pulled for me. I have a job. Usually, I enjoy it. Anyway, it's what I do."

I heard a sigh and I knew what he was thinking. First, I'd shocked him by choosing the Marines instead of the Navy upon my graduation from the Academy. His romance was with the big ships, but I never could relate to anything that didn't respond to wind and wave. When I was wounded in combat and prematurely retired from the service, he'd considered it a worse tragedy than I had. He pulled every string to get me the kind of position a disabled war hero deserved. When I rejected his efforts, he was mystified. The truth was that it took me a while to adjust and to realize that a bottle wasn't the solution to my problems. I lost a wife who'd married an able-bodied man, and if her image of me was changed, so was my own. I came through it all right, though, and made a new life. The last thing I needed was to go home where people would make allowances because I'd been wounded and, more important, because I was the Captain's son. I heard him on the other end of the line now, clinking his glass, and I knew he was pouring another drink, probably standing there on the front porch in his immaculate white slacks and blue jacket, staring out at the dunes.

"You know, sometimes I get lonely," he said and it took me by surprise. The idea of the Captain confessing to such tenderness. "It's been thirty years since your mother went. Thirty years last week."

So that was what accounted for the call. I'd been small when my mother died; I only remember brown hair, a soft voice, and a smile that meant nothing could go wrong. Then one day she was gone. I followed him from station to station then, growing up fast, under a succession of nannies. Most of the time he wasn't around, but I got letters describing his various ports of call. I suppose he'd even been a commander at one time, but even then he'd had his own ship, so he was the Captain, always had been and always would be.

"Twenty years," he said. "Twenty years since they piped me ashore. You know we only had seventeen years together, and half that time I was at sea. I thought we'd have all the years after I retired, together here."

There wasn't anything I could say, so I kept silent.

"I was . . ." He cleared his throat. "I was going through some old letters of hers, boy. Written while I was in Japan, during the Korean thing. Telling me when you first crawled, when you walked. She was proud of you. I'd like you to have them sometime."

"Sure," I said. I didn't like his tone of voice. There

was something alien, as if he was afraid to tell me something.

"Dad, are you all right?"

"Me? Fine. I . . . well, it's just some tests, is all. But I'll come through with flying colors."

"Dad, are you telling me you're sick?"

"Hell no. Just getting old. Navy doctors. They killed more people in the war than the Japs. I don't believe a thing they tell me. I'm fine, son. I was just standing here, thinking about . . . things. It's been good hearing your voice. Look, go on back to what you were doing."

"Dad . . ."

"Talk to you soon." The line went dead and I hung up, feeling suddenly cold all over. The Captain not immortal? It was a heresy. He was the kind of man who lived forever, who'd had a destroyer shot out from under him in the Philippine Sea, who'd taken another almost into Haiphong Harbor to pick up a downed airman in '67. Nothing could kill the Captain.

I changed into my jogging clothes and made myself trot up Esplanade to the Beauregard Monument and back. It's five miles, a distance I can usually do in just forty-five minutes, even with my arm bound against my side. Today, though, my energy seemed to be sapped, and I stumbled through the doorway of the voodoo shop feeling like a wet rag. Less tired, I might have been more alert. Instead, I caught a glimpse of a woman's face, disconcerted behind the thick glasses, and when I turned back to Lavelle's showcase, trying to place where I had seen her before, she was gone.

I showered, shaved, dressed, and broke out a beer, chiding myself for exceeding my limit. My mind went unbidden to the old man on his porch overlooking the dunes and confronting his own mortality. I wanted to call, to tell him not to be afraid, but I knew it would sound foolish. He was the Captain, after all.

I went out onto the balcony and took a seat overlooking the broken fountain. It didn't seem to be working, and old Mr. Mamet, the caretaker, was puttering around with a toolbox and some wrenches. I kept trying to sort out my feelings about the Captain. He'd shown more of himself today than I'd ever seen and it frightened me, because it was a tacit admission of mortality on his part. Of course, I was going up at the end of July. My annual visit. Maybe that's why I felt so bad; maybe it was guilt because I hated it so much, the visiting of old faces and places. Now I wondered if I shouldn't go earlier.

By the time night fell I still hadn't made up my mind, so I sat quietly, listening to the distant rhythm of traffic in the world outside. Hours later, despairing of an answer, I went in to bed. I was drifting through a nonsensical dream of Mayan artifacts and Vietcong snipers when the ringing phone woke me. I fought the sense of dread and fumbled for the receiver.

"Hello?"

"Mr. Dunn? Micah Dunn?"

It wasn't the Captain. I knew that at once. But the voice was vaguely familiar.

"Speaking. Who . . . ?"

"Mr. Dunn, this is Gordon Leeds. We talked earlier today. I'm sorry to call you so late, but I have to talk to you. It's urgent."

"Can't it wait till tomorrow?" I asked.

"No. Really. Please. Can I come to your place in half an hour?"

My brain cleared slightly. "How did you find out where I lived? Who gave you my phone number?"

"I'll explain later. Please." The line went dead.

I glanced down at the bedside clock. One-thirty. I swung myself to the edge of the bed.

I fought my way into clothes and staggered out into the sitting room, put on some coffee to wake me up and

slumped into my chair. What could be so damned important that Thorpe's graduate assistant had to see me in the
middle of the night? And who had told him where to find
me? I hadn't given anybody my address.

Then I realized he wouldn't be able to get in. Lavelle's shop was closed at this time of night, and the only
other entrance was the locked pedestrian gate beside the
driveway doors into the courtyard.

I kicked on my shoes and went down the outside
stairway. The plaza was dark and Mr. Mamet had cut off
the floodlights. A car horn sounded somewhere beyond
the walls, but then the world lapsed into silence. I felt
my way along the brick paving toward the gate and
opened it, looking out onto Barracks Street. There was a
rustle in some trash boxes on the curb and then a cat
leapt away into the darkness. I exhaled, leaning back
slightly against the wooden barrier.

Then I saw him, first just a shadow, rounding the corner at Chartres a block away, then merging back into the
blackness of the buildings as if seeking cover. Leeds was
too far away to see him clearly, but the walk gave him
away, almost mincing at times, then hurrying as if he
might miss his appointment. He was on the opposite side
of the street, and I wondered why he had come from the
direction of Canal, instead of parking a block away, on
Esplanade. The Quarter is not known for its congeniality
at night.

As if eager to answer my question, he stepped off the
curb, heading in my direction, and I moved forward to
meet him.

He had only gone a few steps when the darkness lit
up. Tires squealed somewhere behind him and headlights pinioned him in their glare. The motor's roar re-
verberated through the narrow street like an echo
chamber and I glimpsed the car barreling toward him.

All my senses were alert now and I knew this was no mere drunk on his way home in a hurry.

I yelled a warning at the same time I left the curb, but he didn't hear. Like a fool, he stopped to look behind him and for an eternal instant I caught his profile, terror-frozen in the light. Then bone and metal met and my body took over and I jumped back out of the way, slamming against the gate as the car bounced up onto the curb and roared past inches away.

When I got to him he was going fast and I thought for a moment that he didn't recognize me. Then he raised his hand and held something up for me to see: a dark stone, polished smooth. I took it and said his name but by that time he was past hearing. I got up slowly, pocketing the little relic. It was going to be a very long night.

By the time the cops let me go, it was
half past three. I went with them to the
station, gave a statement to a young detective named Castile, and then drove myself home. I'd
told them the truth, that Leeds had called and asked to
meet me. I'd also told them I didn't know why. When
they asked how I'd met him I said that I'd been asked to
look into security for the museum. Had something
turned up missing? No, I said truthfully, there had been
no such problem to my knowledge. They marked it for
the day shift, probable drunk driver, and I figured they'd
have me in again before it was over, because people just
don't get run over on the way to clandestine meetings
without some eyebrows going up. They weren't going to
mount a massive investigation to solve it, though, not
when there was heat from city hall over a tourist who'd
been raped and strangled near one of the projects.

I hadn't said anything to the cops about the little

stone in my pocket, because I'd wanted to examine it in private. When I got back, I poured out some milk and lit my desk lamp. In the light I could see that it was not just a stone; it was a piece of almost unnaturally dark jade, perhaps two inches long by an inch and a half across. Roughly the shape of a hatchet blade, it had one smooth side with a pair of grooves running lengthwise from one end to the other. It was the other side, though, that interested me. It had been worked to show a face with slanting eyes, below which, cut into the smooth surface, was a series of esoteric designs. I had seen writing like that before, in the display cases at the exhibition, and then, again, in the cases at the Middle American Research Institute. They were Mayan glyphs.

I wrapped the little jade in some paper, stuffed it in an envelope, and brought it into the bedroom, where I placed it in the bureau drawer. I slipped under the sheets and closed my eyes. In my dreams all I could see was the look on Gordon Leeds's face as death sped toward him.

It was eight-thirty when I stepped into the hallway of the Middle American Research Institute. Even without the four flights I felt like two miles of streetcar tracks, and when I saw Gregory Thorpe, standing in his office door with a dazed look on his face, I could tell he felt like the other two miles. They'd gotten to him, of course, and the world of police questions and statements was light-years away from the quiet world of tombs and potsherds.

"What are you doing here?" he blurted and then realized he'd said the wrong thing.

"A better question is what was your assistant doing in the street outside my apartment at two o'clock this morning? And how did he find out where I lived?"

There was movement behind Thorpe and Katherine Degas stepped out into the hallway. "I'm afraid I have to take responsibility for that," she said quietly. "Gregory, you aren't very good at dissimulation, you know. You're too much of a scholar." She said it softly, almost as a compliment. "All this mumbo jumbo about an insurance man and everybody started asking what was going on. I took it on myself to try to calm them down because I knew you had your hands full with this business." I gathered from the way she said it that it wasn't the first time she'd undertaken to solve his problems. "I looked up Mr. Dunn's company on his business card. It didn't exist. So, on a hunch, I checked the directory listings for detective agencies."

"And you came up with a match," I said. "Very smart."

"I try. Anyway, I told Astrid you were a detective and that it was about the artifacts that kept popping up in the exhibits. I was almost certain it was one of the museum people, one of Cobbett's employees, and I just wanted to keep our people from going to pieces. They've all put a lot into this, especially Astrid."

"What about Leeds?" I asked, watching her face for a reaction.

"Yes, of course," she said calmly. "Everybody's worked hard. But Astrid's so high-strung she needed calming. Anyway, I guess she must have told Gordon."

Astrid. Of course. Now I remembered the face in Lavelle's shop.

"Well, Katherine, I don't know, I can't say I'm pleased . . ." Thorpe began.

"I'm sorry. I thought it was for the best, but I guess I overstepped myself. In any case, Mr. Dunn, I'm responsible."

Thorpe sputtered and there wasn't anything for me to say, so I changed the subject.

"Can we talk privately in your office, Dr. Thorpe?"

He nodded and Katherine watched us go down the passageway, then closed the door behind us. Thorpe flopped behind a cluttered desk, his eyes wandering from overflowing bookshelf to volumes stacked waist-high on the floor, as if he were just discovering the intense disorder of his surroundings.

"When was the last time you saw Leeds?" I asked quietly.

He frowned as if I had put an abstruse problem to him. "Well, last night, I suppose. At the function."

"Function?"

He waved his hand dismissively. "A party for the Friends of the Center, at the Cobbetts' house. It was a bore, but there's always the chance there'll be some well-heeled donor. Gordon was there, as were the other members of the crew. Come to think of it, he left early."

"What time would that have been?"

"Eleven. My wife and I left just before twelve. Right after Astrid and her fiancé. She wasn't feeling well. He came back after he dropped her off, I understand."

"Her fiancé?"

"Yes. Decent young fellow. Fred Gladney. Something in oil. I think he's taken by the romance of it all. He adores her. Been a good influence. She's totally wrapped up in her studies. Brilliant girl, but you can study too much."

"And your assistant, Mrs. Degas?"

"Katherine? Oh, yes, of course. I'd forgotten. She was there for a while, but she left at about nine o'clock. Something having to do with her son. She's a widow, you know."

"I don't guess your field assistant was there?"

"Artemio Pech? No, he'd feel out of place. I know some of the old ladies would love to stare at him because he's a Maya Indian, but I wouldn't expose him to that."

"Does he speak English?"

"He gets by. He's picked up quite a bit in the field, just being around us, but we generally speak Spanish to him. He's more comfortable with it, or with Mayan. Though none of us speaks that except Astrid. She's made a special point to try to learn some words and grammar. Damned hard language."

I reached into my pocket and felt the little jade object, still wrapped in the paper, then thought better of the idea and took my hand out.

"Did Leeds get along with everybody?" I asked.

"Same question the police asked. And my answer's still the same: In the lab it's easy to get along. In the field, though, with long days, sickness, insects, the constant togetherness, tempers flare. That's only natural, and it's not worth making a lot of. Gordon could be a pain. He was a year ahead of Astrid and so he was the field supervisor, but, between the two of us, she's the better scholar and student. He tended to go for gut feelings. Bad habit. There was friction at times. But I can't imagine it was serious."

"How about Artemio? Did he resent Leeds?"

Thorpe shrugged. "I wouldn't know. I doubt it. He's a Mayan. They're used to taking orders. It takes a lot to get them really riled."

"What happens then?"

"Oh, well." Thorpe gave a choked little laugh. "Then they rise up and kill every white they can get their hands on, like they did in the Caste War of 1847."

"Cheering thought," I said.

Thorpe stared up at me, his eyes bloodshot. "Look here, Mr. Dunn, do you think this is connected to that business with the artifacts?"

"It seems likely," I said. The little jade in my pocket made it seem even more probable, but my instincts told me not to reveal that yet. "It seems odd that there would be two such things happening and they wouldn't be related."

"My thoughts, too." He nodded. "So I've told the

police about the entire affair. I mean, there's really not any way to keep it quiet now, is there? It has to come out."

"Probably."

"It will ruin me, of course," he said bleakly. "I'll never get another cent of research money. I'll lose my students. Maybe even my directorship."

There was an awkward silence and then he removed his glasses and pressed his fingers against his eyes. "If you'll send me your bill, I'll see that it's paid immediately."

"You want me off the case?"

"I'd hardly say you've done me any good, would you? Since employing you, I've had my student killed, and the very thing I feared, a public airing of the whole business, seems inevitable. Since the police are paid by the public to investigate from this point on, I can't see why I should retain your services. I assumed you had come to that conclusion yourself, and were here to present your bill."

"I'm here because somebody was killed outside my place," I said. "It gives me a personal stake. So if you don't mind, I'll keep asking questions. On my own time."

"Whatever," he said and I knew our conversation had come to an end.

I went out down the stairs and into the quadrangle. It was already hot, and with my lack of sleep I was having trouble putting my thoughts together. Astrid Bancroft had had a possible motive to kill Gordon Leeds. But even as I considered it I knew that was the wrong question. The answers to the murder had to do with the artifacts that someone had brought into the exhibition, the artifacts that had no business being there. Perhaps Leeds had found out who was doing it. There were lots of possibilities, and I still was short of data.

I found her in the laboratory, fumbling with some bits of pottery, her face pale. There was a young man with her, fair-haired and handsome, dressed in a business suit. He was talking to her in a low voice and she seemed to be working at the pottery as if she needed to keep her hands busy.

I knocked on the doorframe to announce myself and stepped into the room. "Miss Bancroft? My name is Micah Dunn. I'd like a few minutes, please."

Their heads jerked up and for an instant I saw fear in her eyes. Her mouth half opened, and then the man with her straightened. His good-natured baby face gave him a pleasant appearance. He wore a blazer coat and a Tulane tie pin of the type alumni associations give away for a nominal donation.

"I'm Fred Gladney, Astrid's fiancé. She's had a pretty bad shock, Mr. Dunn. One of her friends has been murdered and the police were just here. Maybe you could come back a little later."

It seemed a reasonable request, but murder is never reasonable.

"I'm sorry. I know about the murder. That's what I need to ask about."

Gladney frowned. "Are you with the police?"

"No."

"Then I don't think it's the time or the place."

"Yes, I'm afraid it is. You see, Miss Bancroft, I recognized you in Lavelle's voodoo shop yesterday. And when you saw me, you left. I'd like to know why."

Gladney's face registered shock and he looked down at the girl. "Astrid, what's he talking about? What voodoo shop?"

"Lavelle's is downstairs from my office. It was really my office you were looking for, wasn't it?" I asked.

"I . . ." The girl's mouth moved but she seemed to have a problem getting her words together. "Katherine

Degas told me you were a private detective. I was worried something was wrong. I was going to ask you to . . ."

"Then why didn't you?"

"I was afraid. I could lose my assistantship."

"Why? Is something wrong? Did you know about something going on here that shouldn't have been?"

She looked from me to Gladney and he gave me an entreating look. "Mr. Dunn, she's upset. Can't this be discussed some other time?"

As if to reinforce his words, she burst into tears and I realized I wouldn't get anything more today. I nodded assent and walked out.

It must have been the lack of sleep, because I passed the white sedan at curbside and it wasn't until I heard the doors open and footsteps behind me on the sidewalk that I turned around.

"Micah Dunn. I thought it was you." The speaker was a short, wiry man in his forties with thinning black hair and a simian face. Like his younger companion, he was dressed in a rumpled suit, and where his coat hung open I could see the badge stuck onto his belt.

"Sal Mancuso," I said. "You mean they gave you this case?"

"Me and Leon here, that's right. You remember Leon."

"Sure." We shook hands and Leon's eyes shifted away from my left side as if that part of my body didn't exist. He still wasn't quite used to it, but I knew his partner would straighten him out. Mancuso would tell him he was too young for Nam, but if he wanted to see our world, the real one, he could come to the kind of meeting where Sal and I had met.

"Well," Mancuso pronounced, "looks like it doesn't matter about the names now."

"Names?"

"The ones you wanted me to run. I did, by the way. All clean. Now, you got anything for us?"

I told him about my meetings with Thorpe the day before and my conversation afterward with Gordon Leeds. "So you know as much as I do, Sal."

"Maybe a little more." He smiled. "After all, we got the resources of the whole bankrupt City of New Orleans at our beck and call."

"Meaning?"

"Meaning just keep your eyes open and read the papers."

"Thanks a lot, Sal." I left them on the sidewalk and walked back to my car. It sounded as if they were on to something, but they weren't about to share it. All I could do now was continue my own investigation.

I drove back uptown to the Cultural Center and found Jason Cobbett in his office. It appeared that the police had not been to see him yet and that made me think they had already decided who was responsible and were about to make an arrest. He was a bluff man of sixty, with a silk shirt, gold watch chain, and a belly that must have made deskwork difficult. He peered down at my PI card through half-moon glasses and then handed it back with a smile.

"Well, what can we do for you, Mr. Dunn? I'm afraid we don't need a security specialist. Our alarm system is excellent."

"I'm sure it is," I said dryly. "But what I'm looking into isn't museum theft. It's murder."

"Murder?" He frowned and then shook his head so that his double chin trembled. "Dear me. No one I know, I hope?"

"Gordon Leeds, Dr. Thorpe's assistant."

"Gordon?" He came up straight in his chair, his jowls giving him a bloodhound look. "Why, this is terrible. When did it happen?"

"Early this morning. He was run down in the Quarter."

"Run down? By a car? Then how do they know it was murder?"

"I saw it. Believe me, it was no accident."

Cobbett rose slowly. He started to close the door, and then turned back to me. "Why haven't the police been here then? Why are they leaving it to a private detective?"

"The police are used to easy solutions. They go for the obvious, and in a couple of days they usually have the guilty person. After that, it becomes unlikely they'll ever find the perpetrator. They aren't stupid. It's just that their resources are stretched thin. I assume that in this case they think they know who did it."

"My Lord." He took a step toward me and when he spoke again it was in an exaggerated whisper. "And you don't agree, is that it, Mr. Dunn?"

"I'd just prefer to cover all bases. It happened outside my apartment. I take that personally."

"And quite rightly so. Please consider me at your disposal. This must not be unavenged. Gordon was a very fine young man, from what I'd seen of him. He took his work very seriously, a commendable quality."

"I understand he was at your house last night, along with Professor and Mrs. Thorpe and some others?"

"That's true. I hope . . ." He frowned again and then smiled. "Of course not. Forgive me for what I was thinking. I know you have to ask these questions. There's absolutely no reason for me to take them personally, is there?"

"Not if you're innocent," I said evenly.

"Innocent?" His eyes bulged slightly and then he broke into a giggle. "For a moment I thought . . . Well, never mind. My house last night. Yes. We had a little function, Adele and I, for the opening of the exhibition.

We wanted to bring Professor Thorpe together with some of the sponsors of the exhibition. Naturally, we invited the members of the field team. There was Gordon, and there was Mrs. Degas, Thorpe's secretary, and that strange young woman, what is her name? Astrid Bancroft, and her young man, Frank something or other . . ."

"Fred."

"Yes, I suppose so. Not an archaeologist. He stayed until two o'clock." Cobbett shook his head disapprovingly. "Then there was Mrs. Porrier, the president of the Friends of the Cultural Center. Old money," he confided in a lowered voice. "And Esther Weingarten, the executor of the Weingarten Foundation; and Marcel Thidobeaux, whose husband is the chairman of First Commercial. And, of course, Jules St. Romaine. His son Claude was supposed to be there, too, but . . . Well, so long as they send their checks." He managed a chuckle. "They were all people who'd supported the exhibit, don't you know? I was trying to get them together with Gregory, but I'm afraid it was pretty much a lost cause."

"Oh?"

"The man is so maladroit *socially*. Stands there like a wooden Indian. I'm sure he's a genius in the field, with his Indians and students, but if you ask me, he'll never last at the Institute."

"I thought he'd been there for some time."

"At the Institute, he has. But only as a professor. He only stepped in as *director* this last year, when the old director got a better offer somewhere else. That was a real loss; a second-generation archaeologist, too." Cobbett leaned toward me. "He was the one who really started the work at Ek Balam. When he left, they should have done a search, gotten someone from the outside. But Gregory was right there and available. A mistake, mark my words."

I remembered Thorpe's question about my arm and I mentally placed him in a salon with a bevy of society matrons. Cobbett was right. If he was expected to woo blue-haired dames, he was the wrong man.

"Was Leeds by himself last night?" I asked.

Cobbett thought for a moment, then nodded. "Matter of fact, he was. In fact, I've never seen him with anyone else. Seemed a rather solitary young man. Intent on his work, I should say."

"How was Leeds last night, at the party? Did you notice anything different about him?"

"Different? Oh, you must be talking about the business with Thorpe. I hope no one's blown that out of proportion. It was nothing, really, just a difference of opinion."

"They had an argument?"

"I'd hardly call it that. It was something about the importance of planctary phenomena to the Mayan priesthood. Thorpe was being dogmatic, claiming the ordinary people had no appreciation of astronomical phenomena and that's what kept the priests in power. Young Leeds was just holding for a more open-minded position. But Gregory wouldn't have any of it. Made some cutting remark about graduate students being the wisest species of creatures. Meant it as a joke, of course, but Leeds just went red in the face and turned away. Come to think of it, he left not long afterward."

"Interesting."

"Oh, come now. Conflict between teachers and students is as old as Socrates. Most students feel they're intolerably oppressed. I wouldn't read anything into it."

"No. But what about museologists?"

His face went blank. "Pardon?"

"Museologists and archaeologists. They fight, too, don't they?"

"Oh, I see someone's been filling your head with some nonsense. That's all ancient history."

"How so?"

"Because, my dear Mr. Dunn, archaeologists started *out* as collectors, and, despite all their pretensions, many still *are*. All the great classical archaeologists—Schliemann, Carter, to mention a few—dealt in artifacts. More recently, archaeologists have tried to distance themselves from that image by passing ethics codes. At the same time, they forget that museologists have been policing themselves as well. Oh, every so often we find the odd curator who buys a black-market item, and when it happens it makes headlines. But we mustn't forget that there are also archaeologists whose discoveries are fabricated. I can assure you that everything was perfectly aboveboard here."

"What about appraisals of smuggled artifacts?"

"Smuggled artifacts?" Cobbett tisked to himself. "Mr. Dunn, someone has badly misinformed you. I do appraisals, of course. But most are of items that have been in this country for twenty, thirty, or fifty years. Figurines brought across the border by somebody's grandfather before there even *were* antiquities laws. We depend on public support and enthusiasm here. I cannot possibly offend people by assuming a judgmental attitude concerning some item that has been in the closet for the past quarter century. Occasionally I am brought something by a diplomat from a Latin country, something that he has brought in via the diplomatic pouch. My assumption in such a case is that if his country has allowed the item to leave, then it is not my office to interfere. But knowingly abet the trade in illegal antiquities? Never."

"I'm glad to hear that," I said. Then I reached into my pocket and brought out the little jade object.

"Maybe, since I'm here, you could take a look at this," I said, unwrapping it.

He stared down and his hand went down to touch it and then pulled back, as if the stone were hot.

"But that's not Mayan," he said. "That's a jade *hacha* from Costa Rica. Mayan influence, certainly, but not Mayan. Where did you get it?"

"A friend gave it to me," I told him. "Is it valuable?"

He screwed up his face. "A hundred dollars. Maybe a little more or less. Probably part of a cache."

"A cache?"

"A group of burial artifacts. It has the form of a hatchet, but it was never intended for use. Purely ceremonial in function. Actually, that one may not be worth quite as much as I suggested, because the edge is broken off. Lowers the value, don't you know?"

I rewrapped the little artifact in its paper cocoon and put it back in my pocket.

"Thank you very much, Mr. Cobbett. I've learned a lot."

"Have you. Well, I'm sorry to hear about young Leeds. But I can hope that the police will find his killer soon."

"I hope so," I said and went on.

This time, standing in the sun outside the museum, what was prickling me was more than perspiration from the heat. It was a sixth sense, born of experience. Something about the way he had drawn back his hand, a tremor that had passed through his voice.

I knew Jason Cobbett was lying. He had seen the jade before.

5

I had a ten-thirty appointment with a man whose warehouse was being pilfered. Nothing exciting, just a routine investigation. I asked him if he was more concerned with prevention or with finding the guilty party. He said the best prevention was to make an example, and besides, he didn't want any thieves working for him. Then he said if I'd bring the culprit in, so he could break his neck, he'd give me a one-day bonus.

I sympathized but said it didn't work that way. When I explained how much it would cost to put a man under cover, he seemed to be having second thoughts about vengeance as well.

"I mean, can't you just place one of those electronic gadgets in one of the boxes?" he asked. "Or use some of that powder?"

"How would I know which box was going to be pilfered?"

He knew I had him there. We talked a little about surveillance cameras and alarms and his eyes kept going to my bad arm. But lots of people did that, and by now I was used to it. It was when he asked me what I thought about the Saints that I knew I wasn't going to get a job from him, at least not today.

I went back to the office, stopping in to ask Lavelle about the jade *hacha*. He looked at it with an expert's eye, turning it over in his hands.

"Cobbett told you right. Chances are this came from a bigger lot. But I haven't seen anything like it lately. There was a Tico named Flores, used to be a consultant to some university program here. He used to bring in the things on a diplomatic passport, but he was recalled about two years ago. He was small-time." Lavelle sneered and handed the object back.

"It couldn't have come from Yucatán, then?"

"It is not likely to have *originated* in Yucatán, because there aren't any jade deposits there. But it could very well have been made to order elsewhere and been *imported* to Yucatán. After all, those are very definitely Mayan glyphs and the face is feline, a frequent Mayan motif."

I thanked him and went up the steps to my office. I fell into my chair, closed my eyes for a few minutes, and then forced myself back to business. There was a message from Sandra on the answering machine that she was taking a couple of days off, followed by a message from the owner of the Riverwalk Express Shoppe congratulating us on the job and asking me to call him about the bill. I had a bad feeling I was about to get stiffed.

Then I played the next message and my stomach went weak. It was a woman's voice, but I recognized it immediately.

"Micah, this is Elaine Murphy. I didn't know whether to call you or not, but I thought I ought to. I had to take the Captain to the hospital. He had a little spell. You know my number if you need to talk. I hope I haven't worried you. Good-bye."

I bit my lip and rummaged through my card file for her number. I found it and dialed but there was no answer. She was probably at the hospital with him, but which hospital?

We had never been close, the Captain and I, and now each of us was missing the intimacy that other fathers and sons had enjoyed. Instead of playing ball, he had sent me postcards from exotic places and color photos of his various ships. I opened my drawer and removed a second album from beneath the one with my yacht collection. It was a long time since I'd opened this one, but now I did, smiling wanly at my name scribbled on the inside cover. How old had I been? Nine years old?

The first postcard was from Crete, some ruins. Mother had taken me to the library so I could read about the discovery of Mycenean civilization and the mysteries of Linear A and B. Under it was a photograph of a Sumner Class destroyer, its bow knifing a stormy sea. It was not his ship, but one just like it, and it was easy for me to visualize the Captain, one hand on the rail, the other holding the camera. A third photo was of him standing before the Parthenon, a lean, fit figure in khakis, ready to fight another battle of Salamis to defeat the evil forces of the East.

The next page was blank and I knew why. That was the year she died. I closed the album and tried to remember what she had looked like but it was hard; something kept blocking her out, as if the memory was too painful. He'd flown home on a Navy transport, and he'd stood there at graveside, rapier-stiff, eyes straight ahead, as if it would be a bad example to betray emotion. I wondered what he was thinking now.

The phone rang out an alarm and I jumped. I

reached slowly out, as if trying to catch a snake, and then I snatched it up and brought it to my ear.

"Yes?"

"Mr. Dunn, this is Katherine Degas, Professor Thorpe's secretary."

I took a deep breath of relief. "Yes, Mrs. Degas?"

"I'm afraid something terrible has happened. I mean, something even worse than before, and I need your help."

I could see her calm but determined face at the other end of the phone, always there, always anticipating a problem. What was it that she had failed to anticipate this time? Before I could answer, she told me.

"Dr. Thorpe has been arrested."

There was a long silence as I tried to digest the news. "The police think *he* murdered Gordon Leeds?"

"It's ridiculous, isn't it? But they have the car and a Lieutenant Mancuso came around with a warrant, so there was nothing we could do. I'm trying to find a lawyer right now, but I thought it best to inform you as well. He wants to talk to you. I know he regrets letting you go this morning."

"It's all right," I said. "Where is he, parish lockup?"

"Yes," she said as if she had tasted something sour. "I'm afraid so."

"I'll go down to see him. But may I make a suggestion?"

"Please do."

"There's an attorney I've worked with. His name is John L. O'Rourke. If you'd like, I'll call him."

"O'Rourke. You mean the old district attorney's son? The protest lawyer?"

"He used to be."

"Well, I suppose . . ."

"Believe me, he's good."

"But excuse me, Mr. Dunn; you're a veteran, a

Naval Academy graduate. Don't you find it difficult to work with someone who evaded the draft?"

"Mrs. Degas," I said, "it was a long time ago."

"Yes, it was. Well, call your Mr. O'Rourke. We'll see what he has to offer."

I'd met John O'Rourke ten years before, after I was dropped by one of the bigger security agencies. It was a bad time in my life, when I was trying to drink my way out of a bad marriage. He'd trusted me with a routine records check and then tried me with an investigation. To my surprise, I found I liked it and in the ensuing decade did a number of jobs for O'Rourke, and, when his own marriage foundered, had been there as he had for me. It seemed strange to be bringing him into a case instead of the other way around, though, and the thought must have crossed his mind as well as my own, for I saw him smile as he unwound his lanky frame from the car he drove only in the most extreme circumstances.

"I hope this is a good one," he said, as we shook hands. "I almost got killed twice coming down here." He took the trolley to work and rode his bike most other places, and if I'd called him a relic of the sixties he would have laughed, because at least he wore business suits these days, even if they seldom fit, and the idealism of twenty years ago had been softened by hard experience.

"How often do you get to defend a professor on a murder rap?" I asked as we walked up the steps and into the parish prison.

"How many times do I get an Agent Orange case—where the victim dies twice?" he joked, alluding to our last case together. I glanced at his long, good-natured face and said nothing; the case had almost got him killed and had been a worse trial for his emotions.

I briefed him as we walked down the hall, past forlorn people waiting on benches and bored deputies carrying papers from one office to the other. The Orleans Parish prison is an old building and the sins that have been confessed in its interrogation rooms would shock a mission priest. The dregs of New Orleans pass through these doors, from sullen, handcuffed robbery suspects from the Desire Project to brawlers from the docks. Even as we walked, an officer was escorting two handcuffed hookers, one white, one black, to the holding cells, and I caught O'Rourke's head giving a little shake.

We came to a green steel door and he turned to me. "So how do you know he didn't do it?"

"Well . . ." I gave a little shrug. "It seems to me he's too inept."

O'Rourke considered for a moment, nodded, and opened the door.

They brought Thorpe into the interrogation room ten minutes later. He was haggard and his hand trembled as he held it out to shake our hands.

"I'm sorry about this morning," he apologized. "I . . . I had no idea . . . I mean that they thought *I* . . ."

"Why do they think so?" I asked quietly.

"My car. They say it was my car. The Buick."

"You didn't notice it this morning? That it had a dent?"

"No. I mean, I live in the University District, on Calhoun. I usually walk to work. The car was in the driveway, as usual. Why would I look at the front end?"

"Where were you last night?" O'Rourke asked.

"At home, of course. I came home after the party and stayed there all night."

"Did you and Leeds get along?" I asked. "I think you had some kind of argument with him at the party last night."

"My God," Thorpe protested, horrified. "I thought you were supposed to be on my side."

"He is," O'Rourke told him, "and so am I, if I'm to

be your lawyer. But these are questions the police
will ask, and the prosecutor will ask, and if it comes to
that, the jury will ask themselves. It's best to anticipate
them."

"I suppose so." He bowed his head. "Never in my
worst nightmares. Arrested." He shook his head help-
lessly. Then an idea seemed to seize him and he looked
up at me through red-filmed eyes. "But you were there!
You saw the whole thing! You can tell them I wasn't
driving the car."

"I wish I could," I told him. "But the trouble is I
couldn't see the driver."

"Oh my God." He bowed his head in his hands.
"This can't really be happening."

O'Rourke and I waited a moment and then I broke
the silence. "Katherine Degas said you wanted me to go
back on the case, is that right?"

"Yes. Anything. I'll pay. Just get me out of this. The
same goes for Mr.—"

"O'Rourke," the lawyer said. "I'm flattered, Dr.
Thorpe, but it isn't quite that simple. I have to decide to
take the case."

Thorpe blinked and I guessed it had never occurred
to him that his case might not be accepted. "Well . . ."

"Tell you what," my friend said smoothly, "why
don't I sit down and we'll talk and at the end of that we'll
decide whether we want to work together or not?"

Thorpe nodded mechanically. "Yes. Of course.
Whatever you think."

I left them and found Mancuso in the crowded office
of the Criminal Division, trying to talk on two phones at
once.

"Is it true Thorpe's car was used?" I asked him. "Is
that what you were talking about this morning when you
were being so cagey?"

"That?" Mancuso smiled, swiveling in his chair.

"That was only part of it. Hey, what you think we run down here, Dunn, some half-ass operation? We do our homework and we got the whole pizza."

"Meaning?"

"Meaning motive, means, and opportunity." He folded his arms, proud of himself.

"Maybe you can spell it out. I don't get going until nightfall."

Mancuso guffawed. He was a good cop, overworked like most, and he was always glad to wrap up a case quickly.

"Okay. First item: Your man Thorpe hated Leeds. Leeds was his student, Leeds had some different ideas, good ideas, I guess, but what the hell do I know about archaeology, right? Anyway, they argued last night about some little technical thing."

"Hardly enough to kill somebody over, from what I heard."

"Course not. Except that it was just one part of a relationship that was headed for a funeral." Mancuso leaned forward, his dark face intent. "Look, that business about the artifacts showing up where they shouldn't. What do you think that was all about?" Before I could reply he answered his own question. "I'll tell you: It was something Leeds concocted to embarrass Thorpe. He knew Thorpe's asshole was so tight he shits once a month. It was his way of getting back. It was a joke, the kind somebody pulls when they haven't got any other way to get at somebody. Christ, man, Thorpe was the *master*. He kept Leeds under his fucking thumb. They all do that to their students, only Thorpe was worse. He was a tyrant and his students hated him. So one of them decided to ruin his reputation. Unfortunately for Leeds, Thorpe figured it out. Bongo. You may have noticed he's a man who takes his shit seriously. Not much sense of humor. Perfect victim for a practical joke. Perfect killer."

"But he says he was at home all last night."

"Sure he does. But his car is smashed up and I'm willing to bet there'll be a perfect match between the paint and the samples taken from Leeds's body."

"What about his wife?"

"What about her? She'd lie anyway, right? I'm more interested in the neighbor who had an upset stomach and was up at one o'clock and heard the side door of Thorpe's house close, then heard the car start up and saw somebody leave."

He smiled, knowing he had scored. "That's the way it goes, bro."

"We'll see," I said and wrote down the neighbor's name. I started out. The two hookers were gone, replaced by a wild-haired figure of indeterminate sex who mumbled unintelligible phrases while two policemen talked as if the prisoner were not there. I went out down the steps into the hot sun and almost collided with Katherine Degas, coming up the steps.

"You've seen him," she said. Perhaps it was her slightly mussed hair, perhaps the slight tremor in her voice, but all at once I caught a glimpse of a vulnerability that had been hidden before.

"Yes. John O'Rourke is with him now."

"Do you think he has a chance?"

I must have shown surprise at the plaintive tone of her voice because she looked away, embarrassed.

"Well, it's too early to say very much," I equivocated. "There's a lot of background work to do. But I think there're some things the police haven't looked at."

I thought of Jason Cobbett's reaction to the jade, but it was premature to say anything about it. "By the way, he mentioned his wife. Where would I find the second Mrs. Thorpe?"

"At the house, I expect," Katherine said with evident contempt. "I expect she's busy having hysterics."

"You sound like you know her pretty well."

"I do. I've known Cora since she was one of his students. She's quite a bit younger than he is, you know. He married her shortly after Roberta died. She's very pretty." She spoke as if it were the best that could be said for the woman.

"And given to hysterics?"

"Histrionics." I could tell she felt she had said enough, so I let her give me the address and left. The faithful secretary, passed over for the younger woman. It was not a new story. But then, neither is murder.

The University District adjoins what
was once the town of Carrollton, a
short train ride upriver from the down-
town Vieux Carré. In time the train gave way to a streetcar, and the town of Lafayette, closer to downtown,
became the Garden District. Rich people live in the
Garden District; the University District, on the other
hand, is home for university employees. There are shade
trees and it has an air of gentility. The homes are convenient to the streetcar line on St. Charles, and to Tulane
and Loyola universities. There is a spacious park across
from Tulane, named for John James Audubon, and the
New Orleans Zoo, once a fetid horror, is recognized as
one of the best in the South.

All in all, a nice place to live, I thought, as I pulled
up in front of the white Victorian two-story on Calhoun.
Like many other of the houses on the block, it dated
from the turn of the century. There was an iron fence in

the front, and azaleas that looked a little beaten down by
the heat. The driveway was on the left and beside it was
another house of the same vintage, this one boasting a
fresh coat of bright-yellow paint and neo-classical pillars.
One of the green-shuttered windows looked out on the
side door of the Thorpe house and I guessed this was the
one through which the neighbor had seen a shadowy figure leave.

Despite the storm clouds already roiling the sky, the
neighbor house had a sprinkler playing across the front
lawn and I had already formed an impression of the
owner as I went up the sidewalk and lifted the big brass
knocker.

The man who opened the door did not disappoint
me. Dressed in a vest and silk tie, Albert Beasley gave
the impression of a man who had just left his brokerage
to come home and issue instructions to the staff. Maybe
sixty-five, he had neatly combed gray hair and black pat-
ents of the kind you hardly see anymore. But most remarkable were his thick lenses, so that I wondered how I
appeared to him as he squinted at me from the dimness
of the house.

"Mr. Beasley?" I asked. "I hope I'm not disturbing
your lunch."

"Lunch? No, sir, it's after two o'clock," he said
courteously. "If I were to eat, I would have eaten two
hours ago. But the fact is that I didn't eat, that I can't
eat. My stomach, you know." He touched his midsection
and smiled. "How may I help you?"

"My name is Micah Dunn. I'm an investigator working for Dr. Thorpe. I'm trying to find out what happened
last night. If you need to verify me, you can call Lieutenant Mancuso, with the police department."

Beasley pursed his thin lips. "Mancuso, Mancuso.
Oh, yes. I remember now. That Italian policeman." He
said it as though it were important to make the point,

lest Mancuso be confused with someone else. "Well, I told him everything I saw. Was there something else?"

From over his shoulder I caught the interior of the house, almost pathologically neat. But something else wafted out with the odor of mothballs, like a hospital smell, and I had to repress a shudder.

"Maybe you'd just tell me again, sir," I asked.

The old man heaved an exaggerated sigh. "Very well. It was just after one o'clock. I know that because my bedside clock said so. My stomach was hurting, and so I rose for some medicine. I put on my robe and went into the kitchen. It looks out on the driveway there."

"Yes, sir."

"I was washing my glass. You can't take anything from the cabinets without washing them. Cockroaches, you know. And the exterminator sprays that stuff all over. I washed the glass and I heard something outside, so I looked out through the window. It was dark, but I saw someone come out, *slip out* is a better expression. They went from the side door to the car and got in. I thought it odd, but not unheard of. I thought perhaps someone was sick. As I was ill myself, I realized there was nothing I could do, so I took my medicine and went to bed. When I awoke this morning, the police were there, examining the car."

"So you didn't hear the car come in last night."

"No. I was asleep."

"And you couldn't see who it was that went out."

"My eyesight, as you may have noticed, is not very good."

At least that was in our favor.

"Do you know the Thorpes very well?"

"We do not socialize, if that is what you mean. I am retired from Myerson, Woodworth, and Hawkins. You may have heard of them. Public accountants."

I indicated I had. They had half the business in the city and were as arrogant as a multinational oil company.

"Professor Thorpe bought this house in 1977, during the Carter inflation, when real estate prices were headed upward. He paid fifty-five thousand, and even in today's depressed market I'm sure he could get a hundred. Where he lived before, I don't know, but I understand he bought the house within months of his marriage." I sensed that he wanted to say more but was hesitant, so I waited, and after a few awkward seconds he spoke again: "She was twenty years his junior, you know. A student." Did I only imagine the disapproving little shake of his head? "A flighty girl. I assume he was taken by her. I must say I've never spoken to her more than a few times. He seems to have somewhat more substance."

"Do they get along?"

"Mr. Dunn, was it? Mr. Dunn, I do not eavesdrop on people, or monitor what goes on in their bedrooms. If you are asking if they have screaming matches in the middle of Calhoun Street, the answer is no. But, for what it may be worth, I find it very difficult to believe that Professor Thorpe killed anyone, as the police evidently maintain."

"Why is that, Mr. Beasley?"

Beasley's lip curled down in disdain. "My God, Mr. Dunn, the man is a university professor. People who teach in universities are incapable of doing *anything*."

I nodded and thanked him. "I hope your stomach is better," I said.

He gave a stiff little bow. "Thank you. But I think that extremely unlikely. You see, I am eaten up with cancer. My physicians refuse to tell me, but I know. I don't expect to have more than a few months. I am spending my remaining days cataloging my possessions and assigning them to my heirs."

I left him to his task and heard the door close behind me. I went next door, through the iron gate and up the steps. There was no car in the driveway and no answer to my ringing and I realized that Cora Thorpe was probably down at the prison by now. But even as I stood there I heard the squeal of tires and a blue Mazda whipped into the driveway and a straw-blond woman got out. She wore designer sunglasses, gold earrings and bracelets. Her clothes were casually elegant and I guessed Thorpe let her run wild in the boutiques. Maybe early thirties, she was slight of build and I imagined that as a coed she had awakened Thorpe's protective instincts as well as his passion.

"Mrs. Thorpe?" I said as she froze on seeing me.

"Are you from the police?" she asked in a little girl's voice.

"No. I'm helping your husband. My name is Micah Dunn. I'm assisting his lawyer."

"His lawyer?" She looked surprised. "Where did he get a lawyer? Is that something Katherine did?"

"Your husband was arrested for murder," I said. "Don't you think he ought to have an attorney?"

She removed her sunglasses and I saw fear in her blue eyes. "I . . . Well, yes, of course. I just thought . . . I thought it was some mistake, that he'd take care of it, explain to them, and they'd let him go."

"It's a little more serious than that," I said. "Somebody used your husband's car in a hit-and-run. Didn't you notice that when you went out this morning?"

She shook her head quickly. "No. I never drive that car, just my Mazda."

"Did you and your husband come straight home from the Cobbetts' party last night?"

"Why, yes, of course. Well, almost." She bit her lip and I saw a fine bead of perspiration on her forehead.

"That is, we stopped at a bar on Magazine for a night-cap. Alfredo's. Sometimes we go there after parties."

"I know the place," I told her.

She nodded. "We used to go there a lot when we were dating. Gregory likes it. He's so sentimental."

"When did you leave there?"

She gave a little shrug. "Quarter to one."

"And you went straight home?"

"Of course. Gregory isn't the kind to stay up partying all night. It's too hard on him, at his age."

"And when you got home you both stayed there all night?"

She looked away. "Yes. Of course."

"The man next door says somebody left at about one o'clock."

A little flicker passed through her face. "That old . . . Well, if it's important, I wasn't feeling good and I asked Gregory to go down to the K&B at Broadway and St. Charles and get me some Alka Seltzer. Neither one of us was thinking clearly. He went about two blocks and then he remembered it was closed at that hour."

She came across the lawn then and up the steps, swinging her hips slightly as she walked. I could imagine the serious archaeology professor, suddenly bereft by the loss of his wife, losing his perspective and falling for her. I could even understand his still being infatuated ten years later.

"Do you want to come in?" she asked, fitting her key in the door. "It will be a while before Gregory gets home. I could fix you some coffee. He always has me buy the specialty kind. Or I could give you something stronger?"

"Mrs. Thorpe, I don't think you understand: Your husband isn't coming home today and probably not to-morrow."

She gave a weak little laugh. "Of course he is. Gregory will straighten things out. And you said there was a lawyer."

I left her, making a note to check Alfredo's in a few hours, when the night bartender was on duty. I went home, arriving just before the rain started, and fixed a quick sandwich with bologna and some of the French bread from last night. Then I nerved myself to call Mrs. Murphy's number, but there was still no answer. I could start with the different hospitals, of course, but I'd feel like a fool if it was a false alarm, and if it were serious they would surely have called by now.

I took a call from a woman who wanted somebody to follow her husband, but after five minutes she stopped making sense and I knew she'd never pay because when it was over with, if he hadn't turned out to be the reincarnation of Bluebeard himself, she'd decide I was part of the conspiracy. I referred her to a competitor who'd done me a bad turn and was grateful to put down the phone. I leaned back in the chair and closed my eyes. I must have dozed because the next thing I remembered was the cold ringing of the phone. I snatched it up, afraid of what I was about to hear, but it was only O'Rourke and I relaxed.

"He's not the most personable client I've ever had," the lawyer said. "But, for what it's worth, I don't think he did it."

"Any special reason?"

"He couldn't tie his shoes without help."

I smiled to myself. Everybody had the same opinion about Gregory Thorpe, but maybe we were shortchanging him. "He managed to secure major funding and run an archaeological project for five years," I said. "That must tell us something."

"No, it doesn't," O'Rourke declared. "You've met Mrs. Degas. I took some time to talk to her afterward.

She's the one who's been running the show. She types his grant applications, keeps his appointments, sees to his customs clearances, handles the logistics, and runs everything with an iron hand. She even went down to help him in the field last season. Not as a field hand, you understand. Just a short two weeks' visit to bring him some equipment, get him to sign some papers, and so on. And she didn't especially get along with young Leeds."

I settled back in my chair. "Are you thinking of putting her on trial instead of Thorpe?" I asked.

"Do you have a better candidate?"

I thought of the blond woman I had left a few hours before, the woman who was so sure her husband could fix anything, and then I thought of the fat museum curator who had so obviously told me a lie.

"I don't know. I think I'll check out Thorpe's movements when he and his wife left the party. His wife says they were at a place called Alfredo's, on Magazine."

"I know the place," O'Rourke said with distaste. "Don't order the muffalettas. Bread's stale and the bologna's third-rate."

I smiled to myself. He had been searching for the perfect muffaletta sandwich as long as I'd known him and a few times he'd come close, but each time his ideal had eluded him. I assured him I would accept his culinary judgment and rang off. Then I forced myself up. The evening bartender would be on by now, and the sooner I talked to him the better. It was already Wednesday and by the weekend he would have forgotten, unless the Thorpes had done something unusual to catch his attention.

I slipped down the stairs and watched Lavelle palm off a shrunken monkey's head as the only remains of a famous Jivaro chief. When the tourist had left I cleared my throat and he jumped.

"You shouldn't *do* that," he accused.

"What was the chief's name?" I asked.

"Look, if it makes them happy, what's it to you?"

"David, you're a real humanitarian."

"I told you about that name . . ."

"I'll stop if you'll answer me a question." His eyes narrowed as if he weren't sure he wanted me to go any further but I left him no choice. "If you wanted to spend a bundle on pre-Columbian artifacts, where would you go in this town?"

His eyes flickered as if he weren't sure if I had a buyer or was asking from some ulterior motive. "I have a few selected items," he said. "If you're being on the up-and-up."

"No, I mean a *serious* buy," I told him. "Say if I wanted to unload a cache of jade *hachas.*"

He sniffed. "There are *hachas* and *hachas.* And I do not appreciate your relegating me to the status of some discount brokerage. However, if you were a man of more means, considerably more means, and of infinitely higher class and breeding, you might go to Oswaldo Ordaz. I say *might.* But he has a certain reputation."

"Mexican?" I asked.

"Cuban. He's also an immigration lawyer. He finds the two professions complementary."

"Where do I find him?"

Lavelle's brows went up. "Find him? What do you think you can do, go knock on his door? The man lives in Pass Christian, Mississippi, for Christ's sake. Commutes over sixty miles each way. And I don't mean he drives it himself. He has a chauffeur. Has offices on the twentieth floor of the Trade Mart. You don't go see him. He sees you."

"Then how do I get him to see me?"

"Somebody puts out the word that you have something to sell or to buy. But not me," he hastened to explain. "I know you, and you have some hidden agenda. I don't want to take the fall for you."

"Is he that heavy?"

"*I've* never dealt with him. I don't like his way of doing business. There're all kinds of nasty rumors."

"Then how can I get in to talk to him?"

"The same way as in all business. Word-of-mouth. Somebody that deals with him, that he trusts. He doesn't take clients right off the street."

Smart man, I thought, and filed it away for future reference.

Outside, the rain had quit and vapor rose up from the sidewalks, turning the air into a steam bath. I rolled up my car window, turned on the cool, and put a tape in the player. I inched my way through the Quarter and across Canal and reached Alfredo's in fifteen minutes. It was a dim little hole-in-the-wall that served a neighborhood crowd and had a television going full blast in the kitchen to keep the cook from getting lonely. It was close enough to suppertime, so I ordered a Michelob and a Reuben sandwich. The bread was dry, but the bartender was talkative. He remembered the Thorpes: a young woman who made his eyes roll and his tongue hang out, and a middle-aged guy with thin hair and a tired look. In fact, it was probably the tired bit that caused the argument. Nobody threw any punches; it was just that when he served them she was mad at him and he looked like he wanted to stick his head back in his shell. The barkeep thought she was giving him hell for wanting to go home when there were other bars they could hit, but he hadn't listened that closely.

I thanked him and left a big tip. Maybe things were starting to fall into place, but I couldn't be sure. I headed back to Tulane, found a university directory in the Student Union, and called Astrid Bancroft. She answered with a tremor in her voice and it didn't get any steadier when I told her who I was.

"I'd like to talk to you, if I might. It may help Professor Thorpe," I explained, taking a chance.

"But I don't know anything," she protested. "I really don't understand."

"I won't take much of your time," I promised.

"Well . . ." She seemed to consider it and then capitulated. "All right." She gave me her address and I told her to expect me in ten minutes.

She lived on Zimpel, in one of the old homes that had been converted into four-plexes for students. The green paint was peeling and the house sagged to one side as if it had given up on life. The lawn needed mowing and I guessed the owner was a slum landlord who would run another generation of students through before the structure toppled completely, and then the plot would be bulldozed, and if he had the bribe money to get the zoning changed, he'd build a doctor's office.

I knocked on the weathered door because I didn't know if the bell would work. When I was beginning to think she'd skipped out on me, the door opened and we were facing each other.

She nodded shyly and invited me in. Her hair was bound by a blue ribbon and she had changed into a long Mexican folk dress and a white frilly blouse, and I realized she possessed a dimension beyond the one I had seen so far in the laboratory.

I took a seat on the ratty sofa and she sat down in a stuffed chair that was probably older than she was.

"What do you want?" she asked.

"I wanted to ask you a few questions about Gordon Leeds," I said. "You were students together. You knew each other fairly well. Was he a hard worker? Did he have boy-girl problems? Was he easy to get along with?"

"We all worked hard," she said. Her brown eyes

darted over to mine and then away. "He was a perfectionist. But we got along. As far as any girls, I don't think he had a girlfriend."

"He must have known something was wrong, or you wouldn't have been so anxious to come talk to me after he told you Thorpe had hired a detective."

"Everything was at stake," she said. "I have a promise to publish my dissertation. Do you know what would happen if it turned out the data couldn't be relied on? All our careers would be ruined."

"And he thought there was something wrong with the data?"

"He never explained. He just said some things weren't where they should be. It scared me and when he told me Dr. Thorpe had hired an investigator, I thought I ought to talk to you. But at the last minute I didn't have the nerve."

"Why didn't you go to Dr. Thorpe?" I asked.

"Gordon didn't trust him. Dr. Thorpe was always putting him down."

"Were you present the other night at the Cobbett home, when Leeds and Thorpe got into an argument?"

She gave a nervous little headshake. "I don't know about any argument. We were all just talking, that's all."

"I see." I could sense her closing up, but I decided to give it one more shot: "Do you know Mrs. Thorpe very well?"

Again the jerky headshake. "No." She looked up at me, her hands clasped in her lap. "Is that all?"

I nodded. "Except for Leeds's address if you have it."

She seemed relieved and wrote it down for me. It was five minutes away, on Cherokee, in one of those blocks that nudge against a black section, the street forming an invisible barrier between social classes.

The house itself was well kept, with whitewashed pillars and freshly painted mailboxes. I went into the hall-way and saw one door that led upstairs, to the top apartment, and one at the end that, according to the Bancroft girl's description, must belong to Leeds. I knocked on the door and then put my ear against the wood, but there was no movement inside. I went back to the mailbox and took out the last few days' deliveries. There was a letter from Harvey Leeds, of Sioux City, Iowa, who by now, immersed in the horror of what had happened, had probably forgotten he had ever written it; there was a circular from a record club; and, finally, there was an ad from the University of Texas Press. I thrust the mail back into the box and as I did so I heard a metallic clink. I reached down and withdrew a key.

There was no police seal on the door to indicate Mancuso considered this a part of his investigation, and it seemed a venial sin to invade the privacy of a dead man. I stuck the key in the door and opened it.

The smell of incense hit me with all its pungence and I had to suppress a sneeze. I closed the door softly and tiptoed across a thick rug I knew no landlord had paid for. The room was meticulously neat and tastefully fur-nished. I leafed through some archaeological journals beside the sofa and then went into the kitchen. The shelves held the usual assortment of pots and pans, and there was a food processor beside the sink. One cabinet held a bottle of Cutty Sark, half gone, and a bottle of Amaretto, with the gift tag still on it, "To G. from K." I opened the refrigerator door and peered in. It needed restocking, and when I smelled the milk it made me gag. I went over to the back door and looked out on the pa-tio. There were a wrought-iron table shaded by a large umbrella and a barbecue pit, but they could have come with the house or been put in by the other tenant. I started for the hallway and stopped. There was creaking from above that indicated the overhead resident was at home.

I slipped into the rear bedroom, which had been converted into a study, and examined the desk. The papers were all neatly stacked, letters separated from academic work. The letters, as I glanced over them, were mainly professional, from other scholars, but one was from an old friend whom Leeds apparently hadn't seen since high school. I opened the drawer and removed a packet of photographs. They showed a group of people against the background of a forest ruin and I recognized a jeans-clad Astrid Bancroft, smiling self-consciously, and the Mayan, Artemio, all gold teeth. I went through the pack, glimpsing Astrid in the laboratory, a Mayan work gang clearing the wall of a building, and one, apparently taken by Astrid, of Leeds himself, pointing to some architectural feature. The rest were shots of Mayan children, grinning at the camera, and village women in their immaculate white huipiles. I put the photos back in the desk, along with the other items I'd removed. I spent another five minutes looking around the study, then moved on to the bath. It is the bathroom that usually tells about people. The medicines they take, their personal hygiene, even their reading material.

I was not surprised to find that the bathroom matched the rest of the house in neatness. There was a candle stump on the top of the commode, in a little ashtray, and the mat had been folded and placed across the side of the tub. The mirror had been wiped recently and the tub had been scrubbed. I went through the medicine cabinet and the shelf over the toilet, but all they revealed was that Leeds was not taking any medications stronger than Tylenol. That much of itself was odd, I thought, because he'd impressed me as a tense man, the kind who might keep a prescription for tranquilizers on hand. But there was nothing, just some Mercurochrome, a small bottle of ipecac syrup, in case of poisoning, and some Band-Aids.

I stared down at the sink and the single tube of toothpaste, and back at the cabinet and it hit me. Of course. What was missing was his toothbrush. Which meant he hadn't spent his last night here.

The bed was made, but from what I'd already seen I knew he'd make his bed every morning anyway. I rummaged in the closet for letters and magazines, anything that might reveal him as a womanizer, or someone with a passion for little children, but there was nothing except an old *American Heritage* and some shoe polish. I went to the dresser. His socks were folded into pairs and his handkerchiefs were divided into two lots, the functional and the decorative. The other drawers were similarly neat and I could imagine the kind of dissertation he would have written, every assertion documented and every reference cited just so. So where was it, this nearly perfect document? It hadn't been in his study, and I doubted he was the kind to leave it in an office he probably shared with two or three other graduate assistants.

I opened the drawer of his bedside table and looked down at a package of condoms. So he was not celibate. But did it mean one woman or several? And was the "K." who'd given him a bottle of liqueur one of them?

I called a friend at the *Picayune* to get the address of the funeral home that was handling the arrangements, then left the apartment, dropping the key back into the mailbox. I drove out to Carrollton and north to Earhart. The establishment was half a mile down and the people in the lobby seemed to belong to a dead woman in another parlor. The one with Leeds's body was empty, but that was probably because it was dinnertime, and I suspected that afterward a few friends would trickle in. My contact at the paper said the body was being shipped home, to Iowa, so tonight would be their last chance. I looked over the signatures in the visitor's book and wrote down the ones I didn't know. Then I went back out into the lengthening dusk. Traffic was still heavy and I was not contemplating the drive home with pleasure. If I'd been more alert I would have seen them coming, but by the time my brain sounded a warning, it was too late. They were behind me, one on either side, and I felt something hard against my back.

"Let's go for a ride," a voice rasped and it didn't take a linguist to know the accent was Cuban.

The car was a white Continental with smoked windows. One man opened the rear door and the other jabbed me in the ribs. I got in.

To my surprise, there was no one in the backseat waiting, but to keep me from getting the idea this was a service of the funeral home, the man with the hard object slipped in next to me and the other one, who looked like Godzilla, got in beside the driver.

"This is nice," I said, "but my car is parked over there. Besides, I'm not a member of the family."

"What?" The one beside me frowned. He was swarthy and squat, with a little too much gut, but he had the gun. He took it from under his coat and rested it on his lap as if to show me in case I had any ideas. It was a Browning Hi-Power, the kind that fires for about a week before you have to reload it.

"You got a big mouth for a one-arm man," he said.

The driver pulled away from the curb and I reminded myself that calm was the best ally I had. Don't let them smell fear, but don't aggravate them, either. "So where are we going?" I asked.

"Empty the pockets," he said, ignoring my question. "Now."

I showed him the contents of my right trousers pocket and then started to reach across my body. He watched me struggle with the left pocket and then grunted in disgust.

"Never mind," he said, patting me down on that side. "Gimme the wallet."

I handed it to him and he gave it to his companion in the front.

"You don't got no gun," he said.

"What do I need a gun for?" I asked. "I'm not the one who goes around kidnapping people."

"Shut up."

I watched the streets of New Orleans pass and wondered at our destination. We were on Broad now, heading for Tulane Avenue and the downtown district. And yet I knew they weren't planning to drop me at my door.

They apparently had lost interest in talking to me and the driver switched on some Latin band music. The two up front started talking to each other in Spanish and my fat companion appeared bored. The gun wavered in his lap as if he had forgotten about it and I considered a grab, but I knew the odds weren't good. And besides, if they'd wanted to kill me they wouldn't have gone about it this way, at the height of the afternoon rush.

Then I saw it in front of us, looming up like a finger against the darkening sky. The Trade Mart Building. Of course.

We swung into the entrance turnaround and I caught a movement of the big front doors. The man who came out was slight and dapper, in a white linen suit with a red silk handkerchief licking out of his pocket like a flame. He had a high forehead, with slicked-down black hair already gray at the temples, and he carried a black attaché case. A younger man hurried to keep up with him, talking as they went, but the man with the attaché case did not seem to be listening. The goon beside me tucked his gun away as if he were about to be caught with his hand in the cash drawer and jumped out to hold the door open and the man in the white suit got in beside me. The fat man's companion was out of the car now, smoothing his coat. The door slammed and the car left the curb, leaving the muscle boys behind. So this was to be a friendly little chat.

"Mr. Ordaz," I said. "Can we give you a lift somewhere?"

He smiled tolerantly and I caught a movement in the corner of my eye. The bodyguards were following in a black Ford.

"So you are Mr. Dunn," he said, offering me his hand.

I shook it. It seemed a good idea.

"Don't tell me," I said. "My reputation precedes me."

"How many one-armed detectives are there?" He shrugged. "Frankly, I have followed your career for some time. Your work in the Agent Orange affair was remarkable. And before that, there was the matter of the state senator and the devil cult." He offered me a cigarette but I declined. "You seem to do better with one arm than most men do with two."

"I do the best I can," I said.

He gave a little chuckle and exhaled a cloud of smoke. "America has been good to me. I came here after the Communists took my country. I fought in the Bay of Pigs, was captured, escaped by cutting a major's throat, and hid out in the sierra for eight months. I stole a boat and sailed to Key West. I supported myself at the University of Miami as a janitor, until I had my law degree." He tapped his cigarette into the ashtray in the door. "Through hard work and attention to detail I have become wealthy, and I have tried to use my good fortune to help others. I assist refugees from oppression through the legal maze of immigration. I have made contributions to the freedom fighters in Nicaragua. My son, by the way, has just graduated from the Air Force Academy. You should appreciate that." He put a friendly hand on my knee and looked me in the eyes. "You fought for your country. You sacrificed for her. You work for yourself and you owe no man outside of your own blood. We have a great deal in common, Mr. Dunn."

"I'll tell you whether I agree with that when you tell me what happens to some Salvadoreño peasant who shows up and can't pay your price."

"No one works for nothing, Mr. Dunn. But I have done my quota of *pro bono* work. However, I can see that it will take far more time than I have to convince you." He removed his hand from my knee and stubbed his cigarette out in the ashtray. "So perhaps I should go straight to business. You have something. I want it. I will be happy to pay you a fair price."

"I don't know what you mean," I said.

Ordaz shook his head sadly. "Of course you do. I am trying to be businesslike, but if you force me I can be more persuasive."

"You can't persuade me if I don't know what it is you want."

He sighed. "The jade *hacha,* Mr. Dunn, as you know perfectly well."

It would do no good to go on pretending. "I don't have it with me," I told him.

"Of course not. If you did, we would be spared this charade. Where is it and how soon can you get it?"

"It's in safekeeping," I said. "And as far as how soon, you haven't established ownership. Considering that it's evidence in a murder investigation, I'm not sure you want to."

"I am not the owner, but I was at one time. The piece was inadvertently sold with some other artifacts, to my great dismay. Now, in order to right the mistake, I would like to buy it back. It is not connected with the death of Mr. Leeds, you have my word on that. I merely want to have the opportunity to repurchase it."

"Why?"

"Because I am an aficionado of things Mayan. Now, as to the jade . . ."

"First tell me about the other artifacts, the ones it got mixed up with."

The Cuban's face took on a pained expression. "That cannot possibly matter to you, Mr. Dunn. It is a matter of business. I am only interested in the jade."

"Why don't you call me after this is all over?"

"Mr. Dunn, you don't seem to understand. I am willing to pay you more than the piece is worth. Failing that, I will take it, and you will end up with nothing but some broken bones."

"I thought you'd get around to that. What's to keep you from killing me once I turn it over?"

"Why should I do that when I'm willing to go to so much trouble to avoid being involved in a murder investigation?"

"A point. Let me think about it."

He nodded. "Certainly. You have twenty-four hours, and then we take it. And I can promise it will be more painful for all of us, but especially for you."

"It was nice meeting you, Mr. Ordaz."

We stopped and I got out. I was only about a block

from my car, but my legs felt suddenly weak. When I reached it, my clothes were stuck to my body, but I knew that the perspiration was only partly the effect of the late-evening heat.

On the way home I pondered what I had learned. Ordaz wanted the jade because it could link him to the murder. The jade, he claimed, had been mixed up accidentally with some other artifacts. What artifacts was he talking about? The ones Thorpe had been finding in his displays? Ordaz had not been the one salting the displays; he had better things to do than try to ruin an archaeologist's reputation. That meant whoever had placed the items in the exhibits had gotten the artifacts from Ordaz, or a middleman. But who had placed them in the displays and why? Leeds, because he didn't like his major professor? If so, the finger pointed at Thorpe as the murderer. But suppose it hadn't been Leeds? The girl, Astrid, had the combination to the alarm system. Might she have held something against Thorpe, and had Thorpe seized on Leeds as the culprit? And what about Katherine Degas? She was in love with Thorpe, or had been. And after his wife had died, she had seen Thorpe marry a younger woman. Scorned women make good murderers. If Astrid was guilty, I might be able to shake something out of her, but I knew better about Katherine Degas.

The best way seemed through the artifacts, by tracing them back to whoever had gotten them, and that led me to Jason Cobbett. He had called Ordaz, of that I had no doubt. He had recognized the jade and let it be known that I had it. He could, I decided, stand a little heat.

I parked and went up the back steps to my apartment, from the courtyard, and opened the patio door. Suddenly my senses went on alert. Someone was inside, waiting for me. I could smell the cigarette smoke. Since I had made no attempt to be silent, they had doubtless heard me by now. My only advantage was that I knew they were here.

Then I told myself to stop being paranoid; nobody who was trying to sneak in would give himself away by smoking.

Except that there were some terribly stupid people in the world. I tiptoed forward, toward the communicating door into the sitting room, and waited for a sound, but there was none. I made my way slowly through the doorway and toward my office.

O'Rourke didn't smoke, and he had no key to my place. I flattened myself against the wall and then, taking a deep breath, ducked through the doorway, fist doubled.

"Bang," Sandra said from my chair, with a tiny .25 pointed at me. "Micah, you got to do better than that."

I swore under my breath and relaxed my hand. "Damn it, Sandy, you could've gotten us both killed."

"No, honey. Just you. I'm the one with the gun, remember?" She slipped the automatic back into her leg holster with a laugh and reached for her cigarette. "I'm sorry, baby, I didn't mean to put a scare into you. I figured you'd be coming up the front way and Papa Doc downstairs would tell you. I didn't think you'd mind I picked your lock. I sure didn't want to wait down there with *him*. I don't like the way he looks at me, know what I mean?"

I managed a weak smile. "Sure."

She yawned and crossed her long legs on my desk. "'Sides, it's payday and I need my check."

"I'll write it out," I said, going to my desk drawer. She watched me, frowning, while I wrote out the sum and accepted her worksheet.

"Micah, something wrong with you?" she asked. "You look like the freeway after the Sugar Bowl."

"Nothing," I lied. "Just a little something I'm looking into right now."

"Something you need some help on?" she asked. "I could put off my trip to the Gulf Coast."

"No, thanks, Sandy," I said, handing her the check. Then a thought struck me. Few people knew she worked for me. The beauty of living upstairs from Lavelle was that people coming to see me might just as easily be going to his shop, downstairs. To any of Ordaz's goons, Sandra was just another black woman, easily lost in a crowd. "Tell me something. Do you have a good safe hiding place if I give you something to hold?"

"How big?" she asked.

I indicated with my hand.

"Sure. What is it you want me to hold?"

I opened my desk drawer and removed the jade. "I have to warn you, it could be dangerous," I said.

"Sho'nuf? Well, dis li'l old colored gal'll hafta be keerful, won't she?"

I handed her the jade and she held it up to the light.

"Hey, this is Mayan, isn't it?"

I smiled. "I didn't know you were an art buff."

"It's called a college course," she said. "What you think I am, one of these nativistic types, doesn't care for anything 'cept African masks?"

"Of course not." I pecked her on the cheek. "Thanks, Sandy."

"Anytime, sweetheart, anytime." She swung her hips at me suggestively, batted her eyes, and I laughed. She patted me on the face, flounced across the room to the door, and was gone.

I locked the door behind her and went back to my desk. There was a message on the answering machine and I played it back. It was Mrs. Murphy, giving me the telephone number of the hospital room. I dialed, half afraid of what I would find. It rang four times and then was answered by the hospital operator.

"Captain Dunn," I managed, my throat dry. "He wasn't in his room."

The operator checked a list and then put me on hold. If it was bad, they probably wouldn't tell me anything on the phone. If . . . The operator came back on. "Are you family, sir?"

"His son."

"I see. Well, he's in X-ray right now."

I thanked her and asked for the name of his doctor. Then I got the number from Directory Assistance and tried the doctor's office, but I got an answering service. I left my name and replaced the phone, defeated.

Don't worry about things you can't control; wasn't that what he'd always said? Good advice, if you can manage. I made myself take out the list of names I had copied from the funeral register. Some I recognized, some were strangers: *Thomas Fedders, Karl Hahn, Astrid Bancroft, Fred Gladney, Alice Farnsworth, Katherine Degas* . . .

I stared down at the Degas woman's name, a little question taking shape in my mind. All along I had assumed she was in love with Thorpe, but stranger things had happened than a middle-aged woman's becoming attached to a younger man.

I was still staring at it when I heard the knocking on the door. "Mr. Dunn? Is anyone there?" It was a man's voice, hesitant and yet vaguely familiar. I got up and went over to open the door.

Fred Gladney grabbed my hand and shook it with both of his. "Mr. Dunn, thank God. I was so scared you weren't here. Do you remember me? Astrid's fiancé?"

"Yes, of course," I said, stepping back. "Come in, Mr. Gladney."

He rushed in, his face pale and his clothes disheveled. He collapsed into my chair, breathing quickly, and I guessed he had been running to get here.

"What's the problem?" I asked, taking a seat on the edge of the desk.

He shook his head agitatedly. "It's Astrid. You went to see her earlier."

"That's right."

"She's scared to death. She called me as soon as you left. She's beside herself."

"Why?"

"She's afraid you're going to accuse *her* of killing Leeds. I told her that was ridiculous, that you were just trying to make sense of what happened, but she was almost hysterical." He raised himself slightly to lean forward. "She's such a high-strung girl, Mr. Dunn. All she can think about is her work, and this has upset her."

"Why should she think I'd accuse her?" I asked.

"I don't know. That's what's so crazy." He jammed his hands down into his coat pockets and then brought them out again. "Oh, hell, I guess I might as well tell you, because you'll find out, anyway."

"Find out what?"

"Astrid—well, she had some problems a few years back, when she was in her second year at college. She was concentrating too hard and she had a breakdown. She had to be hospitalized for a while. Nobody down here knew about it. Nobody *would* have if she hadn't told me. I kept telling her she ought to tell people, that it was an illness, just like heart trouble, but she refused. Now she's scared to death you'll find out and think she was holding out on you. That's why I knew I had to come here and explain, to tell you she isn't the kind to do that, even if we hadn't been together all that night."

I regarded him thoughtfully. "What was the nature of her illness, Mr. Gladney?"

"The diagnosis was schizophrenia," he said, and

then: "But it doesn't matter. It's all over with, done. She's completely cured, don't you see? She's brilliant, the best student they've ever had. Her ideas will revolutionize Mayan archaeology."

"In what way?"

Gladney gave me a rueful smile. "I'm not an expert, of course, but since I've been going with Astrid I've had to study it a little so I could understand what she was doing. What it seems to boil down to is a revision of the calendar correlation."

I waited for him to go on.

"You see," he explained, "there's always been a problem in knowing when the Maya started reckoning time. They had a very accurate calendar, but nobody knows just how it fits in with the European system, because when the Spanish arrived they destroyed as much of the old knowledge as they could get their hands on. Up until now, the best bet has been a correlation that puts the end of the Mayan Classic period at about a thousand years after Christ. But there's always been this other correlation, that says everything ought to be pushed back two hundred sixty years. With radiocarbon dating, most people seem to think the first correlation is correct." He raised his hands, eager to explain. "But that's where Astrid's work comes in. The pottery she's analyzing comes from a sealed deposit between the last of the Classic material and the first of the post-Classic, or later, artifacts. Her analysis of the different types represented shows that it must have taken a long period, maybe two or three hundred years, to evolve the different styles. If that's so, then all the dates for Maya civilization will have to be revised."

"But what about the radiocarbon dates?"

"That's one of the things the public never has understood. Take the first radiocarbon dates for the Maya area: They all had to be thrown out when it turned out they were in error. Astrid says archaeologists always tend to throw out dates that don't fit their preconceived notions. And she says there are so many ways a date can be contaminated, you need a whole array of them to be sure about anything, and even then there's usually a plus or minus factor that could make the whole exercise meaningless."

"I see. You seem to have picked up a lot from her, Mr. Gladney."

"I love her, Mr. Dunn. She's opened a whole new world to me. Before I met Astrid, all I could think about was my business. She's shown me a world I only glimpsed in books. And I love her. I love her and I want to protect her."

"Admirable," I said. "Tell me, what does Professor Thorpe think about her theories?"

"Oh. I see what you're getting at. You mean do they threaten him? No, of course not. He's supported her all along."

"How fortunate."

"Yes." He frowned. "Oh, I see what you mean: If Thorpe didn't agree with her ideas, they could threaten his own theories." Gladney got up slowly. "I can't imagine that happening. He's always been very helpful to her. And he's interested in something entirely different, Mayan astronomy."

"Tell me, is she seeing a psychiatrist these days?"

"No. She hasn't for a few years. But she does have a prescription she takes regularly." He tried to laugh. "But it's really unnecessary. She's normal, as normal as you or me. Please don't make her think it's all going to start again."

"Of course not," I said.

"Can I tell her that then?"

"You can tell her I don't intend to rake up the past for no reason."

He grabbed my hand again and shook it feverishly. "Thank God. I tried to tell her. Thank you, Mr. Dunn."

"But I may want to ask her some more questions."

"Of course. I know she'll be glad to help." He got up and moved to the door, then half-turned. "This business has upset her so much. Do you know what will happen if Dr. Thorpe is convicted? She'll have to find some other major professor, one that may not be as understanding. She told me a story about a student here whose professor left for another school. The next professor insisted the student completely redo his dissertation. The student finally gave up and dropped out. It happens often. There's so much jealousy among the professors."

"Let's hope that doesn't happen," I said and watched him go out.

I looked up Cobbett's number and called to see if he would be in, but his wife told me he had left on a business trip. She thought he would be back sometime Sunday, though if she knew his schedule, she wasn't about to give it. I wondered what kind of business trip would take a busy director away in the middle of an important exhibit, but I didn't wonder much, because it seemed fairly clear. I considered my options. I could watch Gordon Leeds's apartment in the hopes that whoever he was having an affair with would show up. Or I could baby-sit Thorpe's wife and see what the mouse did when the cat was in the pound. Or I could follow Katherine Degas. And there was a fourth option: I could stay home, have a beer, and just let the case happen. That one was very tempting. It would get me in a better frame of mind for a while, anyway. But there was the phone, menacing with its silence; the phone that could ring and tell me what I did not want to hear. And besides, there was a man out there who had given me twenty-four hours and I didn't like ultimatums. So I went over the options again. Maybe it was because I liked her. Maybe it was because

she represented an island of sanity in this whole business. Whatever the reason, I decided on Katherine
Degas.

I got out the telephone directory. *K. Degas, 2515
Prytania*. It could be someone else, but Degas was not a
common name, even in French Louisiana. And it was
near the University, near Thorpe's house, and even, I
thought, reasonably close to Leeds's apartment. So I
would swing by and give it two or three hours. Odds
were it would turn up nothing, but random surveillance
also paid off sometimes in unexpected ways. I remembered a detective sergeant who had staked out the house
of a woman he figured would hide an escaped convict.
The convict never showed but he watched a truck pull up
and unload twenty televisions hijacked from an interstate
shipment. Katherine Degas might be the proper, hard-
headed factotum she appeared, but there might be
more—something that I hadn't seen, that no one had
seen, except perhaps a dead man.

8

The address was another old two-story
dating from the twenties, well kept,
with a lawn that was too narrow and no
place to park. I wedged myself into a curbside space two
houses down and rolled down my windows. It was nearly
seven o'clock, not enough darkness to hide in and yet
not enough light to see very well, either. The air was hot
and wet, and when cars passed on Prytania they made
slick sounds on the sticky tar. I adjusted my seat backward a couple of notches and waited.

Once, outside of Da Nang, we had lain on the edge
of a jungle clearing through the dusk and into the night,
waiting for the VC to come down the trail. It was quiet
in the way only death could be, and when it got to just
that moment between dark and night I began to see
shapes in the gloom. They shifted and crept and ducked
through the foliage like ghosts and I kept blinking to see
if they would go away. I knew the point man saw them as

well, because a stiffness went through him. I took out the night glasses then and focused on the shapes and, strangely, all I saw was forest. I knew then we had been out there too long, but I also knew *one* day was too long, so there was nothing to do but wait it out. When I came home, I found out I had developed a habit of waiting. Some people called it patience. It wasn't. It was more fatalism, as if certain things had to be done and waiting was one of them. But the memory of the shapes in twilight was never very far away.

The shape I saw after the first hour, though, was not my imagination, because it slid into the curb, got out of the old Cutlass, and started up the walk toward the house. It was male, but there was little more I could tell about it. It seemed to belong to the house, because it stuck a key in the front door and disappeared inside.

I slipped out of my car, shutting the door softly, and walked over to the automobile the shadow-figure had just left. It was locked, and I didn't want to take a chance unlocking it with a burglary tool to look at the registration. Far easier just to run the plates. I went back to my own car, wrote the license number on the clipboard pad I kept on the front seat, and settled in to wait some more.

A light had gone on upstairs and I saw two outlines pass before the drawn shades. They seemed to be talking and one was gesturing. Then one of the shadows disappeared and the light went out. A few seconds later the door opened and the same figure I had seen earlier ran toward the Cutlass and got in. The car's lights flashed on and the motor coughed into life. The car nosed out of the parking space and then, in a squeal of rubber, shot off down the narrow street.

I had the plate number, so there was no need to follow, but I wondered what had happened in Katherine Degas's house. I edged my door open and then made myself get out. I crossed the street quickly and started up the sidewalk, not sure I wanted to know what I was about to find. I stopped at the big front door with its brass knocker and told myself I still had time to turn around and walk off.

But I was wrong. I had no time at all. Even as I stood there the door opened and Katherine Degas was looking at me, a tired little smile on her face. "Come in, Mr. Dunn," she said. "It's too muggy to be standing outside. You can watch better from inside the house."

There was no graceful way to back off, so I followed her in. The decor was something I would have associated with a woman ten years younger. It was straight sixties, some Beatles photos, a couple of Pat O'Brien's glasses, and a big *Casablanca* poster. She shut the door behind me and folded her hands in front of her.

"Can I offer you something to drink? I'm sure surveillance is a lonely business."

She was just serious enough that I had to smile. "I'd take some coffee," I said. "But tell me, how did you know I was watching?"

"From the upstairs window," she said. "When Scott left I lifted a corner of the shade to watch him go. I saw you get out."

"Elementary," I said, shaking my head.

She went ahead of me into the kitchen. "Now ask me who Scott is."

"I don't have to. You're going to tell me."

"Yes, I guess I am." She took a half-full coffeepot from the coffee maker and poured out two cups. "Sugar or cream?" she asked, as if this were a purely social occasion. I helped myself and thanked her. She raised her cup halfway to her lips and then reached across her body with her other arm, as if to hold herself together, and I realized she was shaking.

"You'll have to excuse me," she said quietly. "It always takes me a little while to get myself together after one of these go-rounds." I watched her turn away then and realized that, with her back to me, she appeared suddenly slight and vulnerable.

"God," she mumbled, then turned back to face me. "Scott, if you haven't guessed, is my son, Mr. Dunn. He's a sophomore at Tulane, in microbiology. I told him to go somewhere else, even LSU, to get out of the house, but he said Tulane was the better school. And, of course, since I'm a staff member, his tuition was waived."

She took a sip of her coffee, and then put the cup down heavily on the table, as if the effort were too much. "He's never liked Gregory Thorpe."

"Is that what the argument was about?"

She nodded. "I'm afraid so. He thinks I'm—well, that Gregory and I are . . ."

I waited. She shrugged and picked up one of the supper dishes that were still on the table. There was only one set, I noticed, meaning she had eaten alone. She went to the sink and scraped the dish into the disposal, then washed it. "Gregory has never been comfortable around children. He used to always get Gordon to do the tours and talk to the kids." Then she turned around to face me again. "That doesn't mean he's not a good man, though. He is. You have to believe that."

I raised my coffee cup. "Good people sometimes do bad things."

"No. Not Gregory. Not that kind of thing. Believe me. He's a truly good man and it will get him sent to prison."

"Will it? How?"

"Because he's so damned dutiful, so . . ."

"You don't have to explain."

"But somehow I feel like I have to. You see, he wasn't always like this. When Roberta was alive, he was different, energetic, with a sense of humor. When she died, it took so much out of him."

I tried to imagine the dour Thorpe as the life of the party, but it was hard, so I veered away.

"You've had a few knocks, too," I commented.

She smiled. "You mean losing Jim? Yes, it was hard, and Scotty was just a year old."

"What branch was your husband in?"

"Air Force. He was a fighter pilot and one day he just didn't . . ." Her voice choked. "Well, none of that will get Gregory loose."

I decided to put the question: "Do you think his wife did it?"

A stricken look passed over her face. "I never said that. For God's sake, don't let him think I suggested that. He'd never forgive me."

"But you don't like her."

"It's hard. I remember her as a student. She was just another silly little coed, hanging on his words, popping into his office before and after every exam. Mr. Dunn, Gregory is the best Mayan archaeologist in the country, maybe in the world. He can cite every work that's ever been written in his field and he's published enough material to provide reading for a graduate seminar. But he doesn't know very much about people. For years I tried to be a buffer, to shelter him, protect him, even, but there was nothing I could do when *she* came along. She was young, uninhibited, and she had some money of her own. Tulane, in case you didn't know, is a rich kid's school. What could I do? What could anyone do? I just had to stand back and watch."

For a moment I got a glimpse into her soul, with its hurt and chagrin, and then the opening closed and she seemed to master herself again. "Shall we go into the living room?"

I followed and took a seat on the couch. She sat

down at the far end, placing her cup on her knees. "Anyway, Scott was trying to lecture me on getting involved. His idea of taking care of Mama, like the old girl can't handle herself." She gave a hollow little laugh and unconsciously brushed a dark curl out of her eyes. "Like I haven't done pretty damned well all these years. As I reminded him. But I guess he thinks when you reach forty you get senile. He wants me to back off, let Gregory hang. I called him an ingrate, reminded him of all Gregory had done to help us, and that was when he came out with his comment."

"What did he say?"

"It doesn't matter. I'd rather forget this all happened."

She didn't have to tell me, I could imagine: the son standing over the mother, reminding her that Thorpe had never done anything for her except to have his way, and that the first chance he got with a younger woman, he took it. Young people could be especially cruel.

I decided to change the subject. "How did Thorpe get along with his wife?"

"I don't know for certain, but I think it was more one-way than mutual. He's still infatuated with her, but I think she's bored. She's not a woman of particular depth, so far as I can see. But then, I guess I'm prejudiced."

"Is she going out on him, do you know?"

I could see her struggling, but her natural probity won out. "I wouldn't know the answer to that," she said quietly.

I felt guilty then, and so I rose, placing my cup on the coffee table. "Thank you for your time, Mrs. Degas."

She frowned slightly. "Do you have to go?" she asked.

I tried to hide my surprise. "Is there some reason I should stay?"

She shook her head. "No. Unless you just want company like I do. You seem to be doing your best for Gregory. I thought maybe that gave us enough in common to share the rest of a pot of coffee."

I smiled. "You're an interesting woman, Katherine."

"I wish everyone else thought so," she said wryly. "But the truth is I'm not. I'm just single-minded in my own way, like Gregory is in his. It's my curse that what I happen to be single-minded about is totally useless. And it *is* a curse. Scott wants me to leave here, go somewhere else. He's probably right. I know there are other jobs. And yet whenever I think about it I get paralyzed. I remember talking to Gregory about it once after Roberta's death. It was a couple of years after I went to work for him, long before he was director and before he'd ever met Cora. I had an offer from UCLA. They have a fine Latin American program. I could sense things weren't going to work out here, at least not the way I wanted, so I went to him and told him I had another possibility. Do you know what he said?"

I waited.

"He said he'd be sorry to see me go but I ought to do what was best for me and he'd write me a good recommendation." She bit her lip. "I should have left. God, I should have left. It was my last chance." Her tone was bleak and there was nothing for me to say, so I turned to look at the wall posters.

"I have a friend who collects these," I said. "This *Casablanca* one is an original, isn't it?"

She smiled with pleasure. "Yes. Before my marriage I went with a fraternity boy. He and his brothers broke into a movie display once and took out everything they had. I know it was a terrible thing to do."

"I've heard of worse."

"Yes." She got up. "I almost forgot about the coffee."

She started for the back but never made it, because before she got to the door the phone rang.

"Excuse me," she said, lifting it. I watched as her expression turned grave. "Yes," she said. "Thank you. I'll see what can be done." She hung up, shaking her head.

"It's Artemio, the Mayan. That was the police telling me he's been picked up drunk and disorderly down in the Quarter. They want me to come bail him out."

"Would you like me to drive you down?"

She nodded gratefully. "Would you? I'm afraid my mind isn't very well focused right now. I can't even think where I put my keys."

I walked her out to my car and headed for St. Charles. The streetlights were on now, and somewhere blocks away I heard the eerie wail of a siren, like some night thing hunting in the dark.

"It's really getting bad with Artemio," she said. "He's had a lot of difficulty adjusting. There was none of this when he was here last year. This will make the third time."

"Is he by himself? No family?"

"Yes." She broke out a cigarette and lit it. "That's part of it, of course. He was just a poor looter when Gregory took him under his wing."

"Oh?"

"I was being sarcastic. I mean he and some of his friends were looting Ek Balam when Gregory first started going there. It's fairly common in the Mayan villages. The people are poor and the sites are sources of income. The government can't guard but a few. Gregory said the best way to protect the site was to put the looters to work as crew members; let them earn money honestly."

"Isn't that risky?"

"Apparently not. The Maya are very loyal. And Gregory loves everything Mayan. I think he'd do more for his workers than he would for some members of his own family. As a result, they'd die for him. Artemio was one of the better crew members. He worked like a Trojan and showed a real interest in the archaeology itself. You have to understand: The contemporary Maya have almost no real sense of what happened in their history. Most of that was wiped out by the Spanish. All they have are myths that they've combined with recent events, so you get a hodgepodge. Artemio was more intelligent than most; he knows how to read Spanish, and Gregory started to lend him books. At the end of the third field season, Gregory fixed it for him to come up as his laboratory assistant. But I think now that was a mistake."

We crossed Poydras, heading for Canal, but somehow my mind was back with the faces of villagers I had thought I'd known, but never *really* known.

"It's a mistake to take somebody out of his natural milieu," Katherine said. "You show him a whole new world, one he can't ever really be a part of. You let him touch it, taste it, dream it, and when you've finished he isn't satisfied with his world anymore, but he'll never be able to really be a part of the new one. Last year it was all new to Artemio. He was big-eyed and full of wonder at it all. This year he realizes he's not a professor at an American university, like he told everybody in his village he was going to be. Instead, he's just a flunky, at the beck and call of graduate students and secretaries. He doesn't speak enough of the language to feel comfortable, and there's nobody here who speaks *his* language."

"No Spanish speakers?" I asked in surprise.

"I mean Mayan. That's his first language. Spanish is

just the *lingua franca*. Contrary to the popular view, most archaeologists are terrible linguists; it's all most of them can do to speak Spanish."

We turned onto Canal. "Gregory was supposed to counsel him but Gregory isn't very good at handling that kind of situation. I guess it will end up with us having to send him back. He didn't have but a few more months left on the grant, anyway. After that, his work permit expires."

I found a parking place just off Conti and we walked toward Royal, passing a knot of boisterous tourists. The headquarters for Vieux Carré District is on the corner of Conti and Royal, a well-lit building with a grille fence that fits in with the surroundings.

Katherine identified herself and the booking sergeant had her fill out some papers and handed her a plastic bag with the prisoner's effects. Five minutes later a buzzer sounded and a thick metal door opened. A young, jaunty policeman came out with the manacled Mayan in tow.

"Tulane's gonna pay for it, huh?" the desk sergeant asked. He shrugged, as if the University were more foolish than he thought.

"What did he do?" Katherine asked the policeman with Artemio.

"What *didn't* he do?" the policeman answered. "How about putting a barstool through a plate-glass window and trying to gouge the eyes out of the bartender?"

Artemio looked up at her with a pleading expression. "I don't . . . hit him first," he stammered and I flinched from the odor of alcohol.

The policeman removed his handcuffs. "I hope you got a place to keep him, lady. It'll take at least a day for him to sober up."

"I'll see to it," she said crisply, once more the efficient secretary. "Meanwhile, I take it there's no cash bond?"

"No, he's in your custody," the desk sergeant said. "You got my sympathy. The summons you signed has the court date on it."

She thanked them and marched the Indian out. As the door closed behind us she took a deep breath, and then turned on Artemio. "Artemio, you stink, do you hear me? *Tu apestas. Bañate.* Do you understand what I'm saying?"

He nodded with shame. *"Doña Catalina, mil disculpas. Es que . . ."*

"No me dices nada," she said angrily. "Just go home and stay there."

"Your Spanish is good," I commented, watching her shoo the drunken man into the backseat.

"Purely sophomore level," she said. "Though I *have* been to Yucatán a few times, and, of course, Gregory has to entertain Latin American scholars frequently."

I wheeled out into the traffic and Katherine hunted up another cigarette. "I told myself I was going to give up these damned things, but it looks like it isn't going to happen."

I moved my head slightly, glimpsing the backseat from the corner of my eye. The Mayan was staring glumly out of the window. The smell of whiskey was overpowering, so I cranked down the window.

"Thanks," Katherine said.

"Where does he live?"

"He has a little apartment on Burthe. He was staying with a faculty family, but he got impossible this year."

As if in answer, a lugubrious wail rose from the backseat and I twisted around. Artemio was crying, pounding his head against the car window.

"Kalaan in amigo tumen in keban," he moaned in

Mayan. *"El profesor es mi amigo.* My friend . . . in *carcel* . . . because . . . me."

"What's that about?" I asked Katherine.

She shrugged. "Oh, he's blaming himself for everything. He's always sorry afterward."

"Que me lleve Dios por el pecado mío," he sobbed.

"Oh, Christ," Katherine muttered. "Now he wants to die." She turned around in her seat. "Well, if God doesn't get you, I will. *Me oyes?"*

But he didn't hear, because the next sound that emanated from the back of the car was a loud snore.

I found the apartment on one of the narrow one-way streets so characteristic of the Carrollton section. I opened the back door of my Firebird and we wrestled the drunken man across the lawn and down the driveway to the little building behind the house. Katherine fished in the plastic bag for his key and then opened it. We carried him in and hoisted him onto the couch that served as a roll-out bed. It was a spare arrangement, a single room with a stove and refrigerator in an alcove, and a bathroom to one side. There were virtually no furnishings, other than a framed photo of Artemio with Gregory Thorpe at an archaeological site.

"I know what you're thinking," Katherine said, "but believe me, compared to a thatched hut, this is a palace."

I nodded and helped her pull off Artemio's shoes. She threw a spread over him and looked down, shaking her head.

"Well, he won't be going anywhere for a while, so it's safe to leave him."

She closed the door behind us and locked it. I had a funny little feeling in the pit of my stomach but I fought it down. The man was out for the count. Like the lady said, there was nothing more to be done.

I walked Katherine to her door. She
unlocked it, hesitated a moment, and
then turned around to face me.

"You're a very nice man, Micah Dunn. If I asked you
to come in I don't know what would happen. I just know
I might be sorry afterward." She offered me her hand
and I took it.

"You're pretty special yourself," I said. "Not many
people would refuse to speak evil of somebody that had
taken the person they love."

"Just a character flaw," she said wryly. "But I want
one thing understood: If it comes down to it, I'll swear
Gregory was with me all night."

I drove away, thinking about her words. I liked Katherine Degas, but likable people commit murder all the
time.

I decided to pass by Thorpe's house. It was ten
o'clock, early yet. If Cora was playing, she might not be

there. Or she might be there with somebody else. It wouldn't be smart, but then she didn't impress me as a very brainy lady.

I parked across the street and waited. There was a light on in the front room and the blue Mazda was in the drive. There were a couple of cars parked in front and I didn't know if they were visitors to the Thorpe house or belonged to other families on the block. I decided to write down the plate numbers and got out. I had finished the last one when I heard someone clear his throat and looked up.

Mr. Beasley was rocking in the swing on his front porch, watching me. "That one belongs to the Lorios, next door," he called dryly. "And the others are from houses on the other side."

I put away my notebook and went up the sidewalk to his house.

"That's a big help, Mr. Beasley."

"She's been inside all day," Beasley said. He was still dressed in his coat and tie and his face bore a faintly supercilious expression. "She hasn't been out to see him. You'd think she'd at least visit him."

"You'd think," I said. "But maybe she's too upset."

Beasley emitted a little guffaw. "Upset? I hardly think so. All that would upset that young woman would be the inability to take her annual trip to Paris."

As we stood there, the side door opened and I saw a figure emerge and get into the Mazda. An instant later the motor ground into life and the lights flashed on. The car shot backward out of the drive and into the street, halted, and then started toward St. Charles.

"Doubtless gone to visit her husband," Mr. Beasley said.

I left him rocking and started off down the sidewalk for my car.

She had a two-block head start and I saw her turn left

onto St. Charles. I had to wait for three cars to pass before I could make the turn and by that time she was lost in the traffic. I swore under my breath and sped through a yellow light at Broadway. I tried to close the gap, but the car ahead of me was maddeningly slow. Ahead, I saw her turn right onto Carrollton and breathed relief. I didn't know where she was going, but it certainly wasn't to visit her husband. I ran the red light at Carrollton and Claiborne and elicited an angry cacophony of honks. The road was wider now, though, and I managed to gain a few cars. But she was moving quickly and if I got stuck at a traffic signal, I'd lose her. I had an idea she was heading for the expressway, and if I wasn't close enough to keep her in sight I could forget it.

Sure enough, she shot across Washington and swerved right, onto the entrance ramp, and I followed, curving upward. Her taillights were growing smaller and I jammed down my own accelerator as I came onto the expressway, heading north.

She opened it out to seventy-five and I had to increase my own speed to keep up with her, hoping there were no police cars in the area.

We were headed north now, toward Lake Pontchartrain. Traffic was light, but there was enough so that I could hope she hadn't spotted me. Something about the way she was driving made me doubt she was aware of anything except her destination. Just ahead now, the expressway swung left, in the direction of Metairie, the airport, and the swamps. She took the curve and seconds later we were into Jefferson Parish. I hung behind her for two and a half miles and then saw her glide over into the right lane. She was heading for Causeway Boulevard.

I exited after her, and by the time we came to the toll booth, I was two cars behind.

Now I knew: Her destination was the north shore of

the lake, where the rich have their cabins, twenty-four miles from the smog of the city.

I saw the two red dots of her taillights grow small as she pulled away from the booth. I paid and started onto the low bridge after her, forcing myself to hold down my speed. The car between us shielded me from her rearview, but if she held to her speed I would lose her. I debated swinging out and trying to close the distance between us, but it wasn't an attractive thought: If a tire blew, there would be no room to maneuver and the car would ricochet down the lanes like an electron in an atom smasher. I would just have to let her go.

But luck intervened and I saw a red light strobe the darkness ahead as a causeway police car left a turnaround, headed after her. A minute later I passed in the outer lane, and the cop was smiling in the glare of his headlights. Maybe she'd talked him out of a ticket.

I came off the bridge and onto the north shore, where the fresh smell of ozone greeted me from the pines.

Mandeville was quiet and I pulled off at the first street and waited. I flicked a switch under the dash, dousing one of my headlights. Now, instead of two lights behind her, she would see the single lamp of a decrepit heap. If she turned, then in the second we were out of sight of each other I would switch the other headlamp back on. Two cars for the price of one.

Five minutes later she whipped past, seemingly unfazed by her recent brush with the law. She made a right at the second light, heading east onto Florida, and I watched her open out the distance between us.

She went on for five miles, then turned suddenly and I slowed as the crossroads shot up in front of me. I was far from town now, with the pine woods on both sides like a dark tunnel. I wheeled left and saw her red lights blink and then go out. I gunned the engine and watched the needle go to ninety. The road was narrow and there was always the chance of a deer leaping out onto the right-of-way, but I hadn't any choice. As I neared the place I'd last seen her I braked and hoped I wouldn't come up on her stopped on the road in the darkness.

But she was gone, as completely as if she'd vanished into the air. I slowed to a stop and then made a U-turn. I drove back slowly the way I'd come and that was when I saw it: a gravel road to the left, with a thin haze of dust hanging in my headlights.

I flicked off my lights and crawled along, painfully aware of the explosions of gravel under my tires.

A half mile later I came to the gate. I opened my glove compartment, took out my flashlight, and played the beam on it. It was a pair of brick pillars with a cattle guard and a sign that said NO TRESPASSING. A barbed-wire fence led from the pillars into the forest on either side. I thought for a moment, then made a decision. Turning around so that I faced back the way I had come, I left the car at the side of the road and got out.

I started along the gravel, stopping every few seconds to listen for noises, but there were none. I'd gone about five hundred yards when I saw the house. Its windows winked through the trees like a pair of friendly eyes but I knew better. I could see her Mazda now, as well as a white Jaguar. I'd check out the Jag and then see if I could find a crack in one of the windows.

I stowed my flashlight in my guayabera pocket and fished out a small notepad and pen. Then, holding the pad against my chest with the heel of my hand, I pushed the button on the ballpoint and copied the license number. I needn't have done it, because it was a prestige plate, with SAINT on it, which showed somebody had a sense of humor.

The house was a log-cabin affair with a sloping roof. A rock tune drifted out from inside and I heard muffled voices. I edged around to the end, where I was covered by darkness, and tried to get a look through the windows, but the curtains were drawn and the room was dark. I crept to the rear and slipped along the back side of the house, to where a white square of light fell on the grass. There was a concrete deck with some lawn chairs, and I threaded my way among them, flattening myself against the timbers and bending my head to look through the window beside the door.

She was standing in the middle of the room, a cigarette in one hand and a glass in the other. She was talking in a loud voice and now and then I caught words like "responsible," "police," and "prison." Against her pleading I caught a deeper voice, from someone out of sight of the window, and I could tell he was trying to quiet her, but he seemed not to be having much luck. As I watched she took two steps forward, but her gait was unsteady and she dropped the glass onto the floor and I heard a muffled oath. A man came into view then, steadying her and gesturing as if to say that it didn't matter. His back was to me, but I could see that he was tall, well over six feet, and young, with longish, curly blond hair. He was wearing a silk shirt and he had the kind of narrow waist and bulging biceps that went with weight lifters. He was holding her with both hands now, gently shaking her, and he was trying to tell her that everything was all right, but now and then I caught sight of her face, terrified, and I could tell his words weren't having much effect. He turned around then and I thought he had seen me, but I realized he was just fixing her another drink. I watched as he poured in vodka and tonic and then, to my surprise, took out a little vial and dropped in a pill. He stirred and then, satisfied, turned back to her and handed her the glass.

I had only seen him for an instant, but I would remember the face: long, with a pointed chin, and the quick, calculating eyes of a con man. He was bending over her now, the soul of compassion, and I wondered if I should break down the door before she took a sip. Before I made up my mind, however, the decision was taken out of my hands. I heard a twig crackle behind me and started to turn but it was too late. Something hit my head and a Roman candle of colors shot through my vision. I tried to turn but my legs buckled and I fell forward into a tunnel.

When I awoke I was staring into the sun. I moved my head and mortar fire began to explode the ground around me. I held still and the firing subsided. I closed my eyes and tried to remember something, anything. I had been shot and I was lying in a paddy, just as I'd always feared would happen. I was hit and the others had left me for dead. I would lie here forever and be carried in the casualty lists as only a name.

But what name?

I reached for my dog tags but I wasn't wearing them. Then I rolled onto my side and the mortar explosions began anew, only farther away. I tried to shove myself upright with my left arm, but it wouldn't work for some reason.

But my body was otherwise functioning, and that meant I could crawl for the tree line, out of the field of fire.

Except that there wasn't any tree line. And there wasn't any sun. I was in a room and the bright light came from a lamp beside a sofa and a blond woman was stretched out on the sofa, apparently asleep.

I got to my knees and then heaved myself up. The room looked familiar, but I wasn't sure I'd ever been in it before. The woman looked familiar, too, but somehow I didn't think we were lovers.

I reached into my back pocket and brought out my

wallet. I stared down at the driver's license and the PI's license and the Orleans Parish special deputy's commission that allowed me to carry firearms.

And slowly it all drifted back.

I had been looking through the window and somebody had dropped a load of concrete on my head. Then they had dragged me into this room. But why?

I went over to Cora Thorpe and felt her pulse. It was regular and she was snoring. So her male companion had slipped her a barbiturate. But he couldn't have been the one who'd slugged me. Where was he? Had he heard the commotion and left?

I took a deep breath and started around the sofa and stopped. A pair of legs were sticking out and when I went around to the other side I had at least one of my questions answered: He hadn't gone anywhere.

He lay face-up, his arms flung to the side and his silk shirt open to the navel, revealing his muscular chest. It struck me as a pose but I realized it wasn't, because he wasn't breathing. There was a small red hole about two inches below his gold neck chain and the blood around the hole was already clotting. I reached down and fished the wallet out of his pocket. His name was Claude St. Romaine, a name I'd heard somewhere before, and he had an address on the New Orleans side of the lake, near the yacht harbor. He had about every credit card known to the civilized world, as well as a wallet-sized colonel's commission on the governor's staff and a business card from a well-known brokerage firm. I checked his front pockets and found a roll of hundred-dollar bills in a money clip and a vial containing several types of pills. I identified Quaaludes and amphetamines, but there were several other ones that appeared to be homemade.

I put his things back in his pockets and started back around the sofa. As I did, my foot kicked something and I looked down.

It was a .25 Beretta, the kind of pistol ladies carry, not especially deadly unless you're within three feet of your target. Which meant St. Romaine had been shot up close.

My watch said I had been out no more than twenty minutes, so whoever was responsible had had plenty of time to leave. And, I thought, as tires crunched the gravel outside and lights flashed into the room, time to return.

I picked up the pistol, because a .25 was better than a Hail Mary, and backed toward the rear door. But before I got there it opened and somebody told me to drop the gun.

The cavalry had arrived.

By two in the morning we had been
through the routine twice, two St. Tammany sheriff's deputies playing the
good guy and the sadist, and I had already used up my
quota of adrenaline. They were getting irked, because I
had dragged them out of bed, making them go all the
way from Covington to Mandeville in the middle of the
night, and, as they kept reminding me, Claude St. Romaine was from a very well-connected family. I got the
feeling they were hoping somebody would blink long
enough for one of them to sneak in a rabbit punch. They
were probably decent-enough men, but they didn't like
deadbeats and they'd exhausted their patience during the
daylight hours.

So I was especially glad when the interrogation-room
door opened and I saw John O'Rourke behind the uni-
formed sergeant, a pained look on his face.

The detectives left, resigned to the due process of

law, and a sleepy O'Rourke took a seat that until moments before had been occupied by one of my inquisitors.

"Micah, what the hell have you gotten yourself into? You know what it's like to have to take that causeway at two A.M.? Covington's a nice town, but not at this hour."

"Probably about like getting hit in the head with a sandbag," I told him.

He squinted and touched my wound. I flinched.

"Have they taken you to the hospital?"

"Are you kidding?"

He shook his head, tisking to himself. "We've got them there. You're entitled to immediate medical treatment."

"It'll wait. Right now I just want to get the hell out of here."

O'Rourke shook his head sadly. "You really are an optimist. These guys are already measuring you for the chair."

"Is this the same John O'Rourke who once plastered an FBI agent and got away with it?"

"That was different. They were too embarrassed to pursue it. With this, nobody's embarrassed about anything. They have you at the murder scene and the gun was in your hand."

"The residue test won't bear up," I protested. "It'll show I never fired the gun."

"Doubtless," O'Rourke agreed. "But you could die in jail before they get the results. Which, as you know, are not always conclusive."

He rested his chin on his hand and gave me a hounddog look. "What the hell were you doing there, anyway?"

I told him how I'd followed Cora Thorpe and how I

had seen the blond man drugging her drink just before I'd been slugged.

"What does she have to say about it all, by the way?" I asked.

"They pumped her stomach and they're doing an analysis now. She's apparently hysterical and they can't get much besides gibberish out of her. Of course, they'll force-feed her questions and answers and write down what she parrots back, but I think I can have her testimony thrown out if it comes to that. At least I hope so."

"So do I. Who *was* this St. Romaine, anyway?" I asked. "I know the name from someplace."

"You should," O'Rourke commented. "He was the son of Jules St. Romaine, who owns the Velmark Building, about fifty oil wells, and some change. Big supporter of the Cultural Center, by the way."

"Of course. Cobbett told me St. Romaine, Senior, was at the party the night Leeds was killed, but Junior wasn't there."

"Well, Claude was never quite up to his father's hatband size, if you get my meaning. Spent all his time on fast cars and faster women, of whom Cora was undoubtedly one. Kept this vacation cabin over here for his girlfriends. He was known to like nose candy, too, from what I could gather from the few people that were awake at this hour, but nothing was ever proved and the boys over here were happy not to look too hard, since the family owns half the land in the parish. Now his old man is outside yelling for the blood of whoever did it, and the sheriff is looking at a marked decline in his campaign war chest if he doesn't oblige. The way they're trying to make it, Micah, you took a contract from a jealous husband. The proof that he's capable of such is evidenced by the fact that he's in jail for murder himself right now."

"I guess I hit myself on the head," I said.

"No. You and Claude had a fight and he got one in. I know it's improbable—the back of your head and all, and none of it'll stand up in court, but what I'm trying to tell you is that you don't stand a chance with these guys. It'll have to be at the DA's level. As an attorney he'll appreciate the weakness in their case. I hope."

"How cheering."

He yawned. "It's hard to be cheerful about anything at this hour. And besides, my stomach doesn't feel good. That place they touted in the *Picayune*? The muffalettas are awful."

"I have a feeling they're better than what I'm going to get here."

"You want it? I think I still got half of it in the car." He got up. "Anyway, first thing is to get your head looked at. Second is for me to talk to the DA. But not now; he won't be very amenable if I wake him up. Can you hold out for five or six hours?"

"Do I have a choice?"

He smiled grimly. "I'm glad you see it my way." He started out and then turned around. "By the way, I guess you know this introduces complications in the case."

"Tell me."

"No, I mean about my role. If it comes down to you versus Thorpe, I'll have to choose. And if I don't represent him, I may not be able to represent you, because of the privilege between Thorpe and me."

And on that note he left.

They took me to the hospital and a somewhat distant nurse dressed my head. The duty intern looked in my eyes and asked if I was having trouble with my vision. When I said no he gave me two aspirins, signed something, and they took me back to jail.

This time, thankfully, they left me alone and I curled up on the bunk, the only person in the cell. I'd slept in worse places, despite the Lysol smell and the snoring of another prisoner down the corridor, and I had confidence in O'Rourke's ability to spring me, but the thought of the bars and the armed deputy outside was not conducive to rest.

I closed my eyes. I kept seeing Claude St. Romaine turning away from the hysterical Cora and dropping that little pill in her drink. And I kept wondering why. What threat did I represent to either of them? Or was I looking at it the wrong way? Was I just a convenient dupe in a plan to get rid of Cora's boyfriend? If I had not come on the scene, what would have happened? Would the pistol have wound up in *her* hand? What did St. Romaine know that made him dangerous?

And somehow, as I lay staring up at the darkness, I found that I wasn't thinking about St. Romaine at all. I was thinking about a lonely old sailor in a Charleston hospital. Damn it, why hadn't I thought to ask O'Rourke to call him? And what if he found out I was in jail? What would that do to his chances for recovery?

I never got an answer because sometime around dawn I drifted off to sleep and, thankfully, I did not dream.

It was just after ten when the two detectives came again and this time they were disconcertingly cheerful for men who had lost most of a night's sleep. It was only then that I realized they were taking me to be booked. I walked through the procedure in a daze, trying to remind myself that it was just their eagerness and that O'Rourke would straighten them out. But where the hell was he? Did he even know this was happening?

They took me back to my cell and left me after a few questions convinced them I wasn't going to blurt out a confession. I lay down to sleep some more, but it was useless. Tableaux kept rushing through my mind: the half-forgotten lady who had been my mother; the Captain sailing a postcard ship; a rice paddy in Nam, and the eternity a split second after the explosion. At noon they brought me some red beans and rice and shoved another prisoner into the cell with me. He was a young man, perhaps thirty, with neatly cut brown hair, and I thought they were unnecessarily rough.

He sat down on one of the bunks and told me he was in for a petty narcotics violation and his old lady would have his bail inside of two hours. He asked what I was in for and I told him.

He commiserated and said he'd be glad to look up anybody I wanted when he got out; that he hated the chicken-shit cops on this side of the lake, they were all bully boys and fifth-grade dropouts. He said if I'd killed somebody it was probably self-defense anyway, and he waited for me to elaborate.

When I didn't he asked a few more questions about the crime itself, as if it were the most interesting thing he'd ever heard, and when I gave back vague answers he seemed to get frustrated. By one-thirty, when O'Rourke came, I was tired of my new friend and wished his colleagues would put him back in uniform, where he could do more good with a radar gun on I-12.

I started to complain to O'Rourke but when I saw his face I knew better. It was even longer than usual and when he pounded the chair with his fist I knew things hadn't gone well.

"What's wrong?" I asked. "The DA over here doesn't believe in professional courtesy?"

"I wouldn't be joking if I were in your place," he said. "The bastards are adamant. They're talking Murder One with aggravating circumstances. You know what that means in this state."

"I'll watch where I sit down," I said, but it didn't

sound funny even to me. "Look, you know I didn't do it."

"I know it, but I also know there are things you haven't told me. So come clean."

I managed a smile and nodded. "Ever hear of a colleague at the bar named Oswaldo Ordaz?"

O'Rourke scratched his head. "There are eight million lawyers in the naked city. Still, the name rings a bell."

I told him about my experience with the Cuban and the jade artifact.

"Do you believe him about why he wants it?" O'Rourke asked.

"You mean that he wants to stay clear of the murder investigation?" I shrugged. "There may be something to it. But I don't think that's the whole truth. A man who's scared of having his reputation blemished doesn't go around kidnapping people off city streets and threatening them with mayhem. I think the jade has some other value, but what it is I don't know."

We lapsed into silence and I found my eyes wandering to the green walls and then back again to my friend. "Okay, John. Do what you can."

"I will." He slapped my shoulder. "Believe me. But it may take some time. There'll be a preliminary hearing Monday and after that the case will go to the grand jury."

"Since grand juries are mouthpieces for prosecutors, that doesn't sound very good."

"No." He frowned. "If it gets that far, I think you can assume an indictment." He raised his hands expressively. "But, Micah, I can't in a million years see you getting convicted. Even if I have to drop off the case."

"I don't want to find out," I said quietly, getting up.

"Me either." We shook hands. "Is there anybody you want me to call?"

"Yes." I gave him the Captain's room number and the name of the hospital. "Don't tell him where I am. Just tell him I'm out of pocket and I asked you to see how he was. He *may* talk to you."

I watched him leave, resigning myself to the course of events. I had another round with the two detectives, but they were only going through the motions, because by now they knew I wasn't about to break. They even seemed to have forgotten their roles, because the one who'd been the good guy yesterday kept telling me about the last convict they'd executed at Angola and how the news stories never gave the full picture. He let me have a step-by-step account, and though my yawn in the middle of it threw him off his stride, I had to admit to myself he'd scored. Of course O'Rourke would find a way to get me free. He was a good lawyer. He could dredge up precedents that had lain forgotten for a century and he could make juries cry. At least, that's what I told myself. But there had been something in his manner that bothered me, as if he weren't too sure himself.

Fatigue, I told myself. He'd driven across the causeway in the middle of the night and then come back again a few hours later. Besides, I was his friend and it was natural for him to be worried. But still I didn't like it.

I fell back onto my bunk, at first oblivious to my cellmate. But I didn't stay oblivious for long. He started on another tack. This time he told me how he'd been roughed up and showed me a bruise to prove it. I wondered what it had taken for him to allow one of his friends to punch him in the jaw. He let me know that somebody accused of murder could expect a lot worse. It wasn't very subtle, but I had to give them credit for trying.

I lay back and some more tableaux went through my mind. Now I saw O'Rourke, bringing me back ten years ago when I'd been down and out, giving me a chance because he had a gut feeling I'd work out. I drifted to thoughts of Thorpe, in his own cell now. What had he been told about what had happened on this side of the lake? I smiled grimly to myself; maybe he'd been right to dump me in the first place. I couldn't help either one of us in jail.

Then I thought about the fat museologist, Cobbett. He knew more than he was telling, but he'd taken off as soon as things had gotten hot. It was Friday afternoon now, and he had made sure he wouldn't be back until Sunday.

And I thought about Sandy and the little jade object that I'd given her wrapped in a piece of newspaper. I hoped she would stay away an extra few days.

I tossed and turned all night. My companion had given up with his questions. His strategy now was to try to keep me awake. He paced, he hawked, he rattled the bars until the jailer appeared and made a great show of threatening him. I turned on my side to face the wall but it didn't do much good.

I tried to block it all out, the way I had when I was in the hospital, and it helped. I woke up Saturday morning feeling like I'd gotten a solid three hours of sleep.

O'Rourke came at nine-thirty. "I called the hospital. Your father had gone home. They weren't happy at all. I tried his number but the line was always busy."

"I have to get out of here."

I watched his jaw muscles tighten. "Micah, I'm working on it. But it'll take time."

I got up to pace the room, regretting for once that I'd given up cigarettes. "John, I can't do anything in here. The answers are outside. The answers are with that piece of jade. I have to get out where I can find them."

"What can I say except to advise you as your attorney, which won't cut any ice, I know. So I'll advise you as your friend. Let me handle it."

"But you've already told me you'll probably have to drop out because of conflict of interest." I shook my head. "You're a fine lawyer, John. The best there is. That's why I don't plead cases. I only do investigations."

O'Rourke unwound himself from the chair. "Okay, okay."

I thanked him and let them shepherd me back to my cell, a broken man. Even the deputies noticed the change and I thought I caught smirks of satisfaction on their faces when they thought I wasn't looking. My cellmate even perked up.

"Looks like you got some bad news," he said.

I ignored him, crawling onto my bunk and turning my face to the cold wall.

There wasn't much O'Rourke could do. Once he'd been a protest lawyer and had risked disbarment with his anti-war activities. He was taking a big chance now, advising two clients whose cases might well conflict. I knew it wouldn't be fair to put him in a worse position.

I reviewed my options and kept getting the same answer, so I closed my eyes and willed the time to pass. It was a long night.

It was about two when I began to groan from the pain. By the time the guard came I was writhing on my bunk. My cellmate blabbered something about how I'd been complaining of the bump on my head. The jailer got me on my feet and I told him I was okay and then fell down. The jailer called for assistance and a couple of deputies dragged me to a waiting car for the trip to the parish hospital.

They might have handcuffed a man with two good arms, even one suffering from a concussion. But it was the dead of night and I was disoriented, muttering incoherent sentences. They sped me to the hospital and helped me into the emergency room, where I lolled against the wall, my eyes unfocused, while they woke up the duty intern. I told them about my terrible thirst and one of the deputies, who was sixtyish, overweight, and kindly, helped me to the water fountain. Then I said I was nauseated and he guided me around the corner to a snack area with a couple of tables and a door that said TOILET. I mumbled thanks and went into the tiny room and as soon as the door closed I made a retching noise and called for help. He opened the door to assist and found me doubled over the toilet.

"Hey, fellow . . ." he started.

I wheeled, hit him in the gut, and while he was still bent over, grabbed his pistol from his holster and prodded him into the little room. Then I wedged a chair against the door and walked away in the opposite direction from which I'd come.

I only made it because the hospital is
on the highway. I was out the front
door before the nurse in the reception
area realized what had happened. Then I raced across
the front lawn, half in shadow, half in the yellow pools of
the arc lamps, tossing the pistol in the bushes as I ran. If
I got caught, so be it, but I wasn't going to get in a gun-
fight with the law in the process. Across the road, less
than a block away, were the lights of an all-night gro-
cery. An eighteen-wheeler was stopped at the side of the
road, just the other side of the gas pumps.

As I started across the road, headlights approached
from the north. I brought my left arm close in to my side
and made myself slow to a walk. The car flashed its
brights and then passed. I did not look to see if it was a
patrol.

I had been gone a minute, maybe less, and now, on
the other side of the highway, I heard shouts. What if

they had seen me? I wanted to run but restrained myself. Maybe it was my imagination. A few more yards now. The little truck stop was just ahead. Once there, I had a chance.

As I reached the parked truck, a siren blasted the stillness. Fortunately, the cab was unlocked. I didn't have much choice; to stay in town would be fatal. So I hoisted myself up and shut the door just as a flash of red scythed the night and a sheriff's cruiser skidded to a stop at the intersection.

I took a deep breath and reached into the sleeping compartment behind the seat.

It was empty.

I slipped into the berth and lay still. Tires spun on the gravel and I heard voices and shouts. I held my breath as footsteps approached from outside.

Then the cab rocked slightly as someone climbed onto the step and I heard the driver's door open. I shrank back in the bunk, willing myself to disappear, and yet knowing that there was nowhere else to go. Someone outside was yelling directions and I recognized the frenzied voice of my erstwhile benefactor, the fat deputy. Lights flashed inside the cab and my skin went cold as I waited for a hand to poke a flashlight into my face.

Instead, the door slammed and I heard keys jingle. The diesel whined into life and I let out my breath, very slowly.

"Good luck," the driver called. Then the rig jolted into movement and I felt us crawling out onto the highway. A radio started playing country music, but the driver switched it off and turned on his CB. He had the police band, because I began to hear calls for assistance in establishing a perimeter of one mile from the hospital on all sides. There was a brief flare and then the strong smell of tobacco smoke drifted back. It burned my lungs and at the same time made me wish that I could join him.

Where was he going? I wondered. He was headed for the interstate, but from there he could go either of two ways, west to Baton Rouge or east toward the Gulf Coast. Or he might head up to Jackson after a few miles, or even back to New Orleans, via the Pass Manchac cut-off.

At this point it really didn't matter. The police seldom put roadblocks on the interstate; it was too dangerous. My best chance was to relax until I got a sense of our direction and make plans from there.

We went into a slow gyre and I had the sense we were headed west. If it was an all-night run, that meant he might not stop until Lafayette or even Lake Charles for coffee. I'd have to slip out then, but without any money it would be hard to find a telephone. I took some deep breaths and reminded myself that whatever happened, it was a damned sight better than staying in the St. Tammany Parish jail.

The driver started to whistle under his breath. After a while he tired of the police band and switched back to the CB. Somebody named Crawdad One asked what traffic was like between Hammond and Bogalusa. Hot Pants Mama answered that it was A-okay, except for some Smokey activity around Covington. A third voice asked for a White Sox ball score and somebody barreling down from Jackson laughed at him and said they were lucky they weren't in an eight-team division. The chatter died out and the driver started singing, this time, disconcertingly, the "Folsom Prison Blues." He was no Johnny Cash, and I thought that every time he wailed that he was "stuck in Folsom Prison," his voice gained a few decibels.

What would he say if he knew an escaped prisoner was only a foot away from his back?

When he finished the "Blues" he went on to an old Kingston Trio tune about a man on the run in the Everglades. I gritted my teeth. We were headed over swamp now, where murderers frequently dumped their victims, and the parallel was too exact for comfort. The hum of the big diesel moved up a half octave and I had the sense that he was opening it out.

"Sheriff Johnstone, why don't you leave me alone?" he sang, and I shut my eyes.

It seemed like forever, but later I figured it could only have been an hour when the rig started to slow down. We were coming to a city and, from the distance, it had to be Baton Rouge. We made a slow arc and I realized we were bypassing the city, and when we started upward I knew we were on the bridge, headed west to Lafayette. We went for a little way and then I felt us edge over into the right lane and the brakes squealed and moaned as we began to decelerate. We were on some sort of exit ramp, and I wondered where the driver was headed. Once, during the trip, I'd smelled hot coffee and realized he was drinking from a thermos. Well, coffee did that to you, so maybe it was a rest stop.

He pulled off the road then and I heard the brakes hiss. The big rig shuddered to a halt and for a few seconds all was silent.

Then the driver brought out the thermos, because I smelled the coffee again. "How about some java?" he asked.

I didn't answer immediately and I heard the seat squeak as he turned around. The curtain moved and he thrust the thermos cup back at me. "Might wake you up some," he said. "But if you don't want it, I'll finish it."

I sighed and accepted the cup, my brain racing through my options. He was a big man with a round face, and from the lights in the parking area I could make out a thin stubble on his chin.

"How did you know I was back here?" I asked.

He shrugged. "Saw you get in. I started to yell at you, but then the Smokeys came running up, asked did I see a one-arm guy, just busted out of the hospital. They was running around like pissants in a shit pile, and I figured anybody who'd pulled one on them couldn't be all bad. Besides, I owe the bastards."

I didn't ask him what he owed, just thanked my stars he had been there when he had. "How did you know I wasn't armed?" I asked.

"Armed?" he guffawed. "That's just it. You *was* armed. *One*-armed. That's what I loved. Here was all these assholes running around like crazy, couldn't even hold on to a man with one arm! I figured you was somebody I had to meet."

"The pleasure's mine," I said fervently. "But you don't need to get involved in my trouble."

"Who's involved? I'm just giving you a lift. How far you want to go?"

"Back to New Orleans," I said.

He squinted at me like maybe he'd been wrong and the cops should have held on to me.

"Podnuh, she ain't worth it, I'll guarantee."

"Maybe, maybe not. I have to go back," I said.

"Your decision. How you aim to do it?"

"I don't know. Maybe you could lend me a quarter. There might be somebody I can call."

He screwed up his face and then opened the cab door. "Stay here. I'll see what good I can do you inside."

He stepped down, the door slammed, and I watched him walk across the parking lot to the coffee shop behind the gas pumps. There were some other rigs in the lot, and some cars. It was almost five o'clock and the sky was already growing lighter. A man with a useless arm would be a giveaway in daylight, so I hoped my unexpected benefactor was having some luck. Then a darker thought seized me: What if he was calling the law right now? What if his little speech had been a clever put-on and he was setting me up? As if in answer, a white state police cruiser emerged from the fog and pulled to a halt beside the building. I went cold all over. The trooper got out and went in. I had a sudden urge to open the door, get out, run. The fog would hide me for a little while. I could head into the cane fields, throw myself flat against the mud.

I put my hand on the door handle and then halted. What if I was wrong? My odds in the cane fields were nil. If the trucker proved out . . . The door opened and he came out, followed by the policeman. It was too late. I had lost the opportunity. Now there was nowhere to go.

Then, as I watched, the policeman laughed and started back for his car, a Styrofoam cup in his hand. The trucker waved and then hitched his pants. He sauntered back toward the cab, in no particular hurry, and then turned to watch the cruiser leave.

He hoisted himself up and pulled the door open. "Had to wait till the Smokey left," he drawled. "Anyway, I think I got you took care of. Fellow inside I know pretty good, name is Red. He's headed for New Orleans with a load of furniture. I told him you was okay, needed a lift. He'll be out in a minute."

"I appreciate it," I said.

He waved away my thanks. "Do the same for me someday. Here." He handed me a pair of bills and chuckled under his breath. "It was worth every cent to see what you done to them fuckers."

Five minutes later a tall scarecrow figure came out and spit onto the pavement. My friend nodded and I wiggled my way into the passenger seat. We shook hands and then I opened the door and swung down.

The tall man waited, digging into a bag of Levi Garrett. I guessed my benefactor had not said anything about my being wanted and I decided not to raise the issue.

"Where you going?" the new driver asked dolefully, popping a wad into his mouth. "I'm heading down 61. I can let you out in Kenner or Metairie, at the motel."

"Metairie's fine," I said.

He nodded and gave his wad a few test chews. He seemed satisfied with the taste and spat. "Okay. Let's go."

It was already light enough to see figures, but the river fog kept visibility to ten yards. I climbed into the seat beside him and fastened my safety belt. He gave me a fish eye, as if I had betrayed my true colors, and started the engine.

After ten miles it seemed clear that he did not want to talk, so I shut my eyes and let my mind wander in and out of dreams. I was on a plane, dropping through the clouds, and I did not want it to land, because when it did I would be back in the suffocating hell of combat. Somehow I knew that if the clouds ever parted, the green world below would be the last world I would ever see. I awoke sweating and saw a sign that said LaPlace.

Twenty-five miles.

It was six-thirty when we passed the airport and the fog was still heavy, like cold smoke, licking over everything. We came to the first in the interminable series of traffic signals and once I looked out the window and saw a Kenner police car, but to the driver I was just another trucker, and he didn't give me more than a second's glance. Ten minutes later we eased off the road at a trucker's motel, and my companion jerked on the emergency brake.

"All right," he said.

I thanked him and he allowed me to shake his hand. Then I took a deep breath and descended into the gray morning.

There was a phone booth at the side of
the building but I realized I didn't have
any change. I looked down at the
money the first trucker had given me. Two fives. I would
have to go inside to get one changed. I didn't like it,
because by now my description was probably on all the
radios, and the desk clerk would have been up all night,
listening, but there was little I could do. I reached over
and placed my left hand in my pocket. Then I walked
into the office.

It was dingy and there were some old *Motor Trend*
magazines on a battered table beside the desk. The clerk
was busy with my driver and I thumbed the magazines
until they were finished. When the clerk turned to me I
handed him a bill and pointed to the cigarette machine
outside. He handed me the change without another look
and I left.

Sandy was out of town and I couldn't involve

O'Rourke without risking his law license. There were two or three ex-girlfriends, but I couldn't be sure they'd be alone or even at the same numbers. Only one name came to mind and I knew it spelled a calculated risk. I raised the phone book and found *Degas, K.*

She might refuse to help. She might even call the police. But I had a gut feeling she could be trusted. I put in my quarter and dialed.

It was the third ring when she answered and her voice was logy with sleep. "Hello?"

"Katherine? This is Micah Dunn. I need your help."

"Micah?" Her voice became instantly awake. "What's happening? I heard on the news they'd arrested you. What happened?"

"We had a parting of the ways," I said. "I'll explain later. Right now I need you to pick me up and bring me to your place."

"Micah, did you escape from jail?"

"It's better for you not to ask questions. Please, Katherine: I need your help."

"Where are you? I'll be there as soon as I get dressed."

I gave her the location and hung up the phone, hoping I'd made the right decision. But in reality I didn't have many choices.

I slipped back into the shadows, as pale streamers of dawn streaked the eastern sky.

My God, what if her son was with her? Wasn't he staying in the house? I hadn't even thought of it, but if it was so . . .

Surely she would have said something.

A police car came slowly down the highway and stopped at the traffic signal twenty yards away. I stifled my urge to head for the shadows, turning back to the phone booth and pretending I was making a call. Thirty seconds later the light changed and the cruiser started off again. It was six o'clock and the night shift was thinking only of getting home to bed.

It seemed like forever and I was beginning to wonder if she'd changed her mind. But then the brown Toyota made a left turn at the light and nosed into the parking lot. She saw me and reached over to open the door.

"You look like death warmed over," she said. "What did they do to you?"

"Chinese water torture," I cracked. "Look, Katherine, I really appreciate this."

"It's okay. But what happened in Covington? It said on the news they were holding you for killing some rich man." Her face darkened. "It also said Gregory's wife was there."

I recounted what had happened and she shook her head, speeding up to pass a slow cab.

"It gets stranger and stranger."

We came to Carrollton and turned right. The city was waking up now, a few people coming and going on the street, and a scatter of cars hurrying people to early jobs.

"So what's the game plan?" she asked. "Or is there one?"

"The game plan is sleep," I said. "I need to get my brain into thinking shape and right now I'm about to pass out. By the way, is your son . . . ?"

"Scott has his own apartment, thank God. He only comes around to raise hell with me for not being wiser in my old age."

"I hope your neighbors won't be awake," I said, fighting the dreams that kept wanting to carry me away. "I'd hate to ruin your reputation."

"Oh, don't worry about that," she said. "It's about time I did *something* to shatter that image."

She parked in front and a quick glance did not reveal anyone else on the street. I hurried up the walk after her and stumbled in gratefully, glad to hear the big front door close behind me.

I collapsed onto the sofa. "I have to warn you that you may be charged with harboring a felon," I said but didn't hear her reply because I was already asleep.

When I awoke I was in a strange room and the covers were over me. I stared at the ceiling and tried to make sense of the chandelier-type light fixture. I was not in prison, I was not in my own apartment, and I certainly was not where I had fallen asleep.

I turned on my side and saw a small framed photograph. The military officer in it looked familiar, but it wasn't me. Beside it was a clock, its red digits burning in the darkness: 2:00 P.M. I threw off the covers and sat up. Someone had removed my shoes and unbuttoned my shirt. The sheets smelled of perfume, but I smelled of sweat and dirt.

Stepping over to the window, I peered through the blinds. It was a bright June day, and as I watched, a car passed along Prytania, headed uptown.

I let the blind drop and went to the door. A folk ballad from the sixties floated up from below. I went out onto the landing and looked down. There was no one in sight, and no sound of voices other than the record, which I could see rotating on the turntable.

I tiptoed down the stairs and was halfway to the bottom when a key turned in the front door and the door opened.

Katherine smiled faintly, removing her sunglasses and stooping to put a heavy brown paper bag on the floor. "Well. I thought I could slip out for a few groceries, but I can see I'm wrong." She picked up the sack and started into the kitchen with it. I followed. "So how are you feeling?"

"Better," I said. "At least I think so. How did you get me upstairs?"

"I wrestled you. You woke up—halfway." She put the sack on the table. "I was down to see Gregory this morning. He's in a bad way. This business about his wife has almost killed him. He wants to confess to keep his wife clear, but I talked him out of it, with the help of Mr. O'Rourke. We told him that if *you* hadn't killed this man, and he *couldn't* have, because he was in jail, then it was pretty clear the real murderer had done it." She turned and faced me squarely. "Micah, we've got to clear you so you can find out who really did it."

"So Gregory can get loose."

"Of course."

"I'll do my very best. Right now, though, I'd give a lot for a bath and some clean clothes."

"No problem. The bathroom is upstairs and there are some towels on the rack. I've put some of Scott's old clothes at the foot of the bed. You're about the same size."

I thanked her and went up to get clean. It was afternoon, I was rested, and I had found a safe house, not a bad accomplishment with the police forces of half the state looking for me. But I still could not come up with any course of action. I could try to confront Ordaz, but he was too well guarded, and I still might not get anywhere. I *couldn't* go anywhere near Thorpe's wife yet.

That left only Cobbett. It was time to apply the pressure.

But Cobbett would be out of town until tomorrow, and there had to be something I could do today. I had the feeling that the girl, Astrid Bancroft, knew more than she was telling, even if she didn't realize it, but under the protective eye of her boyfriend she was as hard to get to as Ordaz. And I had no illusions about either of them not tipping the police if I showed up.

Leeds. I had to find his girlfriend, if he had one. I had to find whomever he had trusted, whoever might know about the jade.

All I could think to do was go back to his apartment. There must be something I had overlooked, something that would give me a name, an address, a photograph.

Of course I would have to wait until dark.

Katherine threw on some steaks for supper, explaining that she could do better but I needed a solid meal. She opened a bottle of Cabernet Sauvignon and told me I could have two glasses, no more, because I would need to keep my wits about me. Then she defrosted a frozen cheesecake in the microwave and gave me a piece, for the sugar content, she said.

"What will you look for?" she asked.

"I honestly don't know. But I think it was Leeds who was planting the artifacts and I think there's a good chance he told somebody about it. He must have had *somebody.*"

She nodded. "One would think so. He was a very handsome young man."

Suddenly I remembered the bottle in his cupboard, with the card reading "from K." I gave Katherine a sideways glance. Was it possible?

"But you never saw him with anybody."

"Not that I recall, unless it was with people working on the project. I often wondered why he and Astrid didn't strike up a match. You know, things like that happen in the field all the time: man and woman, isolated, natural urges. But she seems to have been in her own little world until Gladney came along. *He* certainly found her love spot."

We both broke out laughing at her sudden bawdiness

and I thought it was a pity she had decided to waste her life on the likes of Gregory Thorpe.

My thoughts were interrupted by a banging on the door. I jumped to my feet but Katherine put a hand on my arm. "That's Scott. He never uses the bell and he's always losing his key. Go upstairs and wait. I'll see what he wants, though I suspect I know. The automatic-teller card is the worst invention since Saturday-morning cartoons."

I went up the steps and heard the door open below me. Katherine's voice said something I couldn't understand and then I heard Scott's bass, but the words were inaudible. They moved out of the living room and I guessed he was going to raid the refrigerator. I turned toward the window, then saw the framed photo on the bedside table. As I picked it up, I suddenly knew why the man in uniform looked familiar. Though thirty years younger than Gregory Thorpe, his face nevertheless bore a strong likeness to the scholar's. The man in thc photograph was Katherine's husband. She had lost him and then ended up working with a man who resembled him.

It was a cruel trick for fate to play, I thought, setting down the photo and turning back to the doorway.

The voices from downstairs were louder now. They seemed to be having an argument. I caught a few curse words from Scott and fought the urge to go down and slap him for his insolence. Then, as I watched, he strode out of the kitchen and through the living room to the front door. Its slam shook the house and a few seconds later Katherine came out of the kitchen, her face pale and her hands clenched in front of her.

I came out onto the landing. "What is it?" I asked.

She shook her head. "No . . . nothing. Just the usual give-and-take between stodgy old mother and sage twenty-year-old."

I went down the steps and took her arm, guiding her to the couch. "It was more than that, wasn't it?"

She nodded. "He was harping on the business with Gregory again. He's convinced I've been having an affair with him." She smiled wistfully. "I have to admit I would've if Gregory had ever looked at me as a woman. Anyway, Scott wants me to drop Gregory. He says he's an Ivy League nerd who's never done any work in his life." She shook her head. "Ever since last summer, when Scott went down to work offshore, he's been the world-weary workingman." She shook her head quickly, as if she wanted to rid herself of a bad memory. "Well, that's my problem. It doesn't have anything to do with you." I watched as she underwent the transformation from vulnerable mother to capable, determined defender of the man she loved. She went to the desk in the corner and took out a flashlight. "You'll need this," she said, handing it to me. "And if you're caught, the secretary will disavow all knowledge."

I smiled and she dangled her car keys in front of me. "Here. What does an old fogy like me want with these on a Saturday night?"

I reached for them and then my hand closed over hers. We looked into each other's eyes and then she dropped her gaze and I released her hand.

"Good luck," she told me.

It was just dark enough to blur faces. I wedged myself behind the wheel of the Toyota and reminded myself I'd have to shift as well as steer with my good hand, hardly an ideal situation. I edged out into the street and flicked on the lights. Then I headed across St. Charles to Leeds's place.

It hadn't changed. The key was still in the mailbox and there was the same incense smell when I went in. I flicked on the flashlight and started with the living room, taking every book down from the shelf, examining the inside cover for a name or an inscription, and then shaking it out for notes.

Halfway through I stopped. Some sixth sense warned me to check the street, so I slipped over to one of the windows and looked out.

All was quiet, except that someone had parked in the empty space a car length behind the Toyota. Probably a neighbor, I told myself. But the sixth sense kept yelling danger.

It had saved me a few times in Nam and I knew better than to disobey it, even if it meant blowing the whole job. I tiptoed to the kitchen, opened the back door, and stepped out into the patio. A smell of barbecue came from nearby, spicing the muggy air with mesquite smoke and cooking beef. I closed the door softly behind me and walked around to the side of the house. The barbecue smell was coming from over the wooden fence closing off this backyard from the one behind. But the yard of the house next door was separated from this by nothing more than a waist-high cyclone fence. I went to it quickly, hoping there would not be a dog. Using the limb of a camphor tree, I pulled myself up and then jumped down into the neighboring patio.

I walked alongside this house, stopping at a window. A television was going and somebody inside laughed loudly. I ducked under the window and made it to the front.

I waited, and as I watched, a car passed slowly down the street, its headlights lancing the line of vehicles parked at the curb. For a bare instant the lights stabbed through the glass of the car parked behind mine and I realized my sixth sense had been right: There was somebody inside.

While I was trying to decide my next move, another car approached down the narrow one-way street. Even in the darkness I could see that it was white, with the blue crescent device on the door that advertised New Orleans' finest. It swung in at the curb, the lights went out, and two figures got out. They opened the trunk and took out shotguns and then started for the front of the house.

I bent over and, using some azalea bushes to hide me, made my way to the sidewalk and then darted to the cover of a camphor tree. I heard pounding on the door and knew it would only be a few seconds before half the neighborhood was standing on their front porches. As if in confirmation, the porch lights of the house I had just left glared on and I heard the door opening. I took a deep breath and walked quickly across the street, hoping I would remain unseen in the commotion.

I had a choice to make: Walk away or attack.

A brief image of the Captain flashed through my mind. He was standing on the bridge of his destroyer, the shells whining past overhead and the spray stinging his face, and he was telling them to launch the torpedoes.

I decided to attack.

It was a calculated risk, but no worse
than the other option. I slipped alongside the parked cars, coming up on the
driver's side of the vehicle with the watcher. It was an
older model, and when I glimpsed the plates I had to
stifle my surprise. Perhaps, though, I should have
known.

The driver was too intent on the drama across the
street to notice me until I had jerked open the front
door. When he turned to confront me I had my hand in
my pocket, my finger aimed at his midsection.

"Move over," I whispered. "Make a sound and I'll
blow you in two."

The surprise caught him off guard and he slid over
docilely.

The police were both on the front porch now and another car had pulled up behind the first one. The second
one began to play its spotlight on the parked vehicles

and I forced my captive down in the seat as the glare played over us. It hovered for what seemed eternity and I pushed farther down into the seat, and then the light moved on to the next car. Doors slammed and I heard a disgruntled exclamation. The first car started away and the man beside me stirred, but I reached out with my hand and grabbed him by his hair, forcing him down into the seat. He gave a little yelp but the second police car was moving away now. I let go and moved back to an upright position.

"All right, Scott, now maybe you'll tell me why you followed me from your mother's house," I said. "And why you called the police to tell them I was here."

It was a rugged face that turned toward me, with fashionably long brown hair. He had the square jaw that gave an appearance of determination but I could see in the eyes that he had lost some nerve by being caught off guard.

"You're an escaped killer," he said sarcastically. "That ought to be enough."

"And you're just doing your duty, right? How did you know I was with her? The dishes on the table?"

He nodded. "I knew somebody was there, so I decided to wait outside. When I saw you leave I recognized you because of the . . ."

"Because of my arm. It's okay, I'm used to it."

He relaxed fractionally. "I figured you were hitting on her. I figured you were trying to step in now that Indiana Jones's in jail."

"Indiana Jones? Is that what they call him?"

"Yeah."

"Well, your mother is an extremely attractive woman. She deserves a life of her own. But my relationship with her is strictly professional. For better or worse, she's still pretty hung up on Thorpe. Though I believe her when she says he's never responded."

Scott made a noise of disbelief. Then he turned to face me. "Man, you don't have a gun, do you? You never had one."

"No," I said. "I never did."

"You can't make me stay here."

"Not for long. Though a one-armed man learns a few tricks to defend himself. Want to see one?"

The flicker of indecision in his eyes told the story. "Naw," he said. "So what did you want over here at Leeds's house?"

"I was hoping I could find something to tell me who he hung out with, might have confided in. A girlfriend, for instance."

Scott grunted. "Man, that's a snort."

"Oh?"

"A girlfriend? Sweet Gordie?"

A big piece of reality shifted, took on a different shape. "Gordon Leeds was homosexual?"

"That's the word. He kept it quiet. Discreet is the word. But I went with some friends to a gay place down in the Quarter last year. Curiosity, you know? And there he was, hanging all over some leather-jacket type. He didn't see me and we left. It isn't my scene."

"You didn't tell anybody?"

"No, why should I? If that's how he gets off, let him. Seemed to fit right in with the rest of the crew: Thorpe; that dingy girl, Astrid; and gold teeth, the Mayan."

"You never saw the man he was with in the Quarter that day?"

"No, man. I just wanted to get out before I barfed on somebody."

I reflected. Suddenly it all made sense. "Tell me, you ever hear of Claude St. Romaine?"

"You mean the dude they say you offed?" He shrugged. "He was a big frat rat a couple of years ago. Sigma Chi. Look, man, everybody on campus knew he was pumping Thorpe's old lady. It used to be the talk of the Greeks. Everybody thought it was a blast, you know?"

I thought for a moment, then came to a decision. "I'm going to have to try to find out who killed him," I said. "It's the only way to clear myself. And there's the little matter of who killed Leeds, too. I'm betting they're one and the same. I'm going to leave you here and you can call the law again, if you want. But I'd rather you didn't."

He blinked and then nodded very slowly. "Okay, man. I may be crazy, but I trust you."

I reached out my hand and he took it. We shook and then I left him.

I remembered some of the names in the funeral register. Thomas Fedders. Karl Hahn. Fred Gladney. And there were a few others that I would have to dredge up from my memory if I didn't hit on the first three.

Somehow, I didn't see Gladney in the role. That left Fedders and Hahn.

Was it just a coincidence that one of the names began with a *K*?

I stopped at a phone booth and called Directory Assistance. Karl Hahn lived on Dauphine, a stone's throw from my own apartment. It could hardly be a coincidence. But it would be a risk going there, because I was known in the neighborhood and the cops would all have my description.

I didn't have any choice.

Fortunately, there was a lot of Saturday-night traffic. I found a place down on Esplanade and slipped into the shadows, on the part of the sidewalk nearest the buildings. A little knot of people was gathered in front of the saloon at the corner of Chartres and Esplanade, but they seemed uninterested in just another passerby. I went two more blocks, was propositioned by a hooker, and told

her some other time. I sensed her eyes on me as I walked
away, wondering if she noticed the arm; whether she listened to police bulletins; whether she needed money or a
favor bad enough to hail the next cop car.

I turned at the corner, walked southwest, toward Canal, and then turned right again onto Barracks, the street
named for the barracks John Law built for the provincial
troops. Right now I was more worried about troops of
another sort. I came to Dauphine and stopped. The
place where Karl Hahn lived would be in this block. I
went left, counting the house numbers.

It was a narrow, brick-faced apartment with grilles on
the windows and a step up to an iron-bar door. The
downstairs was dark, but overhead, behind the balcony,
I could see lights in the windows. I went into the entranceway and squinted at the names on the mailboxes.
His name was on the one for the upstairs apartment. I
pushed the buzzer.

There was a long interval of silence and then a voice
croaked against a background of static.

"Who is it?"

I mumbled a reply that I knew would be inaudible
and rang again.

"Who *is* it?" the voice demanded again.

I mumbled again and there was more silence.

Something moved in the corner of my eye and I
shifted my head slightly: A pair of figures emerged from
the corner of Gov. Nicholls Street and turned up
Dauphine, toward me. A passing car caught them in its
lights and I saw the uniforms.

I jabbed the button again.

"Who *is* it?" the voice cried and even through the
static I recognized an edge of panic.

The policemen had crossed over to my side of the
street, were a mere half block away.

"Leeds," I said, hoping the shock would work.

The uniforms were only yards away now.

"What?" The voice in the static was choked.

"Leeds," I said. "Gordon Leeds."

They were almost on me and the one on the inside was looking over at me with awakening curiosity. I pressed myself further into the shadows.

I jabbed the button again as the policemen drew abreast.

The lock clicked as the electronic signal from inside released it and I shoved the grille open, plunging into the merciful blackness. The gate clanged shut behind me like a prison door and I realized my escape could be only temporary. But there was no going back now.

On the right a stairway gaped like an open mouth, blacker even than the darkness around it, like a vortex to annihilation. I took a deep breath and started upward, conscious of the gun-shot creaking of my feet on the boards. The stairwell smelled of dust and I had the suffocating sensation that the walls were about to close around me.

What if Hahn was the murderer? What if I was walking into a trap?

Suddenly, as if in answer, the doorway above me jerked open, blasting the stairwell with light. A stick figure blotted the glare, swaying slightly, its hand pointing at me with a magically elongated finger.

"Stop right there!" it cried, the voice hovering on hysteria. "I've got a gun and I'll shoot, I swear to God."

I froze, letting my eyes adjust to the sudden light.

"It's all right," I said quietly. "I'm not armed."

"I don't know that. You may be lying. You used Gordon's name. You lied about that."

"Then why did you let me in?"

"You can't hide forever. You'd find a way. I know about you people. Gordon told me before you killed him. Well, now the shoe's on the other foot. And I'm going to kill you."

The hand with the gun wavered and I tried to keep my voice steady. "I didn't kill him," I said. "I've been hired by Gregory Thorpe to find out who did."

It caught him by surprise and his body jerked, the hand with the gun waving from one side of the passageway to the other.

"You're police?" he demanded, his voice rising an extra octave.

"Private detective," I said. "I thought you might have some information nobody else had."

There was a moment of quiet while he digested it and I got a look at his features. He had a round face, with a brown mustache that seemed stuck on as an afterthought. His hairline had receded well back on his skull, but he had carefully combed his hair to cover his baldness, at least on one side. He was wearing a wine-colored smoking jacket, but his appearance was of only secondary importance to me right now. I was far more interested in the pistol in his hand. It was a nickel-plated revolver, an old High Standard .22 with a nine-shot capacity, in case you missed the first six times.

"You ought to put that down before somebody gets hurt," I advised.

He looked down at the gun as if he had just discovered he was holding it, and his hand lowered slightly, then snapped back up to center squarely on my chest.

"No, you don't," he said. "If you're who you say you are, show me some identification."

I hesitated and then gave a little shrug.

"Sure," I said, reaching toward my top pocket and taking a step upward at the same time.

His eyes followed my hand as I unbuttoned the top of my pocket and the gun lowered just a fraction. I brought my right hand down suddenly in a quick chopping motion, missing his hand but knocking the gun barrel away. His mouth gaped in surprise and he stumbled backward, into the room. I saw the gun coming up again and this time I kicked out, connecting with his wrist. He grunted, more in outrage than in pain, and the gun crashed onto the floor. I scooped it up a half second ahead of him and let him look down the barrel for a change.

"Good for plinking," I commented, "but my guess is you haven't used this for a long time. Maybe never. It's a bad habit, keeping a gun you don't practice with."

He stood glaring at me, left hand holding his wrist. "It's for protection," he said. "A friend gave it to me. The Quarter is too dangerous these days."

"Your friend's right there," I said, and shoved the door closed. I turned the lock with the same hand holding the gun, an awkward maneuver, and saw sudden realization flood his face.

"You," he said. "You're the one . . ."

"The one-armed man?"

He flinched. "I didn't say that."

"Of course not. You meant to say the man who was wanted for killing Cora Thorpe's lover. And who escaped from the St. Tammany Parish jail."

His lips moved but he couldn't think of anything to add. I could see him better now, in the light. He was in his mid-thirties, older than Leeds, and just slightly puffy around the jowls. He exuded the aroma of cologne and his hair glistened from brilliantine.

"Do we have to stand here?" I asked. "It seems unnecessary."

He nodded assent and sat down quickly on the couch behind him. I took in the rest of the room. It was tastefully furnished, with potted plants along one shelf and a mobile of stained glass hanging from the ceiling. At one end of the room was a giant mirror that made the small living room seem spacious. The furniture was a combination of antique and modern and I could tell that it had been waxed and dusted in the past twenty-four hours.

"Who are you afraid of, Mr. Hahn?"

He bit his lip and I could see that he was trying to make up his mind whether to say anything more.

"Look, you're scared shitless of somebody. You think whoever killed Gordon is coming here to kill you. Now if you'll trust me, maybe we can work this out together. Whoever killed Gordon managed to frame me, because with me out of the way they're safe. With you out of the way they're probably safer. But if both of us know the same thing, killing either one of us won't do them any good. Tell me who it is. Give me something to go on."

The man across from me frowned and then stared down at his slippers. His shoulders heaved and then he started to tremble all over. He started to say something but his voice cracked and suddenly he was crying.

"He told me they were after him," he said through his tears. "He told me that night. He was here. He said he was going to see somebody, somebody that could help him. He said it was only a few blocks away. I offered to go with him but he wouldn't let me. He said it was too dangerous; he wouldn't let me take the risk."

Hahn buried his face in his hands and wept.

"He was going to see me," I said. "But whoever it was got him first."

Hahn wagged his head from side to side, disconsolate. "If I'd have gone with him, just walked alongside . . ."

"There'd be two of you dead now," I told him. "You don't have anything to reproach yourself for. There was nothing you could do."

He looked up through tear-filled eyes. "Do you really believe that?"

"Yes, I do."

He dipped his head slightly in acknowledgment. "Thank you. That means a great deal." He reached into his pocket and brought out a handkerchief and I watched him wipe his face. "I'm sorry. I . . . I loved him, you know."

"I know. And I'm sorry."

Hahn nodded again. "Yes. How did you find out my name? Gordie and I agreed . . . We wouldn't advertise our relationship."

"There was a bottle of Amaretto at his house with your initial. You were the only person with a *K* in his name who signed the funeral register. When I looked up your address it was in the Quarter. It seemed worth checking out." No need, I thought, to tell him about my conversation with Scott.

"I understand," he said, shaking his head slowly from side to side. "We decided to keep everything quiet. No more of the leather-jacket bars that he used to go to when I first met him a year ago. I convinced him they were too dangerous. He agreed. I suppose they weren't any worse than the streets, though."

"Who was after him, Mr. Hahn? Who was he so afraid of?"

"A man," Hahn said bleakly. "He wouldn't tell me his name. He just said it was a very powerful man."

"How did he meet this man?"

"It was an accident. It was all an accident. That's what was so absurd. Everything was an accident. Just the way he found the artifacts. An accident." He stared over at me, demanding my agreement, and I nodded.

"Go on."

"You see, we used to go shopping sometimes. I was helping him furnish his apartment. Some of the things he had in there before we met." He wagged his head again in disapproval. "Atrocious. I make my living as an interior decorator. The furnishings must mediate between the essence of the architecture and the personality of the inhabitant. We were in a flea market near Fat City. I think Gordie was just teasing me. Pretending he was going to buy some perfectly horrible trash. He started talking with the proprietor, a Mr. Tanoos. Lebanese, you know." He shifted slightly in his chair. "They started talking and Gordie mentioned that he was an archaeologist. This Tanoos began to warm up to him, though, of course, I knew he was only interested in making a sale. I wanted Gordie to come along and just when I thought he was ready, this man told him that he had some things that would interest a discriminating person. Naturally, Gordie was curious, so he followed Tanoos into the back and Tanoos went to a big chest he had in one corner of this horribly untidy little office. He opened it and we looked down inside.

"There were several sacks and he lifted them out, one by one, and placed them on the desk there. Then he began to empty them in front of us. Some contained spear points, made of obsidian and flint. Some were fragments of pottery, and there were some little clay dolls. And there was a small object of polished stone that Gordie told me later was an unusual jade.

"Well, I thought it was fairly interesting, because Gordie had taught me a little about Mayan artifacts. But I was hardly prepared for his reaction. He stared down at them as if he couldn't make up his mind what he was seeing, and then he began to examine them one by one. He turned a deathly pale and for a minute I thought he was getting ready to faint. His eyes were bright, like somebody with a fever, and then he asked Tanoos how much he wanted for them.

"Naturally, Tanoos knew he had a victim and I've no doubt whatsoever that he doubled the price. As it was, Gordie wrote out a check for four hundred dollars. I was appalled. I helped him gather up the artifacts and we left. It was only when we got home to my place that he explained what they were."

He looked down at the floor and tried to find his next words. I waited, trying to imagine the scene: Gordon Leeds, the bags of artifacts on the coffee table, checking each item again and again. Because I already had guessed part of the answer.

"They were all from Ek Balam, weren't they?" I asked.

Hahn looked up, surprised. "Yes. They were. He said he remembered excavating some of them himself. But most of them he'd never seen. It was just the style, and the fact that they were associated with other items he *knew* he had dug up, that allowed him to conclude that they were all from the same place. The only thing that wasn't from Ek Balam was the little jade object, but he said it was in the Mayan style. He said they traded a lot of things like that back and forth."

"So what did he do?" I asked.

Hahn waved a hand and the big red stone of his ring gleamed in the lamplight. "He anguished. That's what he did. He knew someone had robbed the site, had actually been smuggling out things while they were working there. Naturally, his suspicion fell on this Indian fellow, the chief of the native crew. But he knew he had to be in cahoots with somebody else, somebody with good contacts, somebody who could set up the deal. He also knew that what he'd bought had to be just a small sample of the less valuable artifacts. Nobody would go to that much trouble for just a few things."

I got up and walked to the other side of the room. The air conditioner must have cut on because suddenly it seemed very cold inside.

"The next day he went back to talk to this Tanoos," Hahn went on, "but Tanoos had left and nobody knew where he was. People didn't seem to want to talk about it. Somebody had gotten to Tanoos and scared him away. I'll remember Gordie's face for the rest of my life, the way he came in that day, bitter, his eyes angry. He told me he knew who'd done it. He knew who'd stolen the artifacts."

"And who did he say it was?" I asked.

Karl Hahn looked me in the eye and when he spoke again his voice was cold. "He said it was his professor, Dr. Gregory Thorpe."

"Thorpe?" I echoed.

He nodded. "Yes. He'd never liked the man, you see. Thorpe was a perfect tyrant. He was Harvard. Superior. Gordie was not of his class, I'm sure. And the man would brook no dispute. A very insecure person, if you ask me."

I nodded, thinking at least that part was probably true.

"But none of that makes Thorpe a thief," I pointed out. "After all, he was risking exposure. His own reputation was at stake."

"Perhaps. But Gordie figured out that it was all a mistake; that probably the artifacts were never supposed to be peddled in New Orleans. It was impossible to find out if more was missing, of course, because, with the exception of a few things in the lab, most of the artifacts are still stored in Mexico. If Gordie stirred up the Mexican authorities, it could endanger the entire future of Tulane projects there."

"But why would Thorpe be doing this?" I persisted.

Hahn shrugged. "Gordie said it was probably his wife. Everybody knows how demanding she is, how all she lives for is a good time. She demands a great deal of upkeep. Gordie figured that Thorpe had just succumbed to his infatuation for her and used the artifacts to raise money he needed to keep her in furs."

"Interesting theory," I admitted. "So what did Gordon do next?"

Hahn raised his hands again. "Well, that was just the dilemma, wasn't it? He had no proof. What could he possibly do? He certainly couldn't confront Thorpe without risking the ruin of his own career. But he had to do something."

"And planting the artifacts in the displays was his way of getting back?"

"It was a psychological ploy, don't you see? He wanted Thorpe to realize in the most direct way possible that someone knew his secret."

"But he wanted to leave him in the dark as to who," I said. "I have to admit it's unique."

"Exactly. Let Thorpe worry about it. The man was on edge already. Just a little more might send him over. At the proper time Gordie planned to leave him a note, anonymous, of course, asking for his resignation before even more embarrassing evidence came out."

I stopped my pacing. "A dangerous game," I said.

Hahn jerked his head in agreement. "I told him that. I begged him not to do it. But he said Thorpe was taking a chance with everybody's future, that he was stealing from the site. You'd have to understand: Gordie had an almost mystical dedication to his work. He identified with the Maya, with the site itself. He saw this as a criminal act that had to be redressed. He was very intense."

"Tell me about what happened just before he died," I said.

"He came in from the Cobbetts' party, excited. He showed me the jade *hacha*. I remember what he said: 'This is what they want.' Naturally, I asked him what it was about, but he refused to tell me. He said it was safer for me not to know. But I remember he said it was all bigger than he thought, that it wasn't just a matter of smuggling. I asked where he was going and he said to somebody who could help."

"Right," I said bitterly.

"Then I read about your being arrested for this murder over there . . ." He waved vaguely toward the lake. "I thought that must mean you were the killer, not Thorpe. So I took out the gun."

"Understandable," I said. "Tell me, did anybody Gordon worked with know about his scheme? Astrid Bancroft, for example?"

Hahn shook his head, "Not to my knowledge."

"And not Katherine Degas, Thorpe's assistant?"

"The Degas woman is a secretary. Gordon did not confide in secretaries."

I went to the window and moved the curtain. The street below was dark, and there was no reason to think the apartment was being watched.

I dropped the curtain and walked back over to the center of the room. I took the pistol out of my belt and laid it on the coffee table.

"I'd put this away, Hahn," I told him. "It's liable to get you killed."

He stared at the floor, hands clasped before him. "I don't care. With Gordie gone, it doesn't matter anymore."

I nodded and went out the door, closing it softly as if

to avoid waking the dead. I heard it lock and for an instant I regretted leaving the gun behind me. I was alone again, and even here, protected from the street by the locked grate, I had a sense of vulnerability. Gordon Leeds had left here only four nights ago, sure he could make it only three blocks. And something had emerged from the night with the finality of perdition.

I shuddered and started down the black stairwell, each footstep echoing like thunder.

Thorpe could have killed Leeds. He had motive and he certainly had opportunity. Leeds had been out to ruin him. It would have been a matter of twenty minutes to leave his house and come here, find a phone booth, make the call that would have sent Leeds out into the deadly night.

But somehow the jade didn't fit in.

Why had Leeds decided he had to get it to me? And why did Ordaz want it so badly? And how had it come into the hands of a flea-market owner named Tanoos, who had since disappeared?

I came to the big iron gate and halted. The street was silent. From somewhere over the rooftops came the mournful sound of a ship's horn. I put my hand on the gate and halted.

Why did I feel that there was someone out there, watching?

I drew back into the shadows and waited. Five minutes went by. Ten.

A man passed, weaving slightly and mumbling to himself as he went. I let the sound of his steps die away and then moved out of the shadows.

I was jumpy, that's all it was. Every sound was a police car, every movement a possible assailant. I took some deep breaths, telling myself I had been in tighter spots.

In Nam I had once had to crawl back for five hundred

yards from a forward observation post that had been overrun. I had survived, hadn't I?

You're a fool, an insistent voice in my mind shot back. There you were just another body, a figure in the dark. Once away, no problem. But here you're on every wanted list in the country.

I had to admit the voice made sense. But I couldn't stand here forever. I pushed the gate open and stepped out onto the street.

The sense of danger was acute now. The little voice told me to flatten back into the shadows, jab the button, get Hahn to reopen the gate. But logic took over, told me not to panic.

I started down the sidewalk, toward Esplanade. Ahead was a street lamp, throwing a pool of light onto the ground. When I passed through it I would be a target. I crossed to the other side, sticking close to the buildings.

I heard a noise behind me and my blood froze. I made myself keep going, refusing to quicken my pace. Imagination, damn it. That's all it was.

There was an open doorway ahead. When I got to it I would take cover, turn around, scan the shadows.

Ten yards, that's all. There was no way they could get a good shot in the darkness.

Five yards.

My spine was tingling.

One yard.

I stepped into the darkness and suddenly hands reached out and grabbed me and I heard a shout.

I flailed away with my right arm and heard a grunt of dismay. Something crashed onto the sidewalk in an explosion of glass and fingers of wetness grabbed my ankle.

"Goddamn," somebody swore. "What the hell's going on? You busted my damn bottle."

The man I had by the neck was cowering, his eyes

wide with fright. His clothes stank and his body was trembling. I let him go and stepped away.

"Sorry," I said.

"What about my bottle?" he demanded. "You broke it. What about my damn bottle?"

I walked away quickly, leaving him to call epithets after me. My legs were soaked and the sour smell of cheap wine assaulted my nostrils.

It was a mistake, a stupid mistake. I had blundered into him in panic and now it was over. So why wouldn't my heart settle down? Why did I still have the feeling someone was behind me?

Esplanade was just ahead. A boulevard that forms the boundary of the French Quarter, it would have people and cars, even at this hour. All I had to do was get there, make it the block or so to the car.

In my mind I heard the roar of the car, bearing down on Leeds; saw him stop, turn around to face it. Except that now it wasn't Leeds they were after, it was me . . .

I was so conscious of the sense of being followed that I missed the shifting shadow a half block in front of me, at the corner. And when I came up to it, it was too late.

The man who stepped out in front of me was the size of a grain silo. If I'd had any thought that he just wanted a match it was banished by the sight of the man next to him. It was one of Ordaz's goons. And if I turned to run, I'd crash into the one they had coming up from behind.

"Mr. Dunn," the smaller goon said, taking a step forward. Like myself, he was wearing a guayabera, and I knew he'd have a gun stuck in his belt, but with the Hulk beside him he didn't need artillery. "You taking a big chance, you know?"

I stopped, the hairs on my neck bristling. "Don't tell me: Mr. Ordaz sent you to rescue me."

The goon gave me a crooked smile. "*Quién sabe?* If

you help him, he will do all in his power. He has instruct'
me to tell you that message."

"Good of him," I said. "But I already have a lawyer."

The Hulk took a step forward and I wondered if he'd
understood anything that we'd said. Whoever was behind me was close now, so close I was expecting a shot to
the back of the neck at any second.

When it came, though, it was from the front. The
Hulk took a single step and then slammed me in the pit
of the stomach with a fist the size of a ham hock. I
crumpled, the breath shooting out of me like air from a
ruptured punching bag. The sidewalk came up, but before I hit it, hands grabbed me, holding me upright. The
Hulk was amazingly fast for a big man and that was un-
nerving. He held me by one hand and the smaller goon
got in my face.

"Mr. Ordaz wants what you got belongs to him.
Now."

"I haven't got it," I wheezed.

"Then you will get it. We will go with you."

I tried to catch my breath. "It's in a bank box," I
said. "I can't get it in the middle of the damn night."

There was a half second of respite and then a knee
like a redwood crashed into my groin and red tracer bullets crisscrossed in front of my eyes. I flew back against
the wall and bounced, feeling my dinner rising up in my
throat. I was on all fours, staring down at the concrete
sidewalk, where a patent leather shoe, extra-large, was
poised to catch me under the chin. And there was nothing I could do.

Not even when the small goon grabbed me by the
hair and pulled back my head, like the holder in football,
giving the placekicker his shot.

The big foot drew back and I gritted my teeth.

And the foot froze, just as the hand holding my hair let go.

"Chinga," somebody muttered and I sensed alarm. My two tormentors had temporarily forgotten me. Something had frightened them, and they were facing behind me. Even as I crawled around to see what they were looking at, there was a muzzle flash from the darkness and a bullet whined off the bricks a foot from the smaller goon's head. He had the big Browning out now, but before he could aim, the muzzle flash came again and he grunted, grabbing his left arm.

It was too much even for the giant. He was half a block away by the time I got to my feet, with his wounded friend close behind. I sagged against the building, relieved.

I knew who it had been behind me all those blocks now, and I was ready to make a novena of thanks. I spit out some of the bile and watched the shape solidify in the darkness.

"Sandy, remind me to give you a raise," I said as she came out into the half-light from a street lamp, tucking the .25 away into her leg holster. "That was some shooting with a lady's gun."

"Luck, Micah. I was scared I was gonna hit you. But I figured you was getting hit enough already, another wouldn't matter."

"Probably right," I groaned. "How did you find me?"

"Why don't we talk about it in the car. Even this little gun makes enough noise to bring out the cops."

As if in answer, I saw a light go on in one of the upstairs apartments. I forced myself upright against the pain and followed her across Esplanade to where her Mustang was parked.

By the time we were pulling out onto the boulevard,

all the lights were on and a few people had come out into the street. They might find a drop of blood or two, I thought, and maybe even a pair of spent casings. But I doubted it. With no body, the cops wouldn't come back till the daytime, and when light came, the evidence would be obliterated.

"I was enjoying myself on the coast when I heard about you being arrested," Sandy said. The windows were down and the sultry night air was whipping me in the face, bringing me back to my senses. "Well, I knew I had to come back and see what I could do. I was outside your place; I thought you might be stupid enough to try to get back there. But the cops had it covered. You know, a white car with an antenna and two guys in suits? Real low profile, right? I told myself, 'Even *Micah* ain't dumb enough to walk into that.'"

"Thanks," I said.

"But then, just as I was leaving, who do you think I see coming out of an apartment on Dauphine? None other than the man Micah himself. So I follow behind. Maybe my eyes are going bad, you know? Maybe this Micah's got a twin. Or leading a double life . . ."

"Funny."

"I thought so. Anyhow, I follow the dude, and what's the first thing he does? He heads into a doorway and tries to pick a fight with some wino. Man, I figure this Micah must've been hit on the head by the cops over in the St. Tammany Parish jail. Then, if all that ain't bad enough, he decides to pick a fight with Frankenstein and his keeper."

"An oversight," I said dryly. "He didn't look so big in the dark."

"Micah, you a real clown."

"I feel like it." Then I told her about the jade and about my interview with Ordaz, and the events of the past twenty-four hours. "I really didn't want to get you involved," I said. "You don't get paid enough for this kind of trouble."

"Paid?" She shot me a killing stare. "Micah Dunn, you think I'm doing this for pay? Because if you do, I'll put your ass out right now and you can walk."

I smiled. "Sorry, Sandy. I didn't mean to insult you. I should have known you'd count yourself in."

"Damn right." We drove on through the night. I'd closed my eyes, letting my thoughts drift and some of the pain wear away.

"I love you, Sandy," I said.

"Sure you do. Now what's the next step?"

"Can we go to your place?"

"I mean *after* that, fool."

"For one thing, I'll need the jade."

She started to argue but I cut her short. "It's the key to this whole business. Whoever holds it is a target. If I'd realized that, I'd never have given it to you to begin with."

Sandy lived in an upstairs condo overlooking the lake. It was the first time I'd been in her place, but I was too exhausted to admire the neo-primitive decor. I collapsed into the big wicker chair and dialed Katherine's number. She answered breathlessly and calmed down when I told her I was all right. I told her where to find her car and when she asked where I was staying obliquely mentioned that I had found an old friend. When I hung up I found Sandy staring at me with a suspicious eye.

"Who is this woman, anyway?"

I told her and her expressive brows climbed even further. "Micah, you getting hung up on this lady?"

"God, no," I mumbled, irritated. "I just like her, that's all. And she helped me when I needed help."

"Gratitude, huh? Listen, friend, I can see that look in a man's eye a mile off. It's made a lot of trouble for me. It means a man's getting ready to do something crazy."

"Sandy, for God's sake . . ."

"No, you listen: What's the first thing you lectured me on when I came to work for you? *Don't let your guard down. Don't trust anybody. Everybody out there's a suspect.* And now you turn around and forget the whole thing. Micah, how you know she's not the killer?"

"Sandy, it doesn't make any sense. What does she have to gain?"

"What does *anybody* have to gain? That's the hang-up. What is it about this little piece of green rock?"

I nodded wearily. "You're right. And I have a feeling that Jason Cobbett has the answer. Trouble is, he isn't back in town until tomorrow. And even then my guess is he'll be hard to dig out, because I've already scared him once."

Sandy smiled malevolently. "Why don't you leave him to me?"

It seemed like an eminently sensible idea. I nodded once and then let her help me to bed. That night I dreamed of the Hulk and his associate with the cannon. The man with the gun kept smiling and I wondered why he was so friendly. And then I realized he was really Mancuso, who took off the mask and told me it had all been a joke. When I awoke in the darkness, though, for some reason I wasn't laughing.

I awoke at ten with the sun in my eyes,
a pain in my groin, and the telephone
bell jangling my frayed nerves. I
reached out for the pink monstrosity beside the bed and
then stopped. How could I know who it was? I looked
around for Sandy, vaguely aware that she had spent the
night on the pull-out couch in the next room. The phone
rang a fourth time and still she didn't come.

I fumbled the receiver to my ear, determined to hang
up if it was someone I didn't know.

But there was no need to have been apprehensive:
Sandy's voice grabbed me over the fiber-optic wires.
"Micah? You still alive?"

"I don't know," I groaned. "Where are you?"

"At the airport, honey. There's a man you want to
see coming in. I came to meet him."

"How did you know when?"

"Do you think all men are as immune to my considerable charms as you are? I happened to find a certain security person who admires a woman of class and warmth. I convinced him that access to certain flight records was of the utmost national importance. And I said I'd go out with him tonight."

"Bless you," I said. "I can get a cab, be there . . ."

"You *are* a fool. Every cabbie in the city has your description. You just leave this to me. I intend to give our friend a free ride. Just call it special delivery."

"Sandy. You can get life for kidnapping . . ."

But it was too late. The dial tone was buzzing in my ear. I replaced the receiver and swung myself upright. It was, I reflected, probably as good a plan as could be concocted under the circumstances. But what if it didn't work? Suppose Cobbett didn't know anything? What then?

I made some toast and looked out the window at the brown surface of the lake. There was really nothing to do but wait.

An hour passed. Two. I stalked from one side of the apartment to the other. Noon melted into evening. I saw sails on the lake and wished I could be with them, with the wind in my face, instead of hiding for something I hadn't done.

I went to the bookcase and scanned the titles, frantic for something to take my mind away. Most of them were texts from Sandy's brief stay at college and among them I found a book by J. Eric Thompson on Maya civilization. I made an effort to skim through it, telling myself that I might find something about the jade, but my mind wouldn't focus. I put the book back and returned to the boats.

It was half past four when I heard movement outside the door. I reached for a flower pot and stepped behind the bedroom door for cover. The lock turned and then the door came slowly open.

"Micah, you there?"

"Sandy." I stepped out into the living room, putting down the pot. I looked around. "Where's Cobbett?"

"Downstairs. Come on, plane was late, this dude's in a hurry to get home."

"You mean he's just waiting?" I asked incredulously.

"Don't have nothing else to do," she answered cavalierly and jounced out with a wave of the head for me to follow.

I followed.

Her Mustang was downstairs and I saw at once that it was empty.

"My God, he's escaped."

"Not hardly." She nodded toward the back of the vehicle.

"Under the blanket," she said and I craned my neck to look into the rear passenger area. There was a red blanket on the floor and even as I stared at it I saw it move. There was a muffled protest from underneath as I lifted a corner. A pair of frightened eyes stared up at me and lips moved incoherently under the adhesive gag.

I shook my head in mixed horror and wonder. "How did you get him in?" I asked, as she pulled away from the curb.

"Easy. I told him I was with airport security, and when we got down to the baggage claim I stuck my gun in his back and told him to keep walking. When the parking lot looked clear I told him to get in the back and then I slipped him a pair of cuffs."

We took the expressway north and then swung east, toward the edge of the city. As we came down off the interstate, I realized where she was taking us: We were headed for what had been an old plantation, until its fields were carved by a grid of streets with names like Abundance, Agriculture, and Industry. One street was

even named for the plantation owner's daughter, De-
sirée.

But it is a misnomer, for there is nothing desirable
about the housing project that the city, in its wisdom,
has placed there. The Desire Street development is a no-
man's land where even the police seldom venture in less
than SWAT strength.

"Sandy, are you sure . . . ?"

She smiled evilly and turned in to park on a street
cluttered by junked autos. She left the motor running,
then swiveled around and whipped off the blanket. "Sit
up, sucker," she commanded, and I reached back and
dragged Cobbett upright. I tore the adhesive strip from
his mouth and he gave a little yelp of pain.

"You," he squeaked.

"I'm glad you read the papers," I said. "Because that
means you know I'm wanted for murder and am a pretty
desperate character."

"That's Micah: desperate," Sandy intoned.

"I will ask you a question and I will ask you once
only," I said. "The first time I showed you the jade you
recognized it. Why?"

He shook his head back and forth, his mouth half
open, but he saw denial would do him no good. "I . . .
you mustn't tell him I told you," he begged.

"Who?" I knew, but I wanted to hear the name.

"Ordaz," he breathed. "Señor Ordaz. But for God's
sake, don't ever tell him. He'll kill me."

"He isn't here and I am. Under what circumstances
did you see it?"

He hesitated, eyes shifting back and forth as if for
some imaginary policeman, but all he saw were graffiti-
splashed walls and cars on blocks. "You have five seconds," I said.

His tongue flicked out over his lips. "All right. He
had this collection, don't you know? Artifacts from a

Mayan site, somewhere in Yucatán. He wanted me to appraise them. I do appraisals. It's not illegal. There's nothing wrong with it."

He coughed, trying to regain some semblance of poise.

"Get on with it."

"Yes. Well, most of it was junk. There was this jade *hacha* or pendant, though, that I thought was rather interesting. It had some Mayan glyphs carved in its center."

"Does that make it valuable?"

"It does if it was a calendrical glyph," Sandy said unexpectedly. "Like if it had a date around one thousand A.D. Maya didn't make any dates after that."

I tried to hide my surprise and reminded myself to get to know Sandy better when this was over.

But Cobbett was already jerking his head back and forth. "No. It wasn't a calendrical glyph. It was something else. Maybe the name of a God. It was fascinating, and I'm not aware of any other black jade just like it, but . . ." He gave a little shrug. "It was worth maybe a couple of hundred dollars, a thousand tops. I gave it and the other artifacts back to Ordaz. And that's the last I saw of them until you showed me the *hacha* the other day."

"You didn't suspect that they came from Ek Balam?"

"They could have come from *anywhere* in the Yucatán. They might have been in somebody's sea chest for fifty years. Happens all the time."

"Then why were you so surprised when I showed you the jade?"

"Because you were telling me Gordon Leeds had been murdered and then showing me something I had no reason to expect you'd have. I knew that it belonged, or had belonged, to Ordaz. I knew that you could not possibly have had it innocently."

Sandy guffawed. "And that's why you took a vacation all of a sudden?"

"I'd had that planned for three months," he protested, his dignity offended.

Sandy and I exchanged looks. It was clear we weren't going to get anything more from him.

"Okay, Cobbett," I said, trying to make my voice hard. "We're going to take you at your word. But by God, if you've held anything back, we'll . . ."

"I swear to God," he declared, tears in his eyes.

I knew what Sandy was thinking: As soon as he could get to a phone, we'd have every cop in the city on us. She gave me an exaggerated movement of her eyes that meant, "Let's leave him here and hope somebody rolls him for his watch." I had a feeling she'd even be willing to blow the horn real loud.

"Listen, Cobbett," I said. "The lady would like to dump you but I don't think we have to do that. So far the cops don't know you're implicated. But if you go to them, you're going to have to explain about the appraisals and about your deals with Ordaz." I shushed him before he could protest: "I know. It's all on the up-and-up. But it won't look like it when it hits the papers. Your directors will take one look and bounce you higher than a basketball. And nobody else will ever hire you. If you talk."

He gulped. "I won't say anything," he said.

Sandy shot me a look that said she thought my softness would be my death, and sighed. She turned out of the parking space, rolled past what looked like a minor dope deal going down between a man with a brown bag and the driver of a Caddie, and took us away. Ten minutes later we were back on the expressway and I unlocked the cuffs. "Out," I commanded, as we slid down an exit ramp and came to a stop at a street corner. The chastened curator scurried away like a frightened gopher.

I turned back to Sandy. "Somehow this isn't what I planned to be doing on my Sunday afternoon."

She fixed me a drink and we sat down before the picture window. "So where from here?" she asked, sipping her piña colada.

"The jade," I said. "Time to give it back."

"Oh, hell, and just when I was getting used to having it to look at."

She went into the bathroom and came back out with the little piece of polished stone.

"Where did you have it?" I asked.

"Secret," she said. "Where only a narc would look."

I took the object and ran my hand over the design cut in its smooth surface.

"We have to find who peddled the artifacts to Ordaz," I said. "It can only have been one of four people: Thorpe, Leeds, the girl, Astrid, or the Mayan, Artemio."

"If it was Thorpe, Ordaz wouldn't need to go to no appraiser to find out the value," Sandy commented.

I nodded. "Ditto the next two. And that only leaves Artemio."

"But I thought you said he was Thorpe's ace boon coon."

"He was also about to be sent back to Yucatán, and he hasn't been very happy about it."

"Hmmm." She raised her glass thoughtfully, eyeing me over the rim. "Why do I get the feeling the Green Hornet's going to ride tonight?"

It was well after dark when we left again. A breeze was coming in across the lake, but it was hot, like a sirocco,

and I was glad for the air-conditioning. I had begged
Sandy to let me take the car, so that I could claim I'd
stolen it if I were caught, but she refused. We drove
down Pontchartrain Boulevard, the bright lights of the
other cars like eyes, probing us, and I kept imagining I
heard sirens. Once a red flasher sped past, in the other
direction, and Sandy laughed quietly as she saw me tense
and then relax.

"Take it easy, Micah. You know the cops in this
town. You old news. They on to the next big story by
now."

I thought of Mancuso and wondered. He was no fool.
He'd have my description in every public rest room in
the state by now. No, he wouldn't forget.

We came to Carrollton and went right, toward the
river, and twenty minutes later melted into the checker-
board of streets that made the Carrollton quarter. The
houses were old and brooding, the trees stately. And the
streets were quiet. We stopped at an intersection and I
opened the door.

"I'll go on foot," I said. "I'll meet you in half an hour
at Burdette and Plum. If I'm not there, get the hell out
of here."

She reached down, handed me the tiny automatic.
"Here."

I smiled and shook my head. "I could never shoot
those things," I said. "It would just get me killed."

I left her at the stop sign and walked away down the
sidewalk.

It was only nine, so there was a chance he wouldn't
be there. In that case, the trip would have been wasted.
But I had to make the effort, because he was the only
one who could have been stealing the artifacts.

I turned a corner and stopped. There was a car double-parked just up the street, across from the house
where he stayed. I ducked my head, hoping it wasn't the

police. The lights hit me in the face and then I was past and I heard somebody laugh. A college kid and his date. I kept walking.

His place was just ahead now, on the left. There was a car in the drive, which meant someone was home, probably the owner or one of the other boarders. I halted, listening. Somebody was playing rock music and I thought it was coming from inside. I went along the side of the house, toward the outbuilding. At first I thought there was a dim light in one of the windows, but then I saw that it was just a reflection from the street. I put my hand on the knob.

The door was unlocked and I pushed the door forward, gently, standing out of the way. It was dark inside and there was no sound, but I sensed someone in the blackness. Sweat was prickling my forehead and I resisted the urge to turn around and walk away. Instead, I felt inside for the light switch, found it, and flipped it on.

There was no gunshot, no blast of dynamite, only light. I waited an extra ten seconds and then stepped through, closing the door behind me.

One look at the body on the bed told me I had found Artemio at home.

I turned him over and flinched as a fog of alcohol hit me. I shook him and he mumbled something in Mayan. I let him fall back onto the bed and glanced around the room. What remained of a bottle of K&B rum was on the table, and I kicked a glass that lay overturned on the floor.

Beside the bed was a little stand that looked like something from a secondhand store. I examined the thin stack of papers atop it. They were mostly comic books and advertising circulars addressed to "Resident." I replaced them and went to the bureau. Judging from the laundry bag in the corner, there wouldn't be much in the drawers, and I was right. A few pairs of socks, some underwear, and a shirt. In the top drawer was a checkbook. The last entry, scrawled in a shaky hand, had been an eight-hundred-dollar paycheck, entered three months before, leaving a nominal balance of three hundred dollars, but from the number of checks used since, I could tell he had lost interest in record keeping. There was also a week-old letter from the bank, advising of a two-hundred-dollar overdraft. What I did not find were a passport and alien resident card, but it hardly seemed strange; they were probably in safekeeping with Thorpe or Katherine.

I replaced the items in the drawers, then went to the tiny closet and looked inside. Some sandals, a raincoat, and, on the shelf, a couple of wadded towels, and a *Penthouse*. The bathroom held a razor, some antiseptic, and a tube of diarrhea pills. There was also a large bottle of very cheap cologne. I shut the door and went back to the sleeping man. I patted down his pockets, but all he had was some change. A battered wallet held three dollars and an ID card in Spanish, plus some receipt tapes from K&B, which I judged from the amounts were liquor purchases.

I felt under the mattress, wondering if he might have hidden something between it and the springs. I had no idea what I was looking for, but anything might help. The mattress heaved like a raft in a sea and the Indian coughed. I eased the mattress back down. I stooped and felt under the bed.

The only things I touched were a single rubber-soled sandal, three of its straps broken at the heel, and a library book in Spanish. I brought the book out into the light and opened it, choking at the dust that rose up from the pages.

It was called the *Relaciones de Yucatán* and was part of a larger, multi-volumed work. I remembered with chagrin the hours I had spent in German class at the Academy when I could have taken Spanish. Well, no sense regretting it now. I flipped through the pages to see if anything might be concealed inside, but there was nothing but a flattened soda straw, which Artemio had evidently been using as a bookmark.

I glanced down at the text he had been reading. The words were all foreign, and I was about to shut it when two words I knew suddenly jumped out of the page at me.

Ek Balam.

I stared down at the page, willing myself to understand, but it was useless. I closed the book, stuck it under my arm, turned out the light, and stepped back into the night.

It was natural for a man to want to read about his land's history, of course, especially when he was employed in the recovery of that history. The book had been checked out of the Tulane library three months before and was now overdue. But that hardly meant more than that Artemio was a slow reader, which, judging by the stack of comic books, he probably was.

I went back to Artemio and shook him until his eyes opened.

"Mashi?" he asked in what I took to be Mayan.

"The artifacts," I demanded. "The ones you stole from Ek Balam. I want you to tell me why."

But his eyes looked past me. He gave me a silly smile.

"Artefactos? Los artefactos? Se los vendí. You want to buy them?"

"I want to know who put you up to it," I demanded. "Who told you where to go to sell them?"

"Sell? *Sí, vendí los artefactos."*

"The jade," I cried in frustration. "The jade piece with the face." I indicated my own face with my hand. "The *hacha."*

His face lit and he nodded, a thin trickle of saliva running down his unshaven chin.

"Ah, sí. La hacha. En el templo Ah. In the temple.

That's where . . ." He made a digging motion with his hands. "I *escavé* the *hacha*. Ek Balam."

"You dug it up in the temple? Which temple?" I grabbed his shoulders, shaking him.

"*Templo Ah*. The temple . . ." His head fell back limply and he emitted a loud snore. I dropped him onto the bed and left.

Suddenly I felt tired and helpless. All along I had asked myself what the Captain would do. When he would have attacked, I had forged ahead. But I was no closer to a solution than before. Now an irrational feeling surged up: All I had to do was go home, somehow make it to the house on the beach. The Captain would take care of everything. And I would take care of him. I fought the urge back and kept walking.

I came to the end of the block. The double-parked car was gone, but there was another one waiting at the stop sign, lights out.

It was too far away to see if it was Sandy. Had I been in the room half an hour? I had lost track of time. I made myself keep walking and as I approached, the headlights of the car flashed on. I froze as the car started forward. The door opened and then, to my relief, I heard Sandy's voice:

"Micah, over here."

I trotted over to the passenger's side and got in. It was not until I had closed the door that I noticed the man in the backseat.

"Micah, I ought to brain you," O'Rourke said.

The tension drained out of me. I turned around and shook my friend's hand. "Damn it, John, how did you get here?"

"Lady came by and picked me up. It's only a few blocks, you know."

"But this could mean your license."

"Nah. I was trying to convince my client to give him-self up. A primary duty of an officer of the court."

"But you're representing Gregory Thorpe. You told me there was a conflict . . ."

"There was. That's why I dropped him."

"You quit Thorpe?"

"Sure." He shrugged. "Why not? They've hit on a better theory of the murders. Why bother a Tulane pro-fessor when they can pin it *all* on a PI? They're going to let Thorpe post bail, because the cops hate like hell to drop charges on *anybody,* but the focus is definitely on *you.*"

"Stands to reason," I said.

"But I do have to tell you," O'Rourke went on, "that what you did was a damned fool thing. Even a lawyer as good as I am is going to have trouble getting you out of this one. Unless you came up with something from your friend's room."

I held up the book. "Nothing but some ancient his-tory. Do you read Spanish?"

He shook his head. "So what's next?"

"You tried to convince me to turn myself in and I told you to go to hell. Now get lost, Counselor."

O'Rourke nodded regretfully. We came to Henry Clay and I got out to let him leave the car.

"Now where?" Sandy asked.

We didn't have that many options. I gave her Kather-ine Degas's address.

We stopped in front and I opened the door. "When I signal, leave," I said. "Mancuso's no fool and he's over-due to pay you a visit. I'd rather not be there. I don't think they'll be looking for me here."

She eyed me knowingly. "You sure that's the rea-son?"

"I'm sure," I said, but I could see she wasn't buying

it. I sighed, walked up to the door and rang. I heard movement and then the door swung open. When Katherine saw me her expression went from surprise to happiness.

"Micah. My God, I've been so worried. I was afraid something had happened to you."

I turned around and nodded to Sandy. The door closed behind me. "I'm sorry," I said. "I thought it was best not to call. I was with a friend."

She stared at me, our faces very close, and I smelled the delicate scent she was wearing. "I thought the police had found you."

"Not yet," I said. "But I can't hide forever."

Her lips opened slightly and she started toward me, then stopped herself. "No." She turned around quickly. "They're going to release Gregory."

"So I hear. I'm sure he's happy."

"I suppose." She looked away. "I didn't want it to be at your expense."

"Things work that way sometimes," I said. "It isn't his fault."

She bit her lip. "You don't know Gregory. When he's under pressure he can say things he doesn't mean."

A warning signal shot through me. "Are you saying he's laying the blame on me?"

"I don't know. I just mean he isn't used to being in this kind of position. It's normal to want somebody else to be the scapegoat."

"It's normal," I said, "as long as you don't throw them an anchor when you see them going down."

I went over to the sideboard, laid down the book, and poured myself a bourbon. The cops never liked to turn anybody loose if there was the ghost of a chance he was guilty. But Captain Lafaux and I had once had a run-in over an arson case and he'd come out looking bad. He hadn't said anything but I knew he'd jump at the chance to get me in the future and now he had his opportunity.

I went over to where she sat and handed her the book. "Does this mean anything to you?"

She took it from me and then opened it. "It's a standard source for Yucatecan ethnohistory," she said. "Gregory's used it on several occasions. Where did you get it?"

I told her about Artemio and she smiled faintly.

"I wouldn't have expected anything else."

Then I brought out the jade and I saw fires of excitement in her gray eyes as she took it in both hands, like the last droplets of water in the desert. She ran her fingers over the dark surface and examined both sides.

"What did Artemio tell you?" she asked.

I explained and she listened, face intent. "What did he say about where he dug it up? *Exactly*."

"Temple. No, *Templo Ah*. Does that make any sense?"

She nodded emphatically. "A lot. *Templo Ah* is Temple A, at Ek Balam. He's saying that's where he found the jade."

"But *where* in the temple?" I asked.

"I don't know, but my guess is that it would be in the center, between the two doorways. That's where Andrews found the clay figures in the Seven Dolls Temple at Dzibilchaltún."

"So far, so good," I said. "But it still doesn't explain why the jade is so valuable."

She looked down at the little face and ran her hands over it caressingly. "The key has to be the meaning of these glyphs," she said.

I told her about Cobbett and she listened with a combination of amusement and horror. "Cobbett said they weren't calendar glyphs."

"He's right. Gregory could tell you, of course,

though I don't know that he could read it. The glyphs are very complex. It was only in the last thirty years, since the work of Knorosov, that it's been realized that many of them stand for phonetic elements. But we still don't have the meanings for a lot of them. It's sort of as if we used several different symbols for each letter of the alphabet."

I turned to the book. "What about this?" I asked. "I found the words 'Ek Balam' in it."

She nodded. "Yes. The *Relaciones de Yucatán* are part of a questionnaire the King of Spain sent to the Spanish landholders in the sixteenth century. Every Spaniard was required to send back a general description of his lands and their history. You can imagine it was a nuisance to most of the Spanish landowners, and they ran out to find the first Indian who was willing to tell them a story. The Spaniards living near Valladolid, in the center of the peninsula, got a story about a great lord named Ek Balam who once reigned in that area. The archaeological site is probably named after him." She broke out a cigarette. "It wasn't more than a few sentences in the book, and nobody knows whether he ever really existed. The old accounts are garbled. A lot of times the Indians said whatever they thought their Spanish masters wanted to hear."

I picked up the little jade artifact. "Ek Balam." I set it down on the coffee table. "Any idea what that means in Mayan?"

She sat back, kicking off her shoes and tucking her feet under her. "I don't know Mayan. Gregory knows quite a bit. The Maya used to take two surnames, the father's and the mother's. Ek Balam would be someone with a father—or is it a mother?—named Ek and the other parent would be Balam. Come to think of it, I think Gregory had an Ek working on the dig. The old surnames still exist."

"But the *meaning*," I persisted. "What do the words themselves mean?"

She shrugged again. "I don't know. We'd need a Motul to know that."

"A what?"

"A Motul dictionary. It's a sixteenth-century dictionary of Mayan, made by a Franciscan friar. It has most of the words in it."

"Where can we get one?"

She frowned. "Now?"

"That's right."

"Micah, it's Sunday night. And even if it weren't, you couldn't exactly walk into a library and ask for one. Only a few copies exist."

"There has to be one at Tulane."

"Sure. In Gregory's office . . ." She frowned as she read my intention. "No, Micah. It's too dangerous."

"You have the key and the alarm combination, don't you?"

The campus was black and the lights of cars on St. Charles died away before they reached us. Katherine fumbled with the keys at the bottom door while the Gothic stones loomed over us. I wanted to tell her to hurry, but I knew she was going as fast as she could in the darkness. I heard her swear under her breath and then what I had feared happened: Footsteps emerged from the dense shadows behind us and a flashlight flicked on. I jerked my head back over my shoulder and saw a uniform.

"Oh, it's you, Mrs. Degas," the patrolman said. "Do you need some help?" He flashed his light on the lock and she slipped the key into the lock and turned it.

"Thank you, Mr. Aucoin," Katherine purred. "I was about to give up."

The policeman tipped his hat. "Any time. Y'all be

careful now." He watched us pass through the doorway
and then returned to his rounds.

"Close," Katherine breathed.

"Very," I agreed, wishing we'd thought to bring a
flashlight. I slid in front of her, against her protests, and
started up the first flight of stairs.

The blackness plucked at my body and the air
seemed to close around us. The heavy institutional smell
of wax permeated the air and our steps echoed off the
walls. We came to the first landing and stopped. The pale
green of an exit sign glowed somewhere off to the left.
Katherine pushed up against me and I heard her breathing. The building seemed deserted. She nudged my elbow to guide me, and I started up the second flight. The
blackness closed around us once more and the op-
pressiveness of the air increased. I felt along with my
good hand, keeping it on the guard rail. We came to the
second landing and then the third.

I remembered that the last flight was a narrow, lad-
derlike series that probably had been designed for work-
men going into the attic. I looked up the tunnel. The
blackness was stygian, but miles above I could see a single dim red bulb burning like a demon eye. Katherine
slipped in before me and I crowded behind her. She was
the only one who had the key to disarm the alarm.

All at once the memory of an NVA bunker sprang
back to clutch me with sweaty fingers of fear. I remembered the fresh earth smell, the faint alcohol scent from
the hospital unit I'd found, the sweet-sick smell of
blood . . .

I stopped, sweat soaking my shirt, and reached up to
loosen the neck of my shirt. There'd been a code book
lying on the table in plain sight, holding down some
maps. I reached for it; then, at the last instant, drew
away my hand, some protective sixth sense telling me to
be careful. When I went back up into the light of day, I

told them about the code book and one of my sergeants volunteered to go back down. He was a veteran, and he knew what he was doing.

But the code book didn't hold a spring detonator. Instead, it was a switch, rigged to charges on the upper level. Later, we dug him out with the bamboo stick still in his hand. The stick and his body were untouched. He'd suffocated.

"Micah, are you all right?"

Her voice brought me back to myself. I took a deep breath.

"I'm fine."

We came to the top and she turned to me. "After I open it, I have exactly ten seconds to disarm the alarm at the panel inside. If I don't, every campus cop on duty will be up here inside of three minutes. Then, after I've turned it off, I have to call in and identify myself."

"Is that a problem?"

"No, I'm on the authorized list. And if anybody asks, I'll say I left something in my desk."

The keys jangled again, but only for a moment. The darkness above moved and I heard hinges give. I followed her upward, into the hallway of the Institute. She walked quickly to a panel in the wall and inserted her alarm key. The blinking red light went to green.

I sensed ghostly shapes around us, hovering in the entrance of the reconstructed temple, peering from the display cases. Here, the wax smell was overcome by the heavier odor of dust and I had the macabre sensation that it was the dust of decayed bones.

There was no novelty in it for Katherine, however, and she went quickly to a wall switch and flipped it on. The hallway was bathed in diffused light.

"I don't want to attract a lot of attention," she explained. "So I just put on the lights at one end."

We went into the narrow hallway that led between

display cases to the director's inner sanctum. She turned on the lights and lifted the phone. I walked along the bookcases, scanning the titles, while she explained to the alarm clerk that she had left something and would only be here a few minutes.

Then my eyes hit it, a thick volume with a cover the color of dried blood. *Diccionário de Motul.*

I removed it from the shelf and laid it on the desk, as Katherine hung up the phone and came to look over my shoulder. I opened the book at random and a barrage of unfamiliar words hit my eyes. I glanced down the columns. Some of the letters were familiar, but some, like a reversed *c*, were not.

"It's from Mayan to Spanish," Katherine explained. "There was supposed to be a Spanish-to-Mayan part once, but it's been lost."

She started to turn the pages, moving slowly. "Mayan has some sounds that the Spanish didn't know, like a *dz* sound, and a *ch* that you kind of bite off, so the Spanish had to invent some new letters, like the backward *c* and the *ch* with a bar through it."

"For somebody that's supposed not to know the language, you seem to know a lot," I commented.

She smiled. "A secretary—and face it, that's what I am, really, no matter what title he gave me to try to keep me happy—a secretary picks up things. I have to read his correspondence and answer a lot of it. I'd be pretty thick-headed if some of it didn't sink in."

She came to the letter *b*. "Let's see. *Balam*. Ah, here it is: of course. *Tigre*. Tiger. That's what the Spanish called the jaguar. Now that I think of it, I think I heard that somewhere. Now let's see what they have for *ek*." She flipped through the pages, stopped, and made a sound of disgust.

"Aagg. That's what's wrong with Mayan," she said. "There are so many words that have multiple meanings." I looked down at the page and saw what she meant: There were no fewer than four meanings for the word *ek,* followed by what appeared to be a page of idioms. She turned to the preceding page and I saw yet another version of the word.

"Well, let's start at the beginning. It looks like *ek* can mean cramps, if my Spanish is right—this sixteenth-century stuff is hard to understand sometimes." She turned to the next page. "It can mean grease. Ah." She pointed down. "It says 'star' or generic name."

I straightened. "So the lord of Ek Balam was named Star Jaguar."

"Yes. At least, that's what I'd bet. But let's see what else the word means: Hmmm. Brazilwood. That doesn't seem to apply. And the last is *cosa negra.* Something black."

I watched her close the big book and brought the little jade out of my pocket, into the thin light of the office.

I unwrapped it and stared down at the enigmatic features. The face was vaguely familiar and I wondered what I had seen that reminded me of it.

"Katherine, what would you say this face represented?"

She took it from me and screwed up her mouth. "Well, it could be anything. Their art was very stylized. But a lot of it seemed to center around a feline motif. This could be a . . ."

She looked up at me and I knew where I had seen the face before: It was in one of the art books on Sandy's shelf.

"A jaguar," I finished. I rubbed the smooth, dark surface with my finger. "A jaguar made out of dark jade. A black jaguar."

"Ek Balam," we said together and stared at each other in amazement. She took the little figure from my hand and regarded it with a frown.

"Of course. The Maya loved word plays and hidden meanings. But there has to be something else, something beyond just the name."

"The glyphs," I agreed, taking the object from her. "But what can they say that's so important?"

She shrugged. "There are only five or six glyphic elements here. That's not much of a text. And if you're right about who this represents, odds are the glyphs are just the name itself."

"Maybe." I rewrapped the jade and put it back into my pocket. "I wonder. Tell me, why would the Maya have buried this to begin with, and why in Temple A?"

"Who knows? Maybe as a kind of dedication offering? Maybe as an offering for good luck?"

"Was the rest of the temple ever excavated?"

"No. Gregory was leaving it for next season. It wasn't one of the more impressive structures. Just a small stone house on a platform a couple of feet high. Probably the temple of some minor god, or maybe the house of a priest."

I thought for a moment. Leeds had wanted me to have the jade. And the day before, Astrid Bancroft had appeared at Lavelle's, looking for me. Suddenly a piece of the puzzle fell into shape.

"Micah, what are you thinking?"

"Leeds may have shown this to the Bancroft girl," I said. "He had a working knowledge of glyphics, right? Maybe he deciphered it and told her what it means."

Katherine chewed at her lip. "That makes sense. So what are you suggesting?"

"It's too late now. But tomorrow, early, maybe you could call her in. Come up with some pretext, like the exhibit, something she won't be suspicious about. You can show her the glyphs. If she's seen them before, her face will show it. If she has, hit her hard. Tell her you don't want any nonsense. Tell her you know she knows the meaning and insist she tell you."

Katherine smiled slyly. "My no-nonsense school-mistress role, huh? The one I use on sophomores and first-year graduate students?"

We left quickly and there was no campus policeman waiting when we closed the big front doors. I checked the street as we pulled in at Katherine's place and was relieved to see that Scott's car was not there. She made coffee and I called O'Rourke. He told me he'd gotten the Captain.

"He wanted to know who I was and why a lawyer was calling him about something that wasn't any of my business. When I tried to explain, he wanted to know why you didn't call yourself."

There was an apologetic note in his voice and I understood; the Captain could be hard to deal with when he wanted.

"Thanks a lot, John. Is there anything new on the case?"

"Nothing really, unless you want to count Cora Thorpe's little gesture."

"What do you mean?"

"She pitched a fit in my office today, claimed I wasn't doing enough. Told me I was fired, which was a little late, since I'd already quit."

"Really broken up, eh?"

"I think she was carrying onions in her purse to help her cry. She almost made me feel sorry for Thorpe."

I replaced the receiver. Cora Thorpe. There was no denying someone had used the Thorpe car to kill Leeds. I thought of the muscular body of Claude St. Romaine, lying on the floor of the cabin, and another piece slid into place. Now, if it would only stay . . .

I started to call the Captain and then stopped myself. A call could be traced and I didn't need to leave any record of being at Katherine's place. Damn. Well, at least he was home, although I had a suspicion it was against medical advice.

"Bad news?" Katherine asked, bringing me a bourbon and water.

"My father's been having some health problems," I said. "Nothing much." I took the glass. Then I told her about Cora.

"I'm not surprised. Do you really think she could have done it?"

"It's possible. But somehow I don't think so, though she probably knows a lot."

"Oh?" She sat down beside me.

"I think she left in Thorpe's car and met St. Romaine. Then he let the killer use the car."

"And he was killed because he knew too much?"

"That's the way it looks to me."

Her hand reached out, touched my arm. "But Micah, who could it be? This Cuban gangster you talked about?"

"Possibly, though his methods seem more direct."

"Well, what about Astrid's beau, Fred Gladney? I know he's a bit of a wimp, but . . ."

"He was at Cobbett's until two A.M.," I said. "And what could be his motive?"

She stared at me for another second, apparently trying to make up her mind about something. Then she exhaled heavily. "I knew St. Romaine," she said finally.

"What?"

Her hand dropped back into her lap. "Oh, not well. But I'd met him a few times. He came up a couple of years ago about making a donation to the Institute. He was pretty well off. He asked that it be anonymous. He didn't want to be bothered by other people asking for money. Technically I broke a confidence by telling you, but what the hell?"

"How much did he give?"

"Two thousand dollars. Peanuts, compared to what he's supposed to be worth. But, like they say, it's better than a sharp stick in the eye. And it entitled him to the newsletter, reports of the progress of the excavation, the usual baloney."

I sat back, holding one more piece of the puzzle. The trouble was that I didn't know where to fit it.

I made a further call, this one to Sandy. She told me she was fine and to quit worrying. I told her to find out everything she could about St. Romaine and his family and then turned back to Katherine, but the couch was empty.

The plumbing rattled in the upstairs bath and I settled in with my drink, trying to fit the pieces together. I was still sitting there when I heard movement on the stairs and turned around.

Katherine was halfway down the landing. She had changed into a negligee and her hair was down around her shoulders. She hesitated and then, as I watched, came down another step.

I rose, my heart quickening. "Katherine . . ."

She raised a finger to her lips and I knew that she didn't want me to spoil the moment by speaking. I went up the steps and halted, inches from her. She reached out timidly and took my hand, then turned around and led me the rest of the way up the steps.

I woke up in the middle of the night, the delicious lethargy of sleep falling away. I had a premonition of disaster. Fragments of dreams raced through my mind. I saw St. Romaine, crumpled on the floor, while Cora Thorpe snored on the sofa. I saw Cobbett cringing in the back of Sandy's car. I saw a terrified Karl Hahn waving a gun he didn't know how to handle. But the dream that had linked it all together was irretrievably gone.

I looked down at the woman beside me. Her face was troubled, and even as I watched she shifted position slightly and her lips mouthed a name.

"Gregory . . ."

It stabbed into me like a knife and I got up and went over to the window. I looked over at my paralyzed left arm. I had come to terms with the injury long ago and usually it did not affect me, but now, for some reason, I felt lacking.

When I awoke, Katherine was already downstairs, dressed. When I came down she gave me a quick smile and then went about preparing breakfast as if nothing had happened. I could see that she was struggling and so I kept quiet, watching her exert the self-control that had first gained my attention. We sat across from each other, drinking coffee in silence, and when the silence finally seemed ready to shatter, she rose calmly.

"Well. I guess you'd better give me the jade if I'm going to confront Astrid."

I had known it was coming and I'd prepared my speech. "I'd rather not," I said evenly and watched the hurt register. I got up and went to her.

"It's not that. It's because the damned thing is too dangerous. Two people have been killed. I don't want a third, especially not you. If Astrid's seen the thing, and if she and Leeds have examined it, she'll know what the glyphs mean."

Katherine hesitated, then nodded. "Of course. You're right." She went to the mirror in the hallway and smoothed her blouse, as I traced the glyphic inscription onto a piece of paper. "I'll call you at about ten or ten-thirty," she said, taking the paper. "As soon as I find something out."

I started to kiss her but somehow the iron self-control got in the way. Instead, I watched her go out and sat back down on the sofa, feeling helpless.

I called Sandy but the line was busy. I paced some more and went to the bookcase. Maybe there was something I could read to help me pass the time. I found a book about modern Maya culture and leafed through it.

What had Katherine told me when this had all started? That she served also in an editorial capacity for the MARI series? That meant she had had a hand in producing all the green-bound volumes. I took down another one. It was an abstruse treatise on Mayan settlement patterns. Another was a survey of coastal Yucatán. And one was a book by Gregory Thorpe, on the significance of astronomical alignments to the ancient Maya. I opened it at random and saw a map of a Maya city, showing projected alignments of different celestial bodies from a central observation point. I put the book back and called Sandy again. Once more the line was busy.

I didn't like it. She was entitled to talk on the phone, but it had been twenty minutes. I paced some more, trying to occupy myself with the pieces to the puzzle.

Ek Balam, the Black Jaguar, had been the mythical lord of the city Thorpe had excavated. A jaguar figure of black jade had been excavated at one of the city's temples. People were willing to kill for the jade figure. Why? I took down the last volume in the series. It was also by Thorpe, entitled *Initial Excavations at Ek Balam, 1982–1987.*

Inside the back cover was a fold-out map and I spread this before me on the coffee table. Each building was designated by a letter and I found Temple A in the central section of the site. I turned the map around, hoping some significant configuration of elements would leap out at me, but nothing happened. I refolded the map, placed it back in the book, and put the book back on the shelf.

I tried Sandy's number again and this time I got it to ring. But the voice that answered wasn't Sandy's. It belonged to a man and I knew it from somewhere.

"Hello? Who's this?" Something about the peremptory tone struck a chord of familiarity.

I hesitated, weighing my options.

"I said who is this?" the voice demanded again.

Finally, my concern for Sandy won out. "Mancuso," I said. "What are you doing there?"

"Dunn? Is that you? Goddamn it, man, you've put your foot in it now."

"Mancuso, damn it, where's Sandy? What's going on?"

"I was hoping you could tell us. We got a call about a hell of a racket going on here. Patrol officers found the place wrecked and blood everywhere."

My breath went out and my legs started trembling. "And Sandy?"

"Your friend's disappeared."

18

Dread swept over me. But at least there was a chance she was still alive . . .

"Micah, are you there?"

"I'm here," I croaked. "Are you tapping the phone, Mancuso?"

"How? I've only been here ten minutes. The bastards knocked the receiver off the hook and the patrol officers didn't put it back until we cleared it." When he spoke again his voice had softened. "Look, why don't you come in and we can talk this over."

"Sure. In one of the interrogation rooms."

The policeman snorted. "Shit, Micah, I never thought you did anything."

"That wouldn't keep you from locking me up. You're too good a cop not to."

"Yeah, I guess that's right. Well, look, at least tell us if you know who's got her."

I hesitated and then made my decision. "I know who's got her," I said, "but I can't tell you who it is. I can't take a chance of having you guys come in like Eliot Ness. He doesn't want Sandy. He wants something I have. If I give it to him, he'll give her back, because he doesn't want trouble any more than the next guy."

"Well, for Christ's sake, man, work with us. We can set up a drop point, stake it out, monitor the exchange, and . . ."

"And what? Arrest me when it's over? It might just about be worth it, but there's still the killer of Gordon Leeds and Claude St. Romaine out there somewhere."

I heard a sigh. "Micah, damn it . . ."

"Later, Mancuso." I hung up the phone, feeling weak. There was no way around it. I had told him the truth: I would have to give up the jade.

I looked out the window. Good. Katherine's car was at the curb, meaning she'd walked the two blocks to the streetcar line. I called her at the Institute. "Do you have a couple of dollars squirreled away somewhere?"

"On the shelf in the closet, in my old handbag. Why? What's happening?"

"Just trying to amuse myself," I said wryly.

"Obviously. Well, make yourself at home. By the way, Astrid will be over in a little while."

"Good."

I disconnected and went upstairs. The money was where she'd said it would be. I found her spare car key on the keyboard in the kitchen, where I'd seen it earlier. I drove to a store on Claiborne that had what I needed. I was back inside of half an hour and set up in the kitchen. It took me another hour or so, but when I was finished I was satisfied.

I cleaned up the mess and went to the telephone. I found Ordaz's number in the business pages and dialed.

At first the woman said he wasn't in. I told her my name and said he was expecting my call. The line clicked and I got thirty seconds of elevator music, and then I heard his voice, fruity and satisfied, as if he was savoring one of life's rare moments.

"Mr. Dunn. How nice to hear from you again. Why is it I had a feeling you would call?"

"Where is she, Ordaz?"

"She? Who, Mr. Dunn? Am I supposed to have something that belongs to *you?* Now, that would be real irony."

"Sandy. You took her. I want her back."

"Mr. Dunn, you confuse me. I'm an immigration attorney. I don't get involved in seizures. Are we talking about a boat?"

I bit my tongue. Everything hinged on what I would say in the next few seconds: "I'm willing to deal," I said.

There was an amused chuckle. "Deal? Deal what?"

"The item you wanted. I have it. I'll give it to you for Sandy."

"Barter? This item for the item you say I possess?"

"That's it."

"That's an intriguing concept, Mr. Dunn. But I wonder if the two items are of equivalent value. Still, the concept has potential."

"Tonight. I'll give it to you tonight. Bring Sandy or there's no deal."

"Tonight?"

"At the Harmony Street wharf, at nine o'clock. You, personally. I don't deal with Mutt and Jeff."

"But—"

I hung up. I hoped I'd hooked him. It was all a big risk, but with Sandy's life at stake, there wasn't much choice.

I turned from the phone in time to hear the door

open and froze. But it was Katherine, taking off her sunglasses and dropping her handbag onto the couch.

"You look guilty," she said. "What did I catch you doing?" She wrinkled her nose. "It smells funny in here."

I looked up at the wall clock. "You're early. It's only just after eleven."

"One of the benefits of running the operation these days. I get to leave when I like." She went to the refrigerator and took out a Coke. "Besides, there's only so much I can take. I got a frantic call from Jason Cobbett just now. He's threatening to cancel the exhibition because of all the publicity. He's already tried Gregory and found him guilty."

"What did you tell him?"

"I told him it was all part of a Mayan curse and that if he had any brains at all, he could get enough PR mileage out of it to make this the new King Tut. I had him going for a second." She took a long swallow. I thought her face looked tired and I wondered how mine must look to her. "Damn it, Micah, I'm getting old. I can only take this for so long."

"I know. Did you talk to the Bancroft girl?"

She nodded. "I don't think she's ever seen the jade. At least, she wasn't sure about the glyphs." She walked back out into the living room and removed a cassette recorder from her purse. "Here: Gregory uses this sometimes for making notes. I recorded our interview. You can hear her yourself."

I pushed the buttons and turned up the volume. There was a second of silence and then I heard Katherine asking the other woman to come in. They exchanged pleasantries. Papers rustled and Katherine asked her to come over into the light.

"This is something Dr. Thorpe has been working on," I heard Katherine say. "I thought if I could get an interpretation of these glyphs, it might move the work along."

Silence, then the Bancroft girl's voice: "I'm not sure. I recognize some of them, but it's not my field."

"Which ones do you recognize?" Katherine asked.

Hesitation. Then: "The first one looks like *ti*, the locative. It means 'at' or 'at the place of.' Then this next one is *Chak,* I think. Yes, I'm pretty sure."

"The rain god?"

"Or the color red. Now this one I don't know, or this one, either, but this one looks like *Yaaxkin. Yaaxkin,* of course, is the dry month, when the fields are burned."

"It doesn't mean anything to you?"

"No. But, like I said, it isn't my field. Sometimes I run into glyphs painted on ceramics, but . . . I'm sorry."

Her voice sounded steadier than I remembered, as if she were fully in control.

Katherine's voice spoke then: "Well, I appreciate your help. I'll save it for Dr. Thorpe."

"Is he being released? There's a rumor . . ."

"I hope so, Astrid."

"It's all a big mess, isn't it? I mean, Gordon being killed and all. Why? All any of us wanted was to do archaeology."

"I know." When Katherine spoke again her voice had become motherly. "I'm sure it will be all right."

"Yes. So how's Scotty?"

"He's fine. I'll tell him you asked."

The sound went off and I pushed the STOP button.

"You see?" Katherine asked, one arm folded across her. "It doesn't make sense. "The place of Red Something-Something-Dry Season."

I frowned. She was right. "Maybe the words have some hidden meaning," I suggested.

"Quite possibly. But I don't know what it would be. Christ, I wish Gregory were here. He'd know."

Yes, I thought, he probably would.

"Well, it'll be over soon," I told her. "I'm going to give Ordaz the jade."

"What?" She brought her arm down quickly, her face showing the shock.

"I have to, Katherine. I called Sandy's apartment and got Lieutenant Mancuso. They've kidnapped her. The only way to get her back is to exchange her for the *hacha.*"

Katherine exhaled. "But how will you prove you aren't guilty? And how will they ever find out who *is?*"

"Well," I said with a wry smile, "I guess the answer to that lies in how much I can do between now and nine o'clock."

She shook her head. "But where will you start?"

I told her about my conversation with O'Rourke. "I think," I summed up, "that I'll start with Cora Thorpe."

I drove past twice and didn't see any stakeout. Her car was there, though, so I stopped a block away and walked up. The noon heat was enervating and I blinked from the glare, feeling like a convict who had just been let out of a dungeon. It was too close a simile for me to entertain without wincing and I was glad when I came to the house with the camphor trees shading the walkway.

This time I didn't see Mr. Beasley, but as I went through the iron-grille gate I caught a flicker of movement at his window curtain. I wondered how long it would take him to call the police.

Cora Thorpe opened the door on the third knock. She was wearing a pantsuit that showed her curves to best effect, with a flowered blouse that did little to conceal her cleavage. When she saw me, her features went from eagerness to disappointment.

"You're not supposed to be here," she said, which I

thought was a curious understatement. I shoved past her into the living room and closed the door behind me.

"You're right," I told her. "The trouble is, I am. And I'm not leaving until I get some answers."

"I think I'll call the police."

"Go ahead. As soon as I leave. If you try it before, I'll yank the damned thing out of the wall."

She eyed me and I could see she was trying to calculate her odds.

"I wouldn't," I said. "Even with one arm I could wring your neck. And I don't think many people would blame me."

She folded her arms, hip outthrust. "So what do you want?" she pouted.

"I told you: I want the answers."

"I don't know what you mean."

"Yes, you do. And the sooner you give them, the safer you'll be. Tell me what kind of game you're playing."

"Game?"

"You're not the kind of woman who's happy waiting for a husband twenty years older to come home and talk about what inscription he's deciphered today. But Claude's dead because of what he knew and you can end up the same way. The more people you tell, the safer you are."

"Nobody's going to kill me," she said. "Now go away."

"I'll go when you've told me what I want to know," I said. "What is it? Thrills? Revenge? Blackmail?"

"Blackmail?" she asked, trying to laugh. "You're crazy."

So I was right.

"Believe me, whoever you've got the hooks into will kill again," I told her, "and the next time the police

come it will be to look down at your body. The next time
Gregory sees you will be in one of the lockers at
Charity." I shook my head. "It isn't a pretty sight, Cora.
No perfume for you down there. Just alcohol and form-
aldehyde. And it's cold.Too cold. Everybody wears a
jacket. But you won't be wearing anything. Just a sheet.
A sheet and a toe tag. And you know the worst thing?
You won't be the wife of the director anymore. You'll
just be a number. A piece of the past. They'll do an au-
topsy like you're a side of beef—"

"Stop it!" she shrieked, her hands to her ears. "For
God's sake, stop it. I'll tell you what you want to know!"

I was just pulling away when the police car arrived. I
turned down Coliseum and was back at Katherine's inside of two minutes. I opened the door and stopped
short. She and Thorpe were facing each other in the center of the living room, the stress evident in their pos-
tures.

"You," Thorpe said.

"It seems to be my day to surprise people," I said,
shutting the door.

"Micah . . ." Katherine began.

"I take it they let you go," I said. "Or did you decide
to imitate me?"

"I posted bond," Thorpe sniffed. "My new attorney
arranged it. A formality. I understand the charges are
going to be dropped, thank God."

"Good for you, not so good for me," I said. "Is this
my cue to go down and throw myself on the mercy of the
court?"

"If you're smart you will," he said.

"Gregory," Katherine broke in. "Micah's as much a
victim as you are. He's the only hope any of us have to
clear this thing up."

"Then why doesn't he call the police and tell them?" Thorpe asked.

"In due time," I said. "Right now there's a matter of finding the real killer and saving another life."

"You don't seem to have done so well up to now," he pronounced. "And your lawyer friend didn't do much for me." He moved away from Katherine, toward the kitchen. "I shouldn't even be standing here talking to you. I ought to call the police."

I sighed. "You do and I'll break your jaw."

Thorpe blinked and I could tell he wasn't used to being threatened.

Katherine stepped between us. "Gregory, Micah deserves your help. He's done everything he could to clear you."

"Like following my wife," Thorpe choked out and all at once I saw what was making him so angry. Without me he would never have had to face the ugly fact of Cora's infidelity.

"If somebody had followed her before, none of this would have happened," I shot back. "Or did you think she was riding around by herself those nights she got bored with the domestic fireside?"

His face went ashen and Katherine looked from one of us to the other, as if trying to decide who would erupt first.

"You keep my wife out of this," Thorpe whispered between gritted teeth. "She had nothing to do with any killings and I won't have her name mentioned."

I thought of the little scheme she had concocted. I didn't feel very sorry for either of them right now.

"Is that why you came here before you went home?" I asked.

Thorpe's mouth worked wordlessly. I nodded to the paper bag of belongings beside the door. "Parish Prison

Suitcase," I said. "Most people don't carry them around any longer than they have to."

"I was just stopping off to notify Katherine. It was business, that's all."

"You don't have to explain," I said. "It's none of my affair." I looked over at Katherine and saw her blush. "Right now, all I care about is getting my friend out of danger and putting the killer in jail. And maybe getting myself off the hook."

"Well, you can do all that," Thorpe said. "Just do it somewhere else."

I took a step toward him and the only thing that saved him was the door opening behind me. I wheeled around.

Scott was standing in the entrance, staring at us.

"Come on in, Scott," I told him. "The professor was just getting ready to throw me out."

The boy looked over at Thorpe and snickered.

"Don't worry," I said. "I'm not going. There's too much to do here."

"Katherine," Thorpe said, turning to her, "this is your home. Do you really want this man to stay here? Do you want him around your son?"

"Scott's a little old to be corrupted by Micah," Katherine said gently. "And, to answer your question, I *do* want Micah to stay." Thorpe went red and started to shove past her but she reached out with a hand to stay him. "And I want you to stay, too. I need you both."

Thorpe shifted his posture, somewhat mollified.

"I don't know what's going on," Scott put in then, "but I think Mom's right. Micah could've killed me a couple of days ago, but he didn't."

Katherine gave him a surprised, grateful look. "Support comes from unexpected quarters," she said fondly.

"Looks like the vote's been taken," I said. "Now let's try to make sense of this." I walked to the other side of the coffee table, so that I was facing Thorpe, with the table between us. "The first thing, Professor Thorpe, is for you to realize that Artemio was stealing from you."

"What?" Thorpe shook his head. "That's totally ridiculous. I saved Artemio. I gave him a chance. Why, before I hired him he was just a *campesino*, a villager. I took him in, worked with him, made him a field boss over the other workers, and brought him to the United States. I even stood for his last child at baptism." He gave a strangled little laugh. "The man's my *compadre*. That's a sacred relationship."

"It is," I said. "I spent a little time this morning reading about it in one of the books on the shelf there. It's so sacred that betrayal is almost unthinkable."

"Which is why he would never have betrayed me," Thorpe declared.

"No, you have it wrong. You're the one who betrayed *him*."

"What?"

"From his point of view. You brought him to the golden land, the United States. You built him up in the eyes of his fellows. He used his experiences to accrue all kinds of prestige with them. Then what happened?" I hesitated, choosing my next words carefully. "In his eyes, you turned around and pulled the rug out from under him."

"But that's absurd," Thorpe blustered. "I don't know what you mean. I was *good* to that man. Even when he got into trouble with his drinking, I always bailed him out."

"Of course you did," I said. "Nobody ever said you weren't a conscientious person. It's probably your most important characteristic. It stands out to everybody that knows you. And in this case it extended to making sure that the immigration laws were strictly followed and that Artemio didn't overstay his work permit."

"Of course. I can't go around violating federal law."

"No. But federal law is not something a person like Artemio understands. In his country, law is something to be gotten around or even disregarded. More important, the tie between two men who are *compadres* obliterates any minor adherence to laws." I lifted my hand to quiet his protest. "Remember, I'm talking from Artemio's standpoint. Professor, I don't think you realize what a disappointed, bitter man Artemio is. That was what fueled his drinking and made him start stealing from you."

Thorpe sighed. "I don't really see how he could have stolen from us. I was very careful to monitor all field-work, and when I wasn't there, Gordon or Astrid was there. The most that could have been picked up were bits and pieces. The very way you put it shows a layman's understanding of archaeology."

Katherine gave me an apologetic look, but if Thorpe caught it, it didn't sink in.

"Unsophisticated people," he lectured, "tend to think of archaeology as a search for treasure. Tombs and temples. King Tut's tomb. And maybe it once was. But in the last thirty years, everything has changed. Today, archaeology is a study of other aspects of culture than simply the most obvious physical remains. In our case, we were looking for astronomical alignments and inscriptions that would cast light on the continuation of the classic Mayan system of time reckoning in eastern Yucatán. No gold, Mr. Dunn. No silver. And precious few artifacts at any one time."

"Of course," I agreed. "But over the course of three years' work you *did* find some figurines and other objects that collectors would pay money for."

"Certainly, but only in the aggregate. I can't imagine any individual piece worth more than a hundred dollars or so. And besides, the Mexican government won't let us bring much out of the country. Most of what we excavate we clean, photograph, and catalog in our lab at Valladolid, after which it's taken to Mérida, to the regional center for the National Institute."

"That's an important point," I said, "because that's the key."

"What are you talking about?"

"I'm talking about systematic theft from the boxes where the artifacts were stored."

Thorpe's eyes bulged. He was sweating now, trying hard not to believe it, and yet smart enough to know I was on to something.

"But that's impossible." He gave a nervous little chuckle. "I think I'd recognize what was excavated at my own site."

"But weren't you frequently away, attending to customs clearances, consulting with your Mexican colleagues, and so forth? How could you be there all the time?"

"Well . . ." He raised his hands, and then dropped them.

"Lceds was there, though," I said. "He was your field supervisor. He *would* have known."

"But we kept records . . ."

"Of course. But how can you tell from a record whether the piece is still in storage in Mexico without having somebody there to verify it? Boxes could be pilfered between the site and the National Institute office in Mérida, or opened at night in the lab before loading, the most valuable pieces taken out. All it would require would be bribery of a guard or a truck driver. It might be years before anybody got around to checking them in Mérida, from what Katherine told me."

"Well, yes, theoretically." He brushed a hand back over his thinning brown hair and turned his back on us. When he turned around again there was something like determination, or as close as he could get to it. "There's one way to find out about this. I'll talk to Artemio. He'll tell me, by God . . ."

I looked over at Scott. "Do you know where Artemio lives?"

He nodded. "Sure."

"Go over there and if he's at home, bring him here. Tell him the professor wants to see him."

"Give me five minutes," the boy said. The door closed behind him and I turned back to Thorpe.

"Bear in mind," I said, "it wasn't big-time theft. It was petty pilferage, because he was resentful, knowing this would be his last trip to the U.S. But I think in the process he saved some items out. The ones he thought were his best, and he smuggled them into the country with him. He figured he could make more without a Mexican middleman. He asked around and found a buyer. He convinced the buyer he could deliver a substantial shipment; all wishful thinking, of course. On that basis the buyer took his offerings, which were relatively worthless, a few hundred dollars at most. The buyer got rid of the merchandise almost immediately." I told him how Leeds had seen the objects in the flea market and had bought them. "Leeds had no idea it was Artemio doing the pilfering. He thought it was *you.*"

The statement hit Thorpe like a broadside and he seemed to wilt. "*Me?* I don't understand."

"Part of it was the normal frustration and resentment a student feels regarding his major professor. But there was more." Thorpe already appeared stricken and, whatever I thought of him, it gave me no pleasure to reduce him further. "Let's just call it a personality thing," I said. "He probably felt you didn't give his theories enough weight. Anyway, he convinced himself that the only way to deal with you was to show you he knew about your alleged thefts."

"Insane," Thorpe mumbled, shaking his head, but

this time I knew he was accusing the dead man, not me. "My God, I never did that boy anything. Why would he turn on me?"

"It might have stopped there, with Leeds's eccentric little game," I said. "But there was one other artifact he hadn't shown anybody."

"Another artifact?" Thorpe cocked his head and I wondered how much was getting through after the initial shock.

"A small piece of jade," I said. "What's commonly called an *hacha*. I suppose Artemio dug it up before he went to work for you, or not long afterward. He kept it as a kind of lucky piece. But then, when his luck started to turn, he decided to sell it. Of all the things he had found, it *might* bring a decent price. After all, it had some writing on it and he knew your people were intrigued by the ancient writing."

"Glyphs?" Thorpe croaked.

"That's right." I reached into my pocket and grasped the little piece of stone. "Artemio included it with the artifacts he sold and the buyer let it go when he unloaded the merchandise on his own buyer. When Leeds saw it, he realized he had something unusual. Not unique, perhaps, but unusual. He set to work trying to make sense out of the writing, meanwhile carrying out his duel with you."

I took my hand out of my pocket, the jade clutched tightly in my fist. "I think," I said, "that one of the points of difference between you and Leeds had to do with interpretation of the glyphs."

"That's true," Thorpe allowed. "He was one of the new bunch. Every bit of Mayan writing has to relate to some event in the lives of the kings or, even, the *people*." His nose wrinkled in disgust. "Members of the old school, like myself, are supposed to be rigidly bound to the discredited belief that the glyphs are only records of celestial and astrological events. That is, reflections of the mythology. The difference is illusory, of course. No one, certainly not I, ever said that—"

"I'm sure. The point, however, is that it took Leeds a little while to figure out what the glyphs on the *hacha* meant. And when he did, it opened a whole new world."

"Oh? And how was that?"

It was my turn to shrug. "I don't know, because I don't read glyphs. But maybe you can tell us." I opened my hand and he stared down in surprise at the jade. He picked it out of my hand and carried it over to the light.

"Where did this come from?" he demanded. "Exactly?"

"Artemio dug it up from the floor of Temple A," Katherine said.

"Temple A?" Thorpe's lips puckered. "Odd. I've always wondered why that little structure was there. Doesn't fit in with the essential symmetry of the site. Well, let's see . . ." He squinted down, holding the jade up to his face.

Katherine joined him beside the lamp. "We think the first element is the locative, meaning 'at,' and the second is 'red' something, followed by the glyph for the dry season."

Thorpe grunted, a man suddenly back in his element.

"Amazing," he declared. "I've never seen anything like this. It's black nephrite. Nephrite is unknown in Central America. This must have come from the West Coast of the United States. The black color in itself is remarkable—it indicates a high quantity of iron oxide. But the style is almost Costa Rican. The stone must have been brought into the Mayan lowlands from the north, traded over an incredible distance, and the artisan who carved it must have come from south of the Mayan area—perhaps installed at Ek Balam as a sort of artist in residence." He shook his head wonderingly. "And these glyphs; it reminds me in many ways of the Tuxtla statuette. But the Tuxtla had a calendrical inscription. This is not calendrical unless you count the reference to *Yaaxkin,* the dry month."

"You can read the glyphs, then?" I asked.

He nodded. "Oh, yes. They're clear enough. I can't imagine why Leeds had any problem. You're right about the *ti.* It means 'at,' and the *Yaaxkin* is clear enough. It is preceded by an element I take to be another locative."

"And the color red?" I asked.

"Simple enough," he declared condescendingly. "Actually there are two glyphs. The second part is unclear, but the combination appears enough in other texts for us to identify them."

"And?" I prodded.

He sniffed and stared over at me with a superior air. "The elements are *Chac Ek.* Red Star. That's the Mayan expression for the planet Venus. Then, the last is a double glyph, the star resting on the head of the characteristic spotted feline face."

"Then the entire message . . ." Katherine started but before she could finish, her front door flew open and we turned to see Scott standing in the doorway, his eyes wide, clothes disheveled.

Katherine started toward him. "Scotty, what . . . ?"

His mouth worked wordlessly for a moment and then he got it out. "It's Artemio," he cried. "Somebody's *killed* him."

I muttered a curse. "Tell me exactly what happened," I ordered.

He slumped against the doorway, his face drained of color. "I parked in front and went around to the back. I knocked but nobody answered. There was a radio playing inside, so I tried the door. It was open. He . . . Artemio was on the bed. I smelled whiskey and at first I thought he was just drunk. Then I saw the blood."

"Oh, Jesus," Thorpe moaned.

"Go on," I said. "How had he been killed, could you tell?"

Scott's chest heaved as he fought for breath. "There was blood on his head, on one side, and it was all over the bed. I think somebody hit him. I didn't see any weapon."

"Murdered while he was sleeping," Thorpe declared. "This is terrible."

I took Scott by the arm and led him to the couch. Katherine had already read my mind and poured him a shot of bourbon. He tossed it down like a man in the desert offered a canteen. I went over to the telephone.

"What are you going to do?" Thorpe asked, alarmed.

"I'm calling the police."

"Oh," he said. Then a crooked little smile twisted his face. "Well, they can't say I did *this* one. I was here all the time. You're all my witnesses."

"Yes," I said with disgust, dialing the number. "You were here." I asked for Mancuso and waited, hoping he would be there. I was lucky. Twenty seconds later I heard his voice.

"Mancuso, listen: This is Micah Dunn. Don't bother to trace this call. I'll be off before you can get the number. Besides, I'm going to tell you where you can find me." I told him about Artemio's murder and gave him the address. I heard him yell the information to an associate and knew a radio car would be on the way. "Now: If you want to know who did it, meet me tonight at ten o'clock at the foot of Louisiana Street. Don't bring an army. If they see you, it'll be for nothing."

"Dunn, what the hell is going on?"

"You'll find out tonight," I promised.

"Jesus," he snorted. "First your lady friend gets snatched, then I have an idiot coming in trying to confess to save his girlfriend, and now *this* . . ."

"What are you talking about?"

"Oh, this fellow Gladney. He's scared to death we're going to lock up his girlfriend because she's got a mental record. He's here now, claiming *he* killed goddamn Leeds, which is a crock, because we've got Claude St. Romaine's prints all over the car. His and Cora Thorpe's and your friend the professor's, but not Gladney's."

"And Astrid Bancroft? Were her prints in it?"

"No, but her compact was. But what the hell? She

says Thorpe gave her a ride the other day and she lost it. We can't send somebody to the chair on that. But the poor jerk's beside himself."

"How long has he been down there?"

"Two hours. Came in just before the professor got sprung. And he'll probably be here the rest of the day, the way he's acting. DA'll raise hell we don't at least *look* at his confession."

"We all have our problems," I said. "Just be there tonight."

"Wait a minute, Dunn. Do you know who did it?"

"Be there," I said and hung up.

All three of them were looking at me. "My God," Thorpe cried. "Do you know who did it?"

"Yes," I said. "And that's why I can't stay here. Mancuso is a good cop. He'll be trying to trace that call. If he succeeds, then a police car will be on the way over. And if I end up back in jail, Sandy will be dead." I started for the door but he reached out and grabbed my arm.

"You mean you're just . . . *leaving*?"

"That's right." I looked down at his hand and he removed it. "I hope I can borrow your car for another few hours," I told Katherine.

"Take mine," Scott offered. "They'll expect to see Mom's outside." He reached into his pocket and handed me some bills. "It's not much, only twenty or so, but you can't go around without money."

"Thanks," I said as he handed me the keys. "As for you," I told Thorpe, "I think I'd go home. Your wife needs you there. She's been playing a dangerous game. You can't blackmail a killer without running a risk of being the next victim."

"Blackmail?" Thorpe's mouth shot open.

"Sorry to disillusion you," I said, "but Cora's a naughty girl."

I went out then and got into Scott's car. Maybe Mancuso was willing to take my word and wait for nightfall, but I couldn't count on it. I found a bar on Magazine where I wasn't known and settled into a back booth, where it was dark. I ordered a beer and a sandwich and watched the TV, hoping the barkeep hadn't been alerted for someone with a limp arm. It was Monday, and the place was almost empty, which meant the bartender had more time on his hands than on a busier day. But he seemed content to ignore me and watch soap operas, shaking his head in disapproval at the machinations of the characters. At four the regulars started coming in. I got up and went to the pay phone in the corner.

O'Rourke's secretary put me through as soon as I identified myself. "I hope you aren't busy tonight," I said.

"Jesus, Micah, what's happening? I've been worried to death."

I told him where I was and he groaned. "They can't do much to the beer," he said, "but stay away from the muffalettas. No olive oil at all."

"I need you to be at the Harmony Street wharf tonight just before nine," I said. "Park on Louisiana, near the ferry. If you see a couple of seedy types in a black Ford, don't worry. I told Mancuso to be there at ten, but you know how antsy cops are. I figure they'll be there at nine-thirty."

"No problem," O'Rourke said. "Am I to assume you're going to turn yourself in?"

"Definitely. Right after I get Sandy loose."

"Oh." He cleared his throat. "Micah, for God's sake, don't try anything tricky."

"Of course not," I said and hung up.

Then I made another call and the person who answered wasn't so happy to hear from me. But he listened to my demand and grudgingly agreed to comply.

"Remember," I said. "One hour."

I had another beer and then went out into the afternoon. It had clouded up and there was a smell of rain, mixed with the rich aroma of coffee from down on the wharves. I got into the car, removing the parking ticket on the windshield, and waited.

He came at exactly four-fifty, a weasel-faced stub of a man with a Hawaiian shirt flapping loose in the sudden breeze. I opened the car door.

"Nice to see you, Harry," I said.

Harry the Hawk threw down his cigarette and climbed in. "Goddamn, I get caught with you, Micah, it's worth three years in the place. And I don't mean the country club at Hunt, I mean goddamn Angola."

"I won't tell your PO," I said. "Cross my heart."

Harry wrinkled his nose. "It'll be three hundred," he said. "I got to pay my supplier."

"Sure. As soon as I get things straightened out."

"Cash," Harry begged.

"Is this the same man I alibied when his PO was trying to arrest him for consorting with thugs?"

"But my story was *true*," Harry whined. "I *was* with you."

"Sure. But I may not have such a good memory next time." I held out my hand.

Harry sighed and reached under his shirt. "Okay, okay." He handed me something cold and hard. "I know you wanted a Colt, but a Smith was the best I could come up with on such short notice."

I looked down at his offering. It was a Chief's Special: snub-nosed, just nineteen ounces, and easy to conceal, but only five shots, which put it at a disadvantage with a Colt in a firefight.

"It'll do," I said, as he handed me a box of .38 ammunition.

When he'd gone I checked the revolver. It was already loaded. The extra shot would have been nice, but it was always the first one or two that counted. I stuck the gun under my shirt and scooped a handful of shells into my pocket, knowing as I did that it was unlikely I'd have a chance to reload.

Then I went back to the bar and waited for night.

An electrical storm started outside and even inside I could feel the blasts of thunder shaking the building. The door opened and some men came in, swearing and laughing, rain dripping off their clothes onto the floor. The bartender greeted them by name and they took stools at the bar. They had Ninth Ward accents and from their conversation I guessed they were longshoremen. A little while later a kid came in and went to the pinball machine. I nursed my beer in the shadows and let the storm pass over, thinking of the rush-hour traffic snarled outside on the freeway, and the fender benders that would have cars lined up two miles from the bridge, all the way back to the Claiborne Street ramp.

I thought of the man in the Trade Mart Building, looking down at it all, and I reflected on the psychology of the new tall buildings with their hermetically sealed glass, which took you up so far above the streets that everything below seemed like a painting, unreal and staged, so that if you did something, dropped a brick on some of the ants below, it was an act without significance.

I thought about the people who had been killed, and why, and I thought about the odd little piece of jade, and about what Cora Thorpe had told me.

When I went outside the rain had quit and wisps of steam clouded up from the pavement. The rich coffee smell of earlier in the day had been washed away by the pungent odor of wet tar mixed with exhaust fumes, as the humid air acted to trap the fumes of the buses and autos.

I drove to another bar a few blocks away, where I could spend the rest of the time without attracting attention. This one was livelier, with a couple of Greek sailors arm-wrestling at one of the tables. I kept to myself in the back, though, and nobody bothered me.

The Captain had taught me always to have a contingency plan ready, so he wouldn't have approved of my situation now. But he had never explained what you were supposed to do when there were no contingency plans available. All I had was the advantage of knowing the battlefield and hoping that everyone else would do what I wanted when the time was right. If they didn't, then both Sandy and I would probably die. The clincher was that we would probably die if nothing was done.

When it was dark I went to a drugstore and bought a flashlight and a cheap digital watch. Then I drove toward the river, parking on Tchoupitoulas and walking across the tracks and up the little entrance drive past the marine-supply store. It was the proximity of people that I hoped would keep Ordaz and his people off balance; the knowledge that the wharf had people coming and going at all hours. But it could also work against me. If the gate had been closed, or a police car had been at the top of the entranceway, to discourage pedestrians, I would have had to pass through the marine-supply store. But for the first time, luck was with me: There was no police car and the gate was open.

The wharf was oddly deserted and I made my way across it, to stand in the shadows, looking out across the river. I could see the lights of Harvey and Marrero, and in midstream was a tug, pushing doggedly upriver toward Baton Rouge, with a string of empty barges. The water level was low, but the surface was dark and menacing and I knew that beneath the swells were currents that could carry a body for miles before it washed up onto a mud bank. The Captain had always disdained rivers. He said the sea was clean and fought fair, while rivers carried man's filth and resented it. I didn't know about the validity of his philosophy, but for some reason even the hot breeze was making me shiver.

I looked down at my wrist. It was almost eight-thirty. If Ordaz was the careful man I thought he was, he would be marshaling his forces now and sending them into position. Then I saw what I was looking for: A tug was moored just a few yards away and it seemed to be unattended. I checked both ends of the wharf for guards and then stepped across quickly, jumping onto the tug and feeling a slight lurch from my weight. My stomach did a small flip-flop, and then I regained my balance. I stole around to the other side of the wheelhouse and crouched down.

Five minutes passed. Ten. A diesel engine huffed its way past along the tracks on the other side of the warehouses.

Ordaz and his men would be off balance, because the wharf was not home territory. They would have to worry about watchmen, late-working longshoremen, and transients hanging around the shadows. So they would be nervous and that would count for something, I hoped.

I closed my eyes. The tug tossed up and down on the waves of a passing oil tanker. Soon now, I thought.

Then I heard it and my blood froze: a chuff-chuffing from downriver that told of a boat battling upstream, close in to the shore. I crawled into the wheelhouse, shielding my body from the river, and waited. It came into view against the glare of the city, and my blood went cold. It was a launch, moving purposefully along the shoreline, without lights. A *launch,* damn it! Why hadn't I thought about the possibility, given Ordaz credit? He was no fool. For just the reasons I'd chosen the waterfront, he wasn't about to come down here at night, to unfamiliar ground. So he had brought a boat, for easy entrance and escape, and *I* was the fool, stranded like a beached fish.

The launch slid alongside the wharf like a shadowy shark and I squinted out alongside the bulkhead of the tug as it moved past, but the most I could make out were a few dark shapes.

It nosed against the dock then, crushing into the old tires that served as shock absorbers, and someone jumped onto the wharf. A rope followed and the man on the wharf looped one end around a post. Then he went aft and caught another line and the launch hugged the dock, its engine idling. It was, I grudgingly realized, a good plan. Ordaz's men would go over the wharf and at the first hint of danger Ordaz would have somebody cut the lines and the launch would be gone.

The first man was moving through the darkness toward the tug now, something angular in his hand. Another body landed, catlike, on the pier, and I flattened myself in the darkness. I heard the footsteps coming along the wharf, toward me, and I edged up the ladder into the wheelhouse, where I could see what was happening. Then something hit the deck below and the boat gave a little lurch. I reached down and brought out the pistol. I could take him out, of course, but if I did, I would have lost, because with the first shot the launch would be gone. I turned my head to look out over the wheel. The second man was at the far end, a black form gliding through the shadows like a phantom. As I watched, he turned to the launch and made a thumbs-up sign.

Then the planks below me creaked. The first man was moving along the deck to the wheelhouse. An instant later his form filled the space at the bottom of the ladder and I knew he was coming up.

This time I got a good look at the weapon in his hands. It was a shotgun, with both barrels chopped and the stocks sawed off to a pistol grip. Within ten feet it would make a hole big enough for a freight train to run through, but right now he was having to hold it in one hand and grab the rungs with the other.

He was wearing a black stocking cap, enough to cushion any blow from above, so I waited. Maybe, I thought, he would get disgusted and stop halfway up. Or maybe somebody on the launch would call him back. Maybe . . .

And then his head appeared through the hatch and we were looking at each other.

For an instant I saw shock and surprise.
Then he started to raise the shotgun,
    but he froze when he saw the .38 two
inches from his forehead.

"Make a sound and you're dead," I said, and he gave
a weak little nod. His eyes fixed on the barrel of the
pistol and I knew he was thinking of what would happen
once my finger started the hammer forward, and how the
158-grain slug would be out of the chamber and plowing
into his brain before he even heard the shot. I moved the
gun slightly and his eyes followed, hypnotized, as I
flicked the cap off his head and then brought the gun
down as hard as I could on his skull.

He gave a little grunt and went limp, rattling down
the ladder to collapse in a heap at the bottom. I followed
quickly, wondering if they'd heard the clatter.

I wrestled him out of his black sweater and slipped
into it. It was a little snug, but it would have to do. Next

I donned his stocking cap. I stuck the pistol in my waist-band, under the sweater, picked up the shotgun, and stepped out onto the deck and jumped to the wharf.

"Oye, Carlos, qué pasa?" someone whispered from the launch.

"Okay, hombre," I said, using the universal word and hoping my voice would pass.

I caught movement from the corner of my eye and saw the man ahead of me on the wharf, near the bow of the boat. I took a deep breath and then I leapt, landing on the deck beside the man who had called to me.

It was just my luck that it had to be the Hulk's play-mate.

The darkness saved me. Before he could react I had the barrel of the shotgun in his face. "Easy," I told him, pointing to the big automatic in his hand. "Drop it on the deck."

He looked around and then slowly leaned over and placed the pistol at his feet.

"Quién es?" a voice called from forward. I decided it was time for me to end the masquerade and answer.

"Ordaz," I called. "Come up and show yourself. I have what you want and I'm still willing to deal."

There was movement forward and I saw the Hulk, a MAC-10 submachine gun cradled in his arms.

"Tell him to drop it," I ordered the man in front of me. "If he fires, you'll be the first one to go."

My prisoner turned around slowly. *"Cuidado, hombre. Bota la ametralladora,"* he rasped.

I'd had a feeling my luck was too good to last. The Hulk's pea-sized brain made a few crude calculations and instead of dropping his weapon he swung it up suddenly and a spatter of bullets whizzed past my head. I lifted the shotgun and fired once.

The blast hit him in the middle and he went over backward, into the water. The man in front of me lunged and I started to club him with the gun barrel. Then I realized it didn't matter, because he was dead.

The man on the wharf was crouching behind a post now and his shotgun tore a chunk out of the launch's hull, a foot from my face. I fired my other barrel at him and threw the empty shotgun away. He was too far away and too well covered for me to feel confident with a pistol, so I hunched down, trying to make my body as small as possible. Then the hatch opened ten feet away and a shaft of light shot out into the light.

"Mr. Dunn, hold your fire." It was Ordaz's voice.

"Tell your man to back off," I called.

"Oye, esperame," Ordaz called in Spanish. *"No dispara."*

The light from the hatch shifted and I saw a raised hand coming up, followed by a head. *Ordaz.*

I aimed the pistol at the center of his body. He came the rest of the way out of the hatch and let go the rail, raising his other hand. He was wearing a white guayabera and light-colored pants and he looked stockier than I remembered.

"I should have known you'd bring an army," I said.

He shrugged. "The wharves are dangerous, Mr. Dunn." He nodded at the body on the deck, in front of me. "Poor Jorge. I suppose I overrated him."

"Where's Sandy?" I asked. "If this is a trick, you die here and now."

"If there is a trick, Mr. Dunn, we both die." He nodded over his shoulder at the man on the wharf, and I knew the shotgun was unlikely to miss again.

"No trick," I said. "I have what you want. But I want to see Sandy."

"Cómo no?" He shrugged and stepped out onto the deck. "Bring her up," he called down the hatchway.

I tried to keep my hand steady, but my muscles had been tensed so long it was difficult. All I had to do was stall; the shots would be bringing people. Then a rumbling crept into my consciousness and I cursed myself for my stupidity. Another train. It would have drowned out the sound of the explosions and blocked any help from reaching me. Sandy and I were as alone as ever.

Then I saw her, coming slowly up through the hatch—first her head, then her face, and finally the rest of her body. She saw me and her face opened in relief.

"Micah . . ."

"Hold on, Sandy. It'll be okay."

But I didn't know if I sounded convincing. Because she stopped halfway up and I knew somebody else was down there, holding her.

"I want her all the way out," I said.

"Very well. Let her come up," Ordaz ordered.

Sandy moved the rest of the way up, swaying as she came, and I realized that hands below were shoving her upward, because her own hands were tied behind her. When she stood in the faint light from the hatchway I scanned her face for signs of abuse. There was a dark welt on her left cheekbone and her eye was swollen.

"If you've hurt her . . ." I warned Ordaz.

He made a face as if the very thought was distasteful.

"Micah, I'm okay," she called and I nodded.

"Untie her," I said.

Ordaz shook his head. "First things first, as you say in English. There is the matter of the item that belongs to me."

"Turn around," I said. "I'll get it."

He frowned slightly and then understanding dawned. He gave me a half-smile and turned his back. I crouched lower to give the man on the dock as little as possible and fished in my pants pocket, holding my pistol in my fingers, and drawing the cloth of the pocket up inch by inch until my free fingers touched the object. I palmed it and resumed my crouch.

"All right," I said. "You can turn around now."

I made my way slowly across the deck and laid the artifact on the gunwale. Ordaz took a step toward it but I cocked the revolver.

"I want Sandy untied and out of here," I barked.

"Mr. Dunn, I have held to my part. You see the girl. Now surely I have a right to examine the artifact."

"Untie her," I said.

Ordaz shrugged and complied.

All along I had known it would come down to this. I turned my head slightly so that Sandy could see my lips in the half-light from the open hatch.

"Sandy, listen to me: I want you to walk very slowly across the deck to the side of the boat. I want you to put one foot up and when I tell you to jump, I want you to jump onto the pier. When you land, get up and run for the tracks. Do you understand?"

She nodded. "You got it," she said, her voice wavering.

I turned back to the Cuban. "All right, Ordaz, come ahead."

He took two halting steps toward the side of the ship, his eyes wavering between the barrel of the pistol and the little object I had placed on the gunwale. His hand reached out, as if to stay the jade from any movement away from him. I counted the seconds, waiting for the moment, but he must have sensed my muscles tensing, because at the last instant he wheeled around toward me, anger in his dark eyes.

I knew that I would not get another chance. "Jump, Sandy!" I yelled and at the same time squeezed off three quick rounds at the shadowy figure with the shotgun.

Everything seemed to happen at once. The shotgun thundered and a wind whipped at my sleeve. Ordaz dived for the deck and something metallic flashed in his hand. There was motion to my right and I could see that Sandy was down, but there was no way to tell if she had been hit. A tongue of fire licked out from Ordaz's position and something branded my cheek. I fired once in his direction and then the shotgun roared again. A fine spray peppered my arm. As in a dream, I saw my hand rise and I pulled the trigger. The figure on the dock gasped and the shotgun fell to the ground. I pivoted toward Ordaz, aware of a small chrome automatic in his hand. I squeezed the trigger of my own weapon and the hammer snapped down on an empty chamber. Ordaz stood up slowly, his pistol leveled at my midsection.

"Mr. Dunn, you really should not have done that," he declared. Mentally, I swore at myself and I swore at Harry, for giving me the Smith. Ordaz took another step toward me. "Now," Ordaz said, "I have to kill you both."

He raised the pistol and I had an instant of regret at coming so close. Then the gun spit fire, but the shot, instead of hitting me, dug into the deck at my feet. There was a second shot, more like a pop than an explosion, and Ordaz stared at me as if he could not believe what had happened. The chrome-plated pistol fell from his hand and he stumbled forward and then collapsed face downward onto the deck.

I lifted my head. A bulky form moved out of the hatchway and stood staring down at the fallen man.

"He was going to kill you," Jason Cobbett said, shaking his head. "Mr. Dunn, I think I just saved your life."

I looked from his smug expression to the tiny four-barreled pepperbox revolver in his right hand and for some reason I did not feel an urge to thank him.

"Cobbett . . ." I rasped.

"You didn't really expect to see me here, did you?" he asked, edging toward the far side of the boat. "But how else was Señor Ordaz going to determine that what he was getting was genuine?" He stepped over the fallen man.

My eyes stole over to the wharf, to see if Sandy had escaped, but there was no movement. "No, Mr. Dunn, it doesn't do any good to look over there. They're all dead. There's just the two of us. The two of us and the jade." He giggled and I estimated the distance between my hand and Ordaz's pistol, lying on the deck.

"I wouldn't," Cobbett warned. "I only have two shots left but I couldn't miss at this range."

He was right. I held fast, feeling suddenly very weary, the wetness on my right arm sticking my clothes to my body. I fought the urge to sit down on the deck and watch from afar.

He was only a foot from the gunwale now, moving spread-legged, like a man who is unused to the sea.

"Cobbett," I breathed. "All along, you . . ."

"Yes," he beamed. "I was the flunky, the museum director that did other people's work. I had to listen to all the praises for Thorpe, what a great archaeologist he was. I was the one who had to make up to the little old ladies, kiss their hands, gush over their hairdos and furs and jewels. And whenever Ordaz called, with some piece to be appraised, I had to jump for my pittance." I took a halting step toward him and the tiny gun came up to center on my body. "But they were nothing compared to *you!*" he cried. "To be kidnapped, treated like some piece of dirt, tied up and threatened . . ."

"Cobbett, listen. The police know we're here. They're on their way right now . . ." The words sounded distant, as if they were echoing down a long tube.

"Then I'd better take the jade and go," he said and, shifting the pistol to his left hand, reached for the artifact.

I took a deep breath and wished my head would stop

spinning. He picked up the jade and held it up to the light. And that was when I made my move.

I shoved forward, raising my right arm to knock him off balance, but my arm refused to work and instead I stumbled against him, sending him against the side of the launch. The launch tipped slightly and he lost his balance. The gun discharged and something branded my leg. I slammed him with my shoulder and we fell against the rail together. He swore, tried to raise the pistol, and I brought my knee up into his groin. The breath gushed out of him and his right hand struck down against the gunwale. His fist opened involuntarily and I saw his mouth gape open as the tiny object fell onto the thin edge of wood. He uttered a strangled cry of protest, grabbed for it, and as the boat tipped, the artifact slid slowly off the edge and toppled into darkness.

"You!" he cried, as much in anguish as in rage. The diversion was all I needed: I rocked into him and, locked together, we went over the side.

The black waters closed over us and I felt his hands claw frantically at my body as we sank into the depths. For an agonizing eternity I lost my sense of direction and panic overwhelmed me. Then his grip came loose and I felt myself being carried away. I tried to reach out, to guide myself, but my arm refused to work and the realization suddenly came to me that I was about to die. For an instant it seemed a very logical outcome and a peace started to settle over me. Then something I'd last felt lying on a stretcher inside an evacuation chopper took over and I kicked out with my legs, hoping I was propelling myself upward and not toward the muddy bottom.

My lungs cried and I fought the urge to open my mouth, suck in the water. I gave a last, feeble flutter with my legs and then, as everything closed around me, my head shot to the surface.

I sucked in the hot night air and tried to get my bearings. Upstream was a burst of lights I couldn't place and as I watched, one of them disengaged and came dancing across the surface toward me. I smiled. It was a spotlight. They were searching for me but they wouldn't find me because I was hiding. The river would hide me. Already I was a quarter mile downstream, and before long I'd be in the big curve that formed one horn of the crescent that gave the city its nickname. By that time I'd be in midstream, of course, and prey to the barge traffic that came and went like cars on a busy highway. Unless the undertow took me first.

Maybe, I thought, that was what would happen. All at once it seemed a funny notion and I laughed to myself. "Cruising down the river," I hummed, "on a Monday afternoon." But no, it was night now. Well, on a Monday *night,* then. A wave washed over my head and I took in a mouthful of water. It tasted of mud and I choked. *My God, what was happening? I was drowning, that's what.* Another wave surged over me and I realized my strength was ebbing and that I was at the mercy of the ugly tow.

The light played on the water, farther away now, and I tried to yell, to let them know I was here, but my words were drowned by the noise of engines.

Engines. My God, a ship was bearing down on me!

I twisted in the water. The hull loomed out of the night like a dark cloud, rushing toward me on wings of death.

My lips opened and I got out a scream, but the hull was only feet away now, plowing up a thin white spume of bubbles. A wave rocked me and I kicked to get away but something was drawing me toward the deadly prow.

I thrashed, trying to free myself of the inexorable pull, but I was moving toward it with a sudden, terrible acceleration. The prow passed in front of me then and I realized I was headed for the side of the hull, where I would be drawn under, to be mangled by the propellers. The hull was above me now and all at once, as I watched, the night turned to daylight and I slammed against the side.

But instead of going under, I was being lifted. Hands were grabbing me, hauling me up, and I dimly realized that what had drawn me forward was a rope, a rope that someone had tossed at something they had seen bobbing on the surface.

Lieutenant Mancuso was staring down at me as they lifted me onto the deck, shaking his head.

"Is he all right?" someone said and I recognized O'Rourke's voice.

"He's a little worse for the wear, but he'll live," Mancuso said. He stooped down, so that his head blotted the light. "Welcome home, yardbird," he said.

They put me in Charity Hospital, in the prison ward, but by noon Tuesday I was moved to Touro, a private hospital in the Garden District. My right shoulder had been peppered by buckshot and my arm was in a sling. My right leg had taken a .22 short in the meaty part of the thigh. I was told I had a new scar on the cheek, where I had been grazed. The doctor at Charity looked at me as at just one more shooting, to get patched up with as few amenities as possible. The doctor at Touro was more congenial, but seemed at a loss for conversation, because few of his patients were admitted for gunshot wounds. And at least one of the nurses kept sticking her head into the room as if to verify that I was real.

I knew that the move was O'Rourke's doing, and an hour after I got to my new room he came through the door, shaking his head, with Sandy behind him.

"You know, Micah, about the only way I got you out

of the Hilton was by convincing them you couldn't go anywhere. Mancuso's captain is pretty hot about all the gunplay."

"So am I," I told him. "Hell, I'm the one that's all shot up."

"Well," Sandy said demurely, "you may be simplifying things a little bit. There *are* five dead people, if you count Ordaz and Cobbett."

"Yeah, but I only killed two of them," I said. "Ordaz's version of a one-man army shot his buddy by mistake. Cobbett shot Ordaz and then fell overboard. It's not my fault he couldn't swim."

"Jesus," O'Rourke muttered under his breath.

"And what about the man I hit on the head?" I said. "They didn't let *him* get away?"

"No," O'Rourke promised, "he's singing like a bird. Seems like he heard Ordaz making plans, and some of his arrangements with Cobbett. Looks like Cobbett's going to get you and Thorpe both off."

"I'll drink to that," I said, "but how do they explain his being out of town when St. Romaine was killed?"

"He was at some conference in Dallas. But there's every expectation that he hopped a return flight under some other name. They're checking it out now."

"Ummm," I grunted, trying to shift myself to a more comfortable position. "Has anybody talked to Cora Thorpe?"

"She's flipped," the lawyer said. "Gone completely catatonic. Just sits there staring."

"The lady always did have a kind of animal cunning," I said laconically.

"What the hell's *that* supposed to mean?"

"Just that for some reason I'm not very surprised."

"I still don't understand about the jade," Sandy said, "but since you went and lost it, I guess I never will."

"Ummm," I said again and closed my eyes. They

took the signal and left. But I didn't sleep, because I had some thinking to do.

At four-thirty the phone rang. I tried to move my right arm, but the sling held it fast, and I swore under my breath. The phone rang a second time and a third. I yelled in frustration and a nurse poked her head into the room.

"The phone," I said angrily. "Could you please pick up the damned phone?"

She was young and redheaded and smiled sweetly. "Of course, Mr. Dunn." She caught it on the sixth ring and brought the receiver to her ear.

"Mr. Dunn's room."

I heard an incomprehensible bellowing from the telephone and she jerked it down abruptly.

"There's some crazy person that wants to talk to you," she said archly.

I smiled in relief and felt some of the anxiety flood out of me. "Please," I said. "Put it up to my ear. It's just my father."

She nestled the receiver against my shoulder and left with a flurry of skirts, unsure what kind of people the hospital was taking in these days.

"Hello, Captain," I said.

"*Hello, Captain?* Is that all the hell you have to say after scaring me to death? Jesus Christ, son, I thought *I* was supposed to be the sick one, and the next thing I hear is your friend, that lawyer you hang around with, telling me you've been shot."

"I'm fine," I said. "But what about you? What about the tests?"

"Bullshit," the Captain snorted. "Navy doctors are the Russians' secret weapon. Tests were fine. They had me scared for a while, I've got to admit."

"You're telling me the truth?" I asked.

"Telling you the truth? On my word as a naval officer!" he swore. "All they said was to cut back on my alcohol a little."

"Which I can tell you're going to do starting tomorrow."

"Or the next day. What do they know?" He cleared his throat and when he spoke again his voice was softer. "No getting around it, though: I'm slowing down. *Have* to cut back. I just can't do it like I used to."

"One of the crosses you'll have to bear," I said.

"Smart ass. Look, you going to be able to come next month?"

"I wouldn't miss it."

"Good. There was a nurse I had while I was at their mercy, a cute little thing, too young for me, but I got kind of friendly with her, you know? And I kind of planted the idea that you might come up and I'd have her out and . . ."

"You really are well," I said. We chatted a little more and then I pleaded fatigue and hung up.

For a long moment I lay staring at the wall, relieved that he was all right. There were times he would lie, but not on his word as an officer. No, things would be all right. In Charleston.

There was just the matter of New Orleans.

At four-thirty Katherine appeared, accompanied by Scott. She handed me a box of chocolates, and when I demonstrated my lack of agility, placed one in my mouth.

"You had us all worried," she said. "They said they took ten buckshot out of you."

"I was worried, too," I said. "But I guess I'm too mean to go."

"Well, I'm glad of that," she said softly. "We all are."

"Yeah," Scott echoed. "But I guess now we'll never know what the jade meant."

"No?" I asked. "Hasn't Thorpe figured it out yet?" Katherine tried to smile and I sensed embarrassment. "He says it's not clear," she said. "He says he'd have to have the jade itself to make sure he read the glyphs correctly."

"Sure," Scott said sarcastically.

"Well," I said, "in that case maybe we'd better give it to him."

Two pairs of eyes stared at me. "What?" Katherine asked.

"The jade," I said calmly. "Maybe we ought to give it to him."

"Have they found it in the river, then?" Scott asked incredulously.

"No," I said. "That would be a waste of time. The currents are too swift."

"Then how . . . ?" Katherine asked.

"Because," I said, "the jade was never in the river. As a matter of fact, it was never on the boat. I never even brought it with me."

Katherine frowned. "Are you serious?"

"Deadly, if you'll pardon the pun. When I was alone at your house I did a little alchemy. Once in a while I've had to take key impressions, so I knew the routine. I made a wax mold and manufactured a replica. A little shoe polish and I managed to get it dark enough to fool somebody at a distance."

Scott slapped his thigh with delight. "You mean what fell overboard, what Cobbett killed Ordaz for was a damned *fake*?"

"I'm afraid so," I said. "And not a very good one. All I hoped for was that in the darkness I could fool them long enough to get Sandy out into the open. Then, with a little luck, while Ordaz was distracted looking at the supposed jade, I'd make my move. It wasn't a very good plan, I'll admit. It was just the best I could come up with."

"Then the real jade . . ." Katherine began.

"Here," I said. "Too many people have been killed over it for me to rest very easy with it somewhere else."

Scott shook his head in wonder and Katherine ushered him from the room. She returned and stood looking down at me, her expression pensive.

"Katherine . . ."

She rose quickly. "I guess I'd better go. The exhibition is in chaos. I have to do whatever I can to help Gregory salvage what can be salvaged."

I sighed and turned to the wall. I wanted it to be over but it wasn't over. I wanted Katherine to tell Thorpe to go to hell, but she hadn't done it. Most of all, I wanted things to be the way they had been a week ago, before Thorpe had called me and turned my world upside down.

Supper was a slice of meat loaf, peas, and potatoes, with some peach slices for desert. I toyed with it, not feeling hungry.

Why? I kept asking myself. What was it about Thorpe?

I yelled for the nurse, had her dial Sandy's number, and got her on the second ring. When I told her what I wanted, she said I was crazy and hung up.

At five I tuned the television to the local news and got an update on the bloody battle at the Harmony Street wharf. Five people had died, including a Cuban attorney the police had long had an eye on for some unsavory business deals. The curator of a local museum had drowned and the police were still searching the river for his body. The best guess was that it was a dope deal gone sour, and the police were questioning a suspect. The other survivor was a local investigator who had es-

caped from the St. Tammany Parish jail. The Orleans
Parish district attorney was reevaluating the evidence
and the investigator had been moved to another location, presumably for his own protection.

It was typically garbled, but that didn't bother me.
For once I had other things on my mind. I tried to reach
the call button to have my tray picked up and failed. I let
out a particularly descriptive epithet as Sandy walked in,
purse swinging jauntily from her arm.

"Well, Micah-man, you look like trouble's in bed
with you."

She moved the tray and then stood over me with
folded arms.

"Micah, I think you're crazy."

"Get in line," I said. "Did you bring them?"

She sighed resignedly and handed me a manila envelope.

"Whatever. By the way, there's a picture in here
from some guy in Florida. Another boat."

"A yacht," I corrected. "The *Cate's Cove II*. Fifty-
three feet long and . . ."

She yawned. "Well, if you're sure you don't want me
to hang around . . ."

"No, thanks," I said. "Go home. Or finish that vacation."

"Sho'nuf. After I clean up what's left of my place."

She left and I opened the manila envelope, struggling
with one hand to tear the seal and slip out the album and
photographs. I worked for the next few minutes pasting
in my new acquisition. When I had finished I admired it,
and then turned back through the pages. I had a whole
section for the '84 Olympic yachting competition. But I
always went back to the America's Cup, because that
was the *one*. I was staring fondly at my faded snapshot of
the *Ranger,* taken before I was born, when I fell asleep.

I hadn't meant to sleep at all, but the combination of

fatigue and medicine had an involuntary effect, and when I awoke the windows showed darkness outside. I could feel the album resting lightly across my midsection, but that wasn't what had awakened me. What had awakened me was a noise. The noise of someone inside the room.

I shifted slightly. "Nurse? Who's there?"

The noise stopped and for a moment I thought I had imagined it. Then the shadows shifted at the edge of my vision. I tried to turn and the album slid off the bed and crashed onto the floor.

"Don't move!" said the voice of the killer.

"I was wondering how long it would take you," I said.

There was a hoarse exclamation. "You *expected* me?"

"Of course. That's why I had the jade brought here. I knew it would bring you out."

"You're insane," he whispered. "Now tell me where it is before I . . ."

"Before you what? Kill me like you did Gordon Leeds?"

"I didn't kill Leeds. St. Romaine killed him, the fool. I just wanted the jade. It was St. Romaine that started this whole damned business."

"But you had to kill St. Romaine. He knew too much. Ditto for Artemio; he was getting remorseful. And that's why you'll have to kill me, too, won't you, Gladney?"

Fred Gladney emitted a choked little sound, as if

someone had punched him. "Just give me the damned jade," he hissed.

"Why? The jade has no value. It's the message on it. And you can't read glyphs."

"But Astrid can. She'll read it for me."

"Then she'll have an accident, I guess."

I could envision his shrug. "Well, you don't think I can spend the rest of my life with an unbalanced girl like that, do you? I tried to take the blame for her, but the police weren't interested. They were far more interested in what I had to say about her mental record. Dull bunch."

"So dull you'll blame my death on her, right?"

"As a matter of fact, that's correct. *Now where is it?*"

"Humor me," I said. "I don't get a chance to be murdered every day. Though it seems like I'm on a roll." I tried to sit up but my sling limited movement.

"How did you find out about the jade originally?" I asked.

"Leeds. He told me, the idiot. He was drunk. He'd had an argument with Thorpe. Something about the argument set him to thinking and he said all of a sudden he had this revelation. He couldn't keep his mouth shut. I let him talk. He told me he'd found this valuable artifact with some glyphs on it and all of a sudden he knew what the glyphs meant. He said they were directions to a fantastic treasure."

"Which was something you couldn't pass up."

"I'd been hanging around Astrid for a year and I'd never gotten anything for it. It was all Claude's idea. He and I were fraternity brothers. Claude started banging Thorpe's wife. At first it was thrills. He'd had Thorpe for a class. He said Thorpe was a turkey. He used to lie there in bed with her after that and laugh to himself about Thorpe studying his artifacts, lecturing while the class slept, and not knowing what was going on with his own wife. Then he got the idea it would be even better to turn some money off it. He didn't need money; the bastard was rich. But it was the idea, see? The fun of it all. He'd try to use Cora as a pipeline to the artifacts. She went along with it."

"Charming lady," I said. "And what about you, Gladney? It wasn't the same thing with you, though, was it?"

"No. I *needed* the money. Do you know what it's like trying to make money as an oil broker in Louisiana right now, with the whole industry in a depression? When I started, in '84, there was hope, but after '86 and the way the ragheads dropped prices . . . Anyway, we agreed to try together. He said Astrid was a flake, that Cora had told him the girl had a mental record. I thought maybe I could talk her into helping me from the inside. But she was pretty hopeless. She wasn't even good in bed."

"She must not have known how lucky she was," I said. "Poor girl. Tell me, which one of you put Artemio up to stealing from Thorpe?"

"He was a greedy little bastard. It didn't take much. I just took him out drinking one night and explained how Thorpe didn't give a damn about him or anybody else. I told him Thorpe would have him back in a Mayan corn-field quicker than he could say *frijoles*. He didn't know a lot of English, but he sure as hell understood *that*."

"I'm sure."

"The trouble was he didn't bring us anything worth stealing. Trash. It was all trash. Claude took it to Ordaz. He'd had some dealings with the greasy bastard before. Ordaz was the one who told him he could make some big money. But when Ordaz saw what he had to offer, he laughed. Paid him a few hundred to keep him on the string."

"Which is where it would've ended if Leeds hadn't told you about the jade."

"Exactly. Now we've screwed around long enough. Where is it? I've killed already. It won't matter to kill you."

"You'll kill me anyway," I said. "Which is why I can't let you do it."

"*What?*"

"Turn on the light," I said. "You'll see the gun isn't very big, but it's pointed straight at your belly."

There was an eternity of silence and then his breath leaked out like air from a punctured hose.

"No," he said.

The light flared on then and I saw him for the first time, three feet away, the ice pick halfway out of his pocket. It was as if the little .25 in my hand mesmerized him, so that he hardly noticed the men shoving through the doorway.

"Put it down," Mancuso said, bringing a magnum to bear on the man in the center of the room. "If his .25 doesn't get you, you can be damned sure this one will."

For an interminable instant Gladney stood rooted, his eyes wavering from one of us to the other. The next few seconds were a surprise that neither of us would ever forget: With a choked cry, Gladney ran, not toward the man in the doorway, but for the window. There was a crash of breaking glass and Mancuso swore as Gladney's body plunged through.

Mancuso lowered his gun and went over to the window. I shut my eyes.

"Jesus," the policeman muttered, looking down.

I managed a weary nod. At last, I thought, it was over.

It was two days later and we were sitting on my balcony, O'Rourke and Sandy and I, looking out over the patio. Old Mr. Mamet, the caretaker, had fixed the fountain,

and now and then a vagrant breeze brought a fine spray
to tease our faces.

I still had the sling, and my right arm was almost as
useless as my left. I caught my two friends swapping
amused glances as I tried to sip my beer through a long
straw.

"Man gonna die of thirst," Sandy smirked. "But I
guess that's better than what he almost died of."

O'Rourke smiled. He was contented these days, he
said, because things had turned out well. The charges
against both Thorpe and me had been dropped, the vil-
lain unmasked, and, most important, he had found a
lunchroom in Arabi, of all places, that served as perfect
a muffaletta as would ever exist. I was happy that he saw
things in such clear perspective.

"Still," Sandy went on, "I don't understand the
whole thing. I mean, you say everything started with this
St. Romaine and Gladney?"

I took a last sip and leaned back. "I guess you could
say that. Or you could say it started with Thorpe and his
personality, and with his infatuation with Cora. Or even
when he met Artemio Pech. But St. Romaine and
Gladney were the triggers."

"Gladney was about to go under," O'Rourke said. "I
did some checking on the company he owns. An office
and an answering machine, with an in-box full of bills."

"It fits in," I said.

"Lots of people that way, though, babe," Sandy said.
"Is that all you had against the man?"

"There was his insistence that the woman he loved
was insane. He seemed to want very badly to spread the
word to everybody he met. Strange behavior for somebody in love, but not so strange if you were looking for
somebody to take the heat. His little confession ploy
with the police was the clincher. He wanted to plant just
the wrong information with them, to convince them he

was trying to save Astrid, and at the same time put the idea in their heads that maybe she was the killer."

"Sandy squinted. "And you *deduced* everything from that?"

"Of course," I said. "And then there was the matter of Cora Thorpe. She told me."

My two friends broke into laughter.

"Then why didn't you go to the cops when you knew who it was?" Sandy asked.

"You mean an escapee who got it straight from the mouth of an accomplice, and a flaky one at that?" I looked over at O'Rourke and he nodded.

"He's right," the lawyer said. "He's lucky I got the sheriff of St. Tammany Parish to drop the escape and battery charges."

"Anyway," I told her, "I was a little more interested in getting you loose. I thought there was a chance he might come back and try to finish Cora, which is why I sent Thorpe over there."

"And Cobbett didn't have anything to do with the plan?" Sandy asked.

"Not really. He was the appraiser Ordaz used. He saw the jade but didn't attach any significance to it until Ordaz got excited about losing it and asked him about the glyphs. Then he realized it must be worth something, and he started to wonder how he could get his hands on it. When Ordaz had him come aboard the launch to verify the piece, he never expected his meek little flunky would be carrying a gun, much less that he'd use it on him."

"I wonder how Cobbett expected to get rid of Ordaz's bodyguards?" O'Rourke said.

"Who knows," I said. "Probably he didn't have any idea what would happen. He never really thought the chance would arise, but when it did, he took it."

"But how did Ordaz find out the jade was valuable?"

O'Rourke asked. "He would never have let go of it if he'd known."

"I suspect that was somebody's big mouth," I said. "Probably Gladney told his pal, St. Romaine. St. Romaine wasn't in it for money. He wanted to be a big shot, to swagger. He probably told Ordaz, after he'd killed Leeds. St. Romaine wanted Ordaz to pay him to get it back. But, like I said, it wasn't the money so much; it was the thrill of the game."

"Sounds like Cora-baby," Sandy mused. "I can't believe that little pinhead was trying to blackmail Gladney."

"Thrills again," I said. "She and her lover, St. Romaine, were a lot alike. Anything for an adrenaline rush. She thought being married to Thorpe would be all Indiana Jones, but she found out he was the wrong man for excitement. She was all ready when St. Romaine made his move. I'll never prove it, but I'd bet it was *her* idea to siphon off the artifacts."

O'Rourke shook his head. "Sweet lady."

"Of course, nobody trusted anybody else," I said. "Which was how she ended up drugged at a murder scene. The way she tells it, St. Romaine called her from the cabin that night I followed her, told her to come in a hurry. She wasn't sure what had happened, but it sounded important, so she went. In reality, it looks like Gladney had convinced St. Romaine that they needed to get rid of her, because she knew too much. That way they could make it look like *she'd* killed Leeds. St. Romaine thought he was luring her to her death, not his own. What he didn't know was that Gladney, nice guy that he was, was holding out on one part of the scheme."

"You mean St. Romaine's death," volunteered Sandy.

"You got it. Gladney's plan was to let it look like a murder-suicide, and blame it on Cora. I stepped into the middle of it and he had to change his plan. Cora got her stomach pumped before the drug did her in and began to put two and two together. She knew it had to be Gladney at that point."

"And that's when she started to blackmail him," Sandy said. "But what was she trying to *get?*"

I sighed. "She's the kind who has to be continually stimulated. Throwing out little hints to Gladney, calling him at odd times, trying to make him jump at her every whim—this was her way of keeping the game alive."

"Good way of getting herself dead," Sandy said darkly.

"Yes," I agreed. "In that respect, she was lucky."

"And she knew from the first her lover Claude had killed Leeds, then, right?" O'Rourke asked.

"She figured it out pretty easily. You remember that Astrid wasn't feeling well and Gladney took her home early? It was the perfect opportunity. Gladney put her to bed and then called, probably from a phone booth. He told St. Romaine to follow Leeds, and then went back to the party, giving himself an alibi. Gladney thought they could steal the jade from Leeds or get it through some form of trickery, I expect. I think he was genuinely upset when St. Romaine, who had taken Thorpe's car and was waiting outside Hahn's place, not only followed Leeds but ran him down. He was at heart a businessman, not a killer."

"Some difference," Sandy said contemptuously. "So Gladney knew Leeds was a little . . ." She raised one limp wrist.

"Right. Leeds had confided to Astrid, who'd told Gladney, of course, without thinking about it. It wasn't so much that Leeds hid it as that he just didn't talk about it or flaunt it. Anyway, Gladney knew he'd be at Hahn's place and that's where he sent his friend to wait."

I took another long sip of the beer. With the straw it

tasted flat, or was it just the sordid tale I was having to recount?

"When you asked me to bring the jade and my pistol along with your boat book, I thought you'd flipped." Sandy declared. "And then, asking me to call up Astrid and tell her you had the stone and you wanted her to come up to the hospital the next day to help you translate the thing . . . You were pretty sure she was gonna tell Freddy-boy, weren't you?"

"It was a chance," I admitted. "But I figured she would, yes. She's not half as crazy as he tried to make out, but she has had problems, and he managed to isolate her even more, through the guise of being protective. He was about the only person she felt she could turn to. Of course, she didn't have any idea he was the killer."

"What'll happen with Cora now?" Sandy asked.

"Extortion and obstruction of justice are both crimes," O'Rourke said. "I understand the DA is filing charges. Matter of fact," he said smugly, "Thorpe has talked to me about defending her."

"Oh, gag." Sandy made a face. "Of course you said no."

The lawyer shrugged. "*Of course* I said I'd think about it. I have to make a living too, you know."

"Well, how's Thorpe going to manage your fee? Tulane's giving him the boot, aren't they?"

"Why? He hasn't done anything but bore students. And the exhibit has been breaking records."

"And he's going to stay with Cora?" Sandy asked, incredulous.

"That's something else," O'Rourke explained. "He's having a good time being noble and forgiving, but it'll be hard to forget what happened. And besides, he has something else to occupy him right now."

"Which brings us to the real question," O'Rourke

said, lifting his Manhattan. "What in the hell do the glyphs on that damned jade *mean?*"

I stopped sipping. "Ah, I was wondering when one of you was going to ask that."

"So?" Sandy demanded, leaning forward in her chair. "Are you going to tell us?"

I smiled. "Why not? Thorpe's got the jade now and he's on his way to Yucatán."

"*Well?*" Sandy persisted.

"The jade," I said, "is a play on the name of the ruler Ek Balam. And the glyphs tell where he's buried."

EPILOGUE

It was nearly dawn and a thin mist hung over the tops of the trees. We stood shivering atop the little mound of rubble, waiting for the sun. From around us came the heavy, earth-laden smell of the rain forest, salted with the strong odor of smoke from the previous day's field burnings. On the eastern horizon the first tendrils of sun were snaking up into the sky and I knew it would be another mercilessly hot May day. I gazed out at the strange world around me. Here and there, against the dark carpet of trees, white forms that had once been pyramids and temples hovered in the mist.

"Not long now," Gregory Thorpe said, consulting his watch. He was dressed for the field: jeans, a khaki shirt, and an ancient straw Panama; while Katherine wore khaki shorts and a white blouse and a safari hat she'd confessed to having ordered from a Bean catalog. The newspeople fiddled with their cameras and recorders and I was wondering why I'd agreed to come. I knew it was

Katherine who'd wangled the invitation and Thorpe could hardly have refused. But just standing with them brought everything back and knowing that I'd helped make this possible was small recompense.

One thing was for certain, though, I thought, as I waited for the sun to appear over the eastern treetops: Thorpe was in his element, oblivious to any shortcomings in his behavior of the previous summer.

A pert woman in her twenties with short black hair, designer jeans, and oversized dark glasses whispered something to the cameraman, who lifted the camera onto his shoulder. A bright light went on, striking the archaeologist in the face, and Thorpe flinched.

"Would you say a few words for our viewers, Dr. Thorpe?" the newswoman began. "About the hieroglyphics and the buried treasure? And maybe touch on the curse of the Balam?"

Thorpe gazed down his nose at her and took a deep, meaningful breath. "In the first place, we are not here to find buried treasure. We are here to open the tomb of the ruler Ek Balam, who lived in approximately A.D. 1400. As for the so-called curse, that is utter nonsense, and repeating such a story does a disservice to archaeology."

"But several people died in making this discovery," the woman persisted.

"People die every day," Thorpe huffed. I looked over at Katherine. She smiled and gave a tiny shrug. I turned back to Thorpe. He'd recovered well from his disappointment with Cora, I thought, partly because of the challenge represented by a new, significant discovery and partly because of a loyal secretary who refused to take no for an answer.

"We'll leave out the curse, then," the woman said with obvious disappointment. "But there *is* a treasure, isn't there? I mean, you've been excavating here for almost a year, just to uncover this single tomb."

Thorpe put on his best pained expression. "We have been excavating here for nine months because archaeology is a painstaking business, contrary to the drivel that is foisted upon the public by the popular press. We have elected to proceed level by level, to the extent possible, recording everything of significance above the tomb itself. As for the treasure, it is probable that the burial is accompanied by offerings, and in many cases these would be of value on the illegal antiquities market, but our main concern is to recover information. In this case the existence of the burial is only secondary, confirming a theory that I have held for some time concerning the practical importance of astronomical phenomena to the Maya."

The defeated newswoman gave a nod for the cameraman to roll.

"Maybe you could tell us about *that,* then," she said.

"Yes, certainly," Thorpe agreed, his body straightening as the camera started to hum. "In this particular case, the clue was a small piece of jade with glyphs on it." He produced the *hacha* and the cameraman struggled to find the best angle. "Here, we have a most unusual situation. A jade ceremonial object of absolutely unique color, black, as you can see, probably selected especially for this ruler and brought here from some other place, possibly Costa Rica. It is sculpted to have a jaguar's face, as a representation of the ruler's name, which means Star Jaguar in Mayan. Since the word for 'star' also means 'black,' and the Maya loved word plays, the black jade was appropriate. The jade was then buried, right where we stand, incidentally, probably as a symbolic interment of the great leader, with a glyphic text indicating the precise resting place of the ruler's actual body."

"And you excavated the jade," the reporter asked, striving vainly to regain control.

"It was found by a worker, yes," Thorpe said obliquely. "Anyway, what is important here is the glyphic text, not who found it."

"And it has to do with the planet Venus?"

"The text," Thorpe explained, "should read as follows: 'Ek Balam, the ruler, lies at the place where the planet Venus appears during the dry season.'"

"Fantastic," cooed the interviewer. "And you were able to figure that out, even before the dry time of the year."

Thorpe gave his best professorial smile. "That was hardly a problem. The positions of the planets and major stars are known for any time of the day and season. It merely requires a few calculations, after which we determined that at the designated time, Venus would appear . . ." He pointed and we followed his gaze to a small heap of rubble half a mile away. There was a collective gasp as we saw the bright star hovering just above Thorpe's finger.

". . . there," he declared in triumph.

"Wonderful," the newswoman declared, then turned to the cameraman. *Are you getting this?*"

"Of course," Thorpe went on magisterially, oblivious to the muttered oaths of the cameraman, who had found at the crucial instant that his mechanism was jammed, "of course, this was simply a bit of theater. A little high drama, shall we say, to make the point. We've held off any further excavations until today. We've already found the sarcophagus, and today we shall open it."

"Not until we can change cameras, I hope," the reporter asked anxiously.

"There'll be plenty of time," Thorpe said grandly. He turned to the rest of us, mere mortals witnessing his victory, and nodded toward the little path at the bottom of the hill. "Shall we go now? We should probably get started before the heat's too terrible."

He picked his way down the rubble-strewn side of the mound, stepping from block to block like a mountain goat, with the members of the entourage falling on one another to follow.

He halted at the bottom and looked back up at Katherine. "Are you coming?" he called.

"In just a minute," she said.

He shrugged and started along the trail.

"You'll miss the main event," I chided.

"It doesn't matter," she said. "He has everything he needs. I realize that now."

I nodded, a spark of hope flickering.

"You know, it's funny," she said, sitting down beside me. "He asked me to marry him when he's free of Cora."

Just as quickly my hope was dashed.

"And?" I asked, my mouth as dry as the fields.

Katherine sighed and wrapped her arms around her legs.

"*And* he even offered me a raise," she chuckled.

"Katherine . . ." I turned to face her and saw her eyes alive with amusement.

"So I told him yes."

"*Katherine . . .*"

"About the raise. And that I'd stay on until this phase of the project is over."

"Damn it." I put my hand on her shoulder and pulled her around to face me and she started laughing.

"Oh, I told him I wasn't interested in marriage," she said and came over against me. "If that's what you wanted to hear."

I relaxed, my anxiety replaced by a calmness.

"It'll do," I growled. "At least for now."

I turned back to the horizon just in time to see the edge of the glowing disk push itself above the horizon. Then I leaned against her and she against me, as we settled in to enjoy the sunrise.